# TIMELESS

## Also by Crystal Collier

Maiden of Time Trilogy:
*Moonless*
*Soulless*
*Timeless*

Short Stories:
*Through the Portal (Heroes of Phenomena)*
*The Fourth Wish (Of Mist and Magic)*
*The Mirror People (Parallels: Felix was Here)*

# TIMELESS

*Book 3 in the*

## Maiden of Time
## Trilogy

## By Crystal Collier

Published by RAYBOURNE PUBLISHING

Copyright © 2016 by Crystal Collier

www.crystal-collier.com

Cover Design by J. Matthew Collier

Summary: Alexia races against her own clock and the birth of her child to stop the Soulless from existing. [1. Fiction. 2. Historical-paranormal. 3. Soulless. 4. Wraiths. 5. Supernatural Creatures. 6. Historical Fantasy. 7. Time Travel. 8. Maiden of Time. 9. Passionate and Soulless. 10. Medieval Times.]

ISBN: 978-1-62983-005-6

*Dear Reader,*

*If you have been with me since Alexia first discovered the mystery behind Moonless nights, you may be saddened to discover that in this novel there is no vicious childlike murderess or socially awkward teen who sees through others' eyes. However, don't despair. These characters have won such a place in my heart that they deserved their own novella: BELLEZZA. Watch for it on Amazon.*

*Wishing you much readerly joy,*

*Crystal Collier*

For Kaily,

who embraces all things girly
and assures me it's okay to
be a hopeless romantic.

*Time holds no meaning to one what is Timeless*
*Yet fissures the world to the old and the new*
*Save them from torment, save them from dyin'*
*Come now, Great Maiden, their fate falls to you.*

—Author Unknown

# Prologue: 1849

Stars burdened the sky. Kiren breathed in the cool night air, barely daring to shift the winds with his presence. His scent had already been detected. The silhouette on the hill reminded him too dearly of the woman he had adored. The woman he'd let go.

He ascended.

Alexia would have loved the sky tonight. She would have leaned into him, tugged his arms around her and gazed into the heavens, turning that adorable smile up at him, forcing his heart to thunder his love for her. But she wasn't here.

The breeze died. A chill settled over him, sinking into his skin and leaching out any hope of happiness. He could almost feel the hunger. The Soulless lust.

Kiren silenced his mind and squeezed the chain in his palm, the false medallion. No familiar energy radiated from this charm. It would offer him no protection, but the Soulless didn't know that. He would exchange it for the real necklace tonight, the one his daughter had carried through the ages and hidden, the same one he'd wrapped around Alexia's neck before she stepped through time and left him here, alone.

He stopped several feet from the woman, focused on her profile.

Her chin lifted, crimson eyes closing. "This is a surprise." Her voice was like a toy boat being held steady on troubled waters, ready to tumble into the cascade the instant it was released.

She was starving.

"You look strong, Sarah." Kiren nodded. "But are you strong enough to battle the hunger while away from scorched earth?"

Her chest puffed out. "I was searching for John."

That made sense. Within the collective consciousness of the Soulless, she would be able to locate her husband on moonless nights.

He waved back the way he'd come, to the inn, to scorched earth and the safety that neutralized her hunger. "Walk with me?"

She followed him.

"Alexia has not returned," he said softly.

"Mmm." The trembling in her voice bordered on despair, but she straightened her shoulders and turned ravenous, crimson eyes on him, eyes that had once been a buoyant olive. "I think she was meant not to return here."

Kiren swallowed hard. Alexia's final words echoed through his mind, driving the desperation that could not be quenched: *"No matter when I am, I will always be yours."*

The woman who so resembled one of the Passionate faced him. "Why have you tracked me down?"

"I am leaving. Leaving for good."

She faced him fully, a quirk in her brow.

"When you find your husband, tell him I am sorry, for everything."

"You are going after her, into the past?"

He bit down, grinding his teeth. If there was any way to save his Alexia from her fate, he would do it. He didn't care that his necklace was missing. He'd have it. Tonight. If it was possible, she would be restored to his care.

# One

# *Five-Hundred Years Back, Five Months Forward*

The ground exploded next to Alexia's foot. She stumbled backward, her broken-sword-turned-dagger clasped tightly in one fist as she scanned the horizon through raining debris. Men writhed across the beach in rawhide jerkins or white tunics bearing red crosses, the chaos of clashing metal like the roar of hungry lions.

Lions. The symbol woven into the enemy's armlets and stamped upon their wooden shields—an emblem that marked them as King Edward's elite killing force.

*Lovely.* Now the enemy had a catapult. Not that their sheer numbers weren't bad enough. On a ship beyond the war-torn beachfront stood the wooden monster that had launched a boulder and scarred the earth next to her.

A jolt in her womb brought her hand up, the babe within pounding to break out and join in the battle. Soon. Very soon her child would enter the world, and her chance to save the Passionate would end. "You will have your time, little one."

Alexia's mere nineteen years were far too few to be with child and centuries away from her husband and home, far too few for her to be in the midst of a war. She clutched the pendant dangling around her neck, heavy metal too dull to hold any monetary value, and focused on the power stored within, pulling at its strength. Golden energy trickled into her fingers, like being filled with sunlight. The world around her slowed.

Weapons crept toward their intended targets, and battle cries thrummed, a rumbling bass.

Five months ago she'd discovered this raggedy band of talented people like herself, the Passionate. Unlike the powerful sub-society of Passionate she'd left behind, these were vagabonds and nomads, a struggling force who gathered others like themselves and fled to safety. They were more suited to living in holes and caves than behind four walls. Many had been rescued from noblemen who enslaved them and used their talents for gain, which brought about the current conflict: too many of the rich had lost their precious prisoners. They begged King Edward to send the Knights Templar—his witch hunters—after their slaves.

Alexia stepped through the slowed conflict, her burlap skirts pulling against her swollen womb like chainmail made for a giant. Dirty faces twisted about her.

Always dirty.

Her own hands were covered in grime, the nails corroded black. What she wouldn't give for a bath in Father's estate!

But Father's estate had not been built yet, and it would not be for another several hundred years. The best she could hope for was a warm rain or chilly river. At least to staunch the smell.

A white haze curled off to her left—one of the Passionate who could transport people across the globe in an instant through mist. Velia. She wrapped herself around a child and would fade to nothing in a heartbeat. The woman had been frantically clearing their band out, carrying them one by one to safety—an effort that would cost her days of sickness and exhaustion.

Alexia was the diversion, along with others who could fight back. She and this battered band had evaded the king's forces for so long, but somehow they'd been tracked to this remote island.

She dragged past another distraction—Amos. Pitch spilled from his fingers, creating a cocoon of midnight that blinded the enemy. Chocolate-hued hair hung to his shoulders, copper skin glowing in the gloom.

With his ability to summon darkness, he had hidden Alexia and their band many times over the months they'd been allies. He was the leader of the Passionate, and a powerful one at that. It was strange working with him. She drew a hand across her neck, remembering how he had slit her throat in the future, how Kiren had saved her with his healing gift.

*Kiren.*

She bit down and pressed forward.

*One battle at a time.*

Alexia reached the water. She had done this only once before, and despite her sweating palms, she stepped onto the near-still swells. Water seeped around her foot like thick clay. The glassy waves reflected her countenance—which she would be able to see if not for her oversized paunch. The waves led to an ocean far deeper than she could breech, and she had never learned to swim.

She hurried forward several yards. A rope ladder dangled from the side of the ship, solid as stone in her grasp.

Kingsmen surged around the catapult in slow motion, loading it with another large boulder as she topped the deck. This was more than Edward's force. These men had been sent by the allied kings and Church to destroy the abominations, but their secret agenda was to capture all Passionate.

Killing for no real reason.

Alexia took a deep breath of crypt-like air, the heaviness that settled in improper time. Now to draw the men away from the catapult so she could dispose of it. She dropped Kiren's pendant, releasing the captive minutes.

Time leapt back into sequence.

Four soldiers jumped and shrieked at her sudden appearance. Swords flashed in the late afternoon rays, bloodied by the sinking sun.

The men rushed her, and she slowed time once more, stepping past them. Next to the machine of death, she eyed the thick ropes and splintering frame. If only she had the gift of fire.

And then she noticed the wheels. Mounted at the cusp of the ship, all the catapult needed was a good shove. She sliced the securing ropes with a single swipe of her dagger. The added pressure once time resumed would do the rest.

Alexia backed up several steps and charged, releasing time a little more with each step. The momentum of her time-inhibited dash added force. She slammed into the catapult with her shoulder. The wood groaned. Wheels squeaked. The machine grated forward.

She doubled over, her body protesting the movement with an intense tightening as she lost her grip on time. Her child should not make an appearance yet. Not for another eight weeks. She needed to be careful.

Men shouted behind her, turning, befuddled. Their swords shook. She faced them full on, challenging the lot.

*Hiss.*

She stopped time completely and whirled.

An arrow hung, mid-flight, only inches from her chest.

She huffed. *How incredibly unkind.*

Alexia stepped away from the deadly tip and squinted through the sprawling limbs on the beach.

There.

A bow dipped as the frozen archer reached for another arrow from the quiver at his back.

She took hold of Kiren's pendant. Warmth flooded into her fingers, filling her with strength, and she crossed the water once more. This was war. Death was expected, but to target the only woman in sight? And one with child? She halted before him, slipped her dagger beneath the bowstring and released time. It snapped.

The man jolted backward and landed on his rump.

She crossed her arms and spoke in old English. The words sounded odd to her, a language she'd practiced with Mae in the future, preparing for this time. Even after months of using them they felt clumsy, but the meaning was what mattered: "Were you aiming for me?"

Crash!

The catapult broke the water and launched a wave over the side of the ship, sweeping three soldiers overboard into dagger-like splinters.

Would it knock one or two of them unconscious? Would they drown? What if one was speared through? She groaned. No more. She would not be the cause of anymore death.

Alexia gathered her strength and reached back through time, into the past five seconds, bracing for the toll it would take. Blackness flashed before her as the world reset. She held time still and stood several seconds, allowing her body to ease into this moment. She did not like going back in time. It was dangerous. Traveling more than a couple moments could alter reality forever, but she had done it when necessary.

The catapult dangled over the edge of the ship, ready to break the glassy swells.

Alexia grabbed the three men. She released the seconds to a slow draw and pulled her enemies to safety. A weight hung at the back of her brain, the exhaustion from manipulating time. Satisfied the wave wouldn't take the men to their death, she let go of time.

The catapult splashed down.

The soldiers stood dazed, water lapping at their feet. One gasped and lifted his sword. Her weapon's hilt felt natural in her grasp, ready to respond to the threat, but the world shifted in her mind.

*She faced a horde of Soulless, their eyes crimson, talons extended to tear the flesh, their hunger insatiable. They had come to take what mattered most to her: Her love. Her soul.*

She blinked the vision free as the blade flashed toward her throat.

Alexia ducked. The sword sheared off a strand of curled dark hair. She fell back. *Kill him,* her inner voice shrieked. *He would do the same to you and all your kind. Protect them by eliminating one more threat.*

It was true. He would come again and again because he believed his cause was just, or because the king's pay supported his family. His hunger was no different than the Soulless.

But she couldn't take a life.

Never again.

She was here to undo all the mistakes of her past, the future, to stop those murders from ever happening and save her dearest sister, Sarah, from succumbing to the worst of fates.

Alexia yanked time to a halt, the air thickening around her. Her clothing dragged at her limbs.

The babe lurched within. She was pushing too hard and the child was warning her. The last thing she needed was to begin labor in the midst of war…and forfeit her life. What she really wanted was Kiren—his peaceful alternatives and confidence. His compassion and steadiness. His ability to read others and guide them toward the best solution. But she had none of those, only her ability to stop the minutes or alter time.

She faced the soldier's threatening weapon, seized his arm, and released time. He jumped.

"There is another way," Alexia said.

Soldiers charged. A tunnel of darkness roared up around them, sealing them into an onyx haze that emanated from the shore. Alexia shoved her attacker into the gloom. Amos stepped through the waves, waist deep, both arms lifted her direction, holding the soldiers within a midnight cloud.

"We are all cleared out!" he shouted and turned his head toward a white silhouette on the shore. Long hair floated translucently behind the mist child, as if she were half in and half out of reality, ready to instantly appear on some foreign continent.

"All?" Alexia called back, waving to him.

Amos motioned her forward. "You are one mighty distraction." He pointed to her baby girth. "But you are wasting precious time and energy."

A soldier stumbled out of the darkness and over the edge of the ship.

"Final retreat!" Amos shouted.

"Take him first," Alexia called to the child of the mist. The Passionate needed their leader safe.

Velia burst into nothingness and faded.

War cries broke through the midnight pitch. Alexia hefted her dagger, the one that had slain numerous Soulless, the one that had stained her soul. But those creatures did not exist here. Only men whose souls were debatably tainted as darkly.

Metal flashed toward her.

She lifted her weapon.

Steel clanged. Her muscles shook under her enemy's blade. She shoved his weapon away, the brush of chilling mist the only evidence that her friend was being swept away to safety. And then the world blanched into whiteness, and she was hurling through nothingness, reminding herself not to breathe.

# Two

# *Machines of War*

Wintry fingers loosened around Alexia's arm.

Haze pulled away, and she stumbled over uneven clods of dirt, weeds tickling her ankles. Decaying stones walled in an overgrown courtyard. Vines crawled over the ancient stones in the haze of pre-dawn, their majesty lost ages ago to war and decline. A stream gurgled nearby, hidden in a veil of trees.

Velia gave her a nod. Even having spent nearly half a year with the woman, Alexia had a difficult time defining her mute friend's features. She couldn't decide if Velia was predominantly mist or corporeal.

Amos stepped between them, facing the hazy woman. "Kindly retrieve the healer."

Velia gave a shallow bow and melted away.

"The healer?" Alexia asked. They had access to a healer, like Kiren in the future, and they'd suffered all this time?

"A hesitant ally." He grimaced. "I daresay he will not be pleased in being brought here, but he is needed." Amos patted her shoulder and turned to a boy of ten years who knelt on the ground, panting, with a gash across his chest. No child should witness the terrors of war and bear its mark. Yet this one had seen enough battle to turn him into a warrior at such a tender age.

Like all of them.

She touched her center. Like her child would.

"Will the child be waybreakin' today?" Regin halted next to her, sliding on a pair of leather gloves as he lifted an eyebrow at the hand on her womb. His black hair was slicked back with sweat from his exertions in the battle.

His was one of the few faces Alexia had recognized after reaching this time. As she'd helped Amos gather in more of the Passionate, she'd come upon Regin in a Jewish stronghold, a secret weapon against the crusaders determined to control the holy city. She recalled meeting him in her own time and being warned of his mischief. No one could make him do something he didn't want. They'd end up snoring in some public location, stripped down to their undergarments while he laughed and made his way across town. He was one of the first to join the Passionate after her arrival in this time—mostly because of his self-declared hatred for the monarchy, the Church, and anyone else who thought themselves mighty enough to dictate people's existence.

"Are you offering to make me sleep through the pain of birth?" she asked.

He chuckled. "Be that what you wish, though missing the babe's first wail would be a right shame." He squirmed. "And I can'na abide gore. You'd be at nature's mercy after I fainted like a wee lassie."

"Is that all it takes? A little blood and the unstoppable Regin falls unconscious himself?" She wiggled her fingers at him. "But you have fought through every battle with us."

He shuddered. "Aye." He tapped the side of his head. "Gravy. I picture...*it* as me mum's gut-gouging gravy. Used to sneak it to the dogs while she served me da." He fastened a cloth about his mouth and nose with a nod to a line of prostrate bodies. "We be testin' me mettle today."

Her stomach clenched. "Are any dead?"

"Aye." He turned. Amos and two others bandaged cuts while whispering prayers for the wounded. "Favian took a blow to the skull while shieldin' the littlins." They both bowed their heads. "Julene received a blade to the gut before Mae could act."

Alexia's head snapped up. "Little Julene?"

Regin nodded.

A child, not yet four years of age, taken. Her stomach roiled. Tears wetted her cheeks, the kind that came far too easily these days. It was hard enough to bring one of the Passionate through childbirth without losing either mother or child, but for one to fall at sword point...

It must be destroying Mae that she couldn't stop it.

Alexia searched the group for her friend and found the woman in the distance, head bowed, arms wrapped around her frail form. Despite her gentle nature, Mae craved death. It was her gift, and her curse. Metal could stop the Passionate from using their abilities, causing a nauseating illness and an inability to focus. It didn't work on Alexia because she was half human, but she'd seen its results. Iron to stop them. Gold to kill.

They'd found a gold cuff in the wreckage of one rescue, and Mae wore it around her wrist at all times. Any other Passionate would be dead, but not Mae. She was too strong. The gold stopped her from draining all life out of the world around her, but it also repelled the Passionate. Not Alexia. She had been helping Mae learn how to control her gift, just as Mae would one day do for her. Most people gave Mae a wide berth...other than Regin. Perhaps he empathized, because he couldn't touch others without putting them to sleep.

Regin approached Mae, his voice a soothing murmur. She looked up, her ice-blue eyes both seeing and beautiful. The woman Alexia had left in the future was blind and one of the dearest people she knew. And Kiren had trusted her entirely.

"The wounded are stable."

Alexia jumped at Amos's baritone. It was nothing like the wheezing rasp she recalled from the future. When he was Soulless. He stood half a head taller than her, his gaze fixed on the distraught Mae and commiserating Regin.

"Gather Deamus for me?" He pointed to the man crouched beneath the trees. "I will talk those two down from the hill. It is time we counseled."

"I wish you safety."

He gave her a smile. "Safer for me than for you."

She shook her head. Amos was a conscientious leader who governed by counseling with the most powerful of the Passionate in all major decisions. He had accepted her upon meeting, and over the months, she'd become his lieutenant.

Deamus knelt in the shadows, clutching scrolls to his chest and panting as if he couldn't catch his breath. Alexia dropped down next to him. The man was awkwardly skinny with a very prominent nose and a quick smile she had instantly liked. He wasn't like the others. Beauty had very little place in him, except for in his soul, and like her, he loved the written word.

She leaned in to catch his gaze as he scoured the ground. "Have you lost something?"

He jolted like he hadn't seen her. Likely, he hadn't. "The magnifiers." His accent had struck her as strange when they first met, slightly guttural, clipping the *e*'s.

He'd lost his spectacles. She hadn't told him yet that spectacles were an invention of a later age. They'd had some difficulty fashioning them out of leather and window shards to her clumsy instructions—with many failures—but the spectacles had made all the difference to her fumbling friend. She pulled them from on top of his head and handed them over.

He blew out a breath. "You rescue me again."

"Beware, Deamus. Much more of this and we shall have to call you a damsel in distress."

He chuckled and sat back, spilling the four scrolls he'd been clutching, then fumbled to gather them up.

She snatched the last one for him. "And what are these?"

He grinned a tuck-lipped, closed-mouth smile, making his cheeks bulge, a child who had done something naughty. "The knight's instructions for our capture."

"And how did you come about them?"

His grin widened and he waved her closer. She leaned. He whispered, "I snuck into the ship before we ran away."

She laughed with him. They might finally discover who was behind all of these attacks and how to stop them. "Bring these. We are to counsel."

The scrolls tumbled from his arms, and he scurried after them again. Alexia pushed off the ground and followed him until he stood, dwarfing her like a parent with a child. He had been the first, the very first of the Passionate she encountered after arriving in this world. Amos accepted him because he came with Alexia, but Deamus's clumsy antics left their leader huffing. She found them endearing.

They joined four others, Amos, Regin, Mae, and Lucian—a man of the orient. Regin waved Alexia to a seat. Deamus crouched and carefully placed his parchments on the ground, tucking his spectacles into place and conscientiously ignoring them as he opened the first scroll.

"No more of this." Tears had cut clean lines down Mae's dirty face. "They are weaker than us. I could have stopped them, all of them. There was no need to…" She covered her face.

Alexia placed a hand on Mae's back, and her friend tensed. The gold bangle staved Mae's hunger, but it couldn't stop her conscience. Alexia knew how her friend suffered under the weight of guilt, how every life she'd consumed hung on her heart. Given the choice, Alexia would never add to that burden.

"And where would it end?" Lucian asked, his voice lilting under his strange accent which cut out *l*'s, *n*'s. "More would come in their place. Should we destroy the whole human family?"

Alexia swallowed hard. Lucian had a gift of premonition. He couldn't see all things, but he caught glimpses of things to come and had steered them away from several tragedies.

"We cannot kill all the humans," Amos grunted, as if that ever was an option.

"Mayhaps just the ones killin' us?" Regin injected, the bandana tied over his mouth and nose muffling his words.

Deamus gasped. He leapt to his feet and held up one of the scrolls, spectacles teetering on his nose bridge as he reread the parchment. He turned the paper, waving it slowly so everyone could see the words. Except no one other than Alexia could read them. She grabbed the communiqué. The slowness with which she read shamed her, but not only was this language newer to her, it was written in a curled script that made it difficult to decipher one letter from the next.

"You see it?" Deamus asked, looking directly at her.

Her cheeks flamed and she read faster, but the words swimming before her didn't make sense. "I do not understand. If what I am reading is accurate, we have a traitor in our midst?"

Regin growled through his handkerchief. "That be how they found us—on the island, in the desert, at the caves…"

Deamus turned the parchment back around, cradling it like a baby as he read on silently.

Regin cleared his throat. "Methinks it may be time for war."

Alexia stared at the man. Regin had been peaceful these many months, a man who would rather lull someone into submission than by force. If he was turning toward this idea… She bowed her head. "Let us not fight the wrong war."

"What war should we be fighting," Lucian faced her, "if not the one for survival?"

9

It was time. She exhaled a heavy breath. "I have been with you longer than I had desired, too long I fear. I had hoped to prevent what is coming without revealing or involving all of you, but it cannot be prevented. You have been patient with me as I withheld my origin and purpose, but I believe it is time to share." She braced herself and lifted her chin. "I am here to stop the Soulless."

# Three

# *Travelers*

Five sets of eyes burned into Alexia, their confusion bubbling to the surface, ready to boil over and bombard her in a firestorm of questions.

Alexia lifted her hand, offering her palm. "Allow me to show you." It was possible to open one's memories to another of the Passionate through physical contact, to *share* one's experiences without uttering a word.

Looks were exchanged and hands reached for Alexia's extended one. Even Deamus abandoned his scrolls. A shudder ran up her arm as person after person touched her open palm, their energy shocking her own, evidence they belonged to the same bloodline. She opened her mind, allowing all of them in through the physical connection. She showed them a condensed truth while omitting faces and details lest the knowledge should upset the future:

*Herself in the year 1768, sixteen and oblivious to the Passionate, a baron's daughter with no hope of a decent marriage other than to increase some gentleman's fortune. The night a child of the Passionate, Bellezza, murdered Alexia's neighbor. How she caught a glimpse of the blue-eyed man who haunted her dreams, and how he returned to kidnap the vicious child. Alexia followed the breadcrumbs and discovered haunted House of Stark. She learned of her half-blood heritage and saved the leader of the Passionate while barely escaping the Soulless: undying monsters who lived only in the darkness and ached to consume her kind. They had once been Passionate, but their essence had been robbed, leaving them hungry to replace it and unable to quench their hunger. They attacked the Passionate on moonless nights, draining them of their vitality, but no matter what they took, it was never enough. Worse yet, every Passionate soul they consumed also became Soulless.*

Alexia paused, allowing the council to digest what they'd been shown. Then she plunged on:

*She had fallen in love, followed by a war with the Soulless, her wedding, the near demise of the Passionate, the child growing in her womb and the hope of preventing the Soulless from coming into existence. Starting with her journey to this time…where she would disappear from existence—probably from dying in childbirth.*

"You are from the future." Amos stumbled back from her.

She nodded. "Five hundred years."

Lucian's eyes narrowed. "You do more than move very, very quickly."

"I control time." Alexia spread her hands in apology. "Though I fear I may have come to the wrong moment to prevent the Soulless from becoming."

"We will not let you die," Mae vowed.

Deamus sagged to his knees, reaching for his precious scrolls.

Regin tugged his kerchief down. "Be my understandin' addled, or can you change the past? Any past?"

She shook her head. "I have failed before, and succeeded, though I have never undertaken such an important endeavor. And in such a state." She indicated her womb. "Changing things is dangerous, but the Soulless must never be born."

In the silence, they listened to children chattering and the murmur of loved ones. If she failed, those voices would fall into hungry hisses and eternally tortured souls. Her fist tightened.

Amos crossed his arms. "What can we do?"

"I have been searching for a way to stop it, but I do not even know the precise moment the Soulless will be created."

They all turned on Lucian. He grunted and took Alexia's hand, focused on the distance, the color fading from his face, lips falling lax. "I see vibrant hues, giant white walls, a crystal palace, lands of fire and lands of ice…"

Paper crinkled.

Deamus's chest rose and fell in quick succession. His mouth opened and closed, then opened again in a mumble.

"What is it you have to say? Speak up," Mae encouraged.

The gangly man tucked his spectacles in a pocket, gaze down. "You, you, none of you would…no. It is not…"

"Deamus," Alexia said, and he focused on her. "Tell me."

"I-I-I thought you came from there. I thought you were here to free me and that we would return…"

New understanding dawned on her as she recalled the moment they'd met:

*Hairs prickled on the back of her neck. The willow tree before her trembled as if the ground were shaking, but Alexia felt no tremors. Warmth pressed against her chest. Warmth, suddenly fire.*

*She grabbed the chain around her neck and pulled the pendant away. The charm glowed yellow, purifying to white.*

*The tree shuddered and bent, like a ribbon collapsing to the ground. She jumped back. It writhed, a branchy snake, and shrank inward. The largest two branches melted into arms. Lumps across the trunk diminished into a robed torso, a long torso. Wild leaves feathered down into strands of dark hair as long as her own.*

*The medallion cooled to a dull gray, buzzing with energy.*

*Alexia tucked the necklace beneath her tunic. Kiren had always kept it concealed, and she thought that a good practice, except when it attempted to cook her. The pendant quivered against her as if it might burst from the power stored within, vibrating like it had before she drained it with her jump through centuries.*

*The man's chest heaved. He braced an elbow on the ground, hair obscuring his face. He lifted a hand, turned it before his face, and laughed. His shoulders froze. A shudder passed through him, and the color bled out of his hair until it was dark blonde. He turned to her, eyes wide. He was a younger man—not many years older than herself. His eyebrows lifted, and his mouth popped open in a vulnerable, almost comical grin.* "You freed me!"

*She conscientiously placed a hand over her hidden necklace.* "Why were you a, a tree?"

*The man sat up, watching her like he expected angel wings to burst from hiding.* "It was an accident, I-I forgot to..." *His cheeks reddened.* "I-it's a long story." *He brightened.* "But you saved me. You have come to take me home?"

Alexia had assumed his home was a hut in some local village. "Where is it you came from?"

Deamus motioned upward.

Alexia followed his aim to the warming sky, stars fading. "From the stars?"

Both hands disappeared behind his back as he considered her closely. Something in his stare solidified, and he leaned forward, lifting an arm and pointing. "There. Out beyond those lights waits another earth, one where...where we live without fear. Only those with *Passionate* blood dwell there."

The idea whirled her head like a top he was spinning just to watch her grow dizzy.

Amos stepped between them. "Tell me about this place."

Deamus backed away, gaze shifting shyly to the ground.

Alexia touched his arm. "Tell me."

"The other land was *created* long ago by a powerful man. There has never been a man more powerful."

To create an entire world... Alexia still couldn't quite fathom it. Only God possessed that kind of power.

"When humanity began destroying...the Passionate, he knew he had to stop them." He brought his fists together and pulled them apart to illustrate. "It would mean separating two worlds. He studied and gathered and worked for decades to make his dream a reality, and at last, he did it."

Alexia gave him a skeptical frown. "Separated two worlds out of one?"

"I heard me somethin' like this story before." Regin scratched his chin. "Weren't there two sons and some kind of battle?"

Deamus stilled and shifted away as if he'd forgotten about his larger audience.

"Do continue," Alexia urged.

"A bridge was erected, a bridge of light that allowed our kind to pass over, but the cost of channeling so much power was the man's life." Deamus bit his lip. His chin shook and he looked away. Quiet accosted them. Alexia wondered if he would continue when he straightened his shoulders, lips puckered in a frown. "He left two sons." He gave a quick nod at Regin. "Both studied his arts and followed in his path, but one was tempted and drawn into dark powers, the kind that consume the soul." A line appeared between his eyebrows. "The other watched over and protected the Passionate—mostly from his brother."

Alexia glanced up at the disappearing stars and shivered, feeling suddenly very small. "And how do you know of this other world?"

Deamus's head tilted, hope shimmering in his gaze. "It is my home."

A shell of silence dropped over them.

*Home.* That single word shot a pang through her chest, seizing her lungs. Alexia's brain stuttered. Her vision shifted to a forested place, unique blooms dotting the small clearing where Kiren stood, gazing upon her with the purest love…

Alexia opened her palm and brushed a finger across the hidden prongs of her wedding ring, a coral diamond with five teardrop petals. Amos had advised her to keep the gems hidden, but she was unwilling to remove the band. It was all she had left.

She gripped Kiren's necklace. She could not be *home.* Not now. Not ever again.

"The bridge opened again not many years ago." Deamus made a path to the sky with one arm. "I passed through from that world to this, searching for the High King's heir, and, and"—he blushed—"became a tree."

He hadn't told anyone but her how that had occurred—that he'd been manipulating the world around him without taking precautions for a backlash. She felt quite solemnly she should keep his secret.

His gaze dropped to her hand, the one attempting to loosen the bolt of pain stealing through her chest. "I have been searching for a way to go back. Alexia, you might have one."

"Me?"

He nodded at her chest.

She pulled her hand away from the charm hidden beneath her bodice, and snapped a quick look between the council members.

"It would be a safe place." Deamus twisted the hem of his sleeve.

"They might never become Soulless," Alexia finished for him. She took a cleansing breath. He assumed she could access the power in the necklace to open this gateway, and perhaps she could. She may very well hold the key to another realm.

Regin untied the handkerchief from his neck. "I like this plan. This is a great plan. We should do this plan, thing."

Lucian nodded along. Mae shrugged.

Deamus straightened to his full, intimidating height and spoke again. "Lucian was describing that world. If he can see it in our future…"

Amos stroked his chin, finally smiling at Deamus. "You think you can open this gate?"

"I…" He ducked and rubbed a hand over the back of his neck. "If the stars align, and I find the right place to open it from, and I can borrow the strength…"

Alexia bit her tongue. Deamus's gift was extremely unique. He could borrow energy and shape it into something completely new. He'd done it once in the desert to turn sand into water when there was none, and when a fire consumed all the bedding in camp, he reshaped stones into bedrolls. Both times, the entire camp was left winded and weak for days.

"It will have to be put to the whole." Amos nodded. "In the meantime, watch the stars and find this place where the gateway can be opened." He bent and snatched the scrolls Deamus had been safeguarding. Deamus bobbed forward after his treasures, but stopped himself as Amos rose. "The rest of us will find this traitor, and not a word of this escapes our circle." He shoved the parchments into Alexia's arms. "You will find us more clues about this person."

"Of course." She nodded.

Mist melted over the ruins.

Amos turned. "Ah! And about time. How long does it take to locate one measly friar?"

Warmth licked the tree line, the tangerine of a promising dawn. Alexia's long-dead but not-yet-born mother had called the sunrise hope. She believed it still—the hope that she would keep the Soulless from existing, the hope that the world would be better because she'd given up her husband, her family, her life.

A man stepped out of the mist, one dressed in a gray friar's robes, but far too young by her account to be a friar.

Ginger hair fell in waves, framing a profile she had dreamed and loved most her life, one it had broken her heart to leave.

But it couldn't be.

Soul-stopping blue eyes scanned the camp and landed on her.

Alexia's heart stuttered and thumped into her throat.

## Four

## Awake

*"You think you can open this gate?"*

The entity snapped awake. It shifted in its shapeless murk, bumbling into the invisible walls of its confinement. Hunger coiled at its center. The time had come, and it was ready to be free. After centuries of stasis, it would finally know true power again. The long night was over, and it was ready to rain on the earth like burning hail from the blackened heavens.

*Yes, open the gateway, little man.*

# Five

# *Ocean Deep*

As if Alexia's thoughts had summoned him, there he stood—the subject of her every dream, every fantasy, every hope. His straight nose, imperial cheekbones, and eyes deep enough to encompass an entire ocean, a blue she'd never expected to see again: the color of the sky right before dawn, the purest azure riddled in specks of light like the fading stars.

Her feet moved before she'd paused to think.

He shouldn't be here.

He wasn't supposed to be here.

He told her he wouldn't be. It was impossible, and yet somehow he must have followed her through time!

Alexia barely contained a happy scream. Her heart thundered through her chest, filling the world with the toll of her happiness. Kiren had found a way. Of course he had found a way. There was no love so full or devoted as his!

His gaze turned to her as she dropped the scrolls, threw her arms around his neck, and pressed her lips to his.

He didn't kiss her back.

Alexia frowned. Why wouldn't he kiss her back? Had he come with dire news, something he needed to communicate right away? Or perhaps he too was astonished, still unable to believe they had found one another.

Something snapped between them, and his hands found her shoulders, his mouth molding to hers. She pressed herself more fully into him, and his grip tightened on her arms.

He jerked free, leaning slightly forward, staring into her eyes while he panted, brows low. His wide eyes swallowed her whole in the expanse of his vast ocean.

But it wasn't love that filled his stare. Confusion. Shock. A hint of fear.

"Kiren?" she whispered.

His mouth dropped open and he shoved her away.

She stumbled to a stop, arms wide to regain her balance.

His mouth formed a rigid line. Jaw muscles flexed as his gaze traveled down and halted on her round center. One fist balled and he took a step back.

She didn't understand. What had happened to him? Had his memories been taken or altered by the journey through time?

Alexia reached for him.

He straightened up, rolling his shoulders away from her, but something wasn't quite right. He still smelled of sweetened oak, his frame every inch the man she remembered...except that stubble shaded his jaw.

His jaw.

Kiren was always clean shaven. When she'd asked him about it, he allowed the hair to grow just enough to show her the bald line along his scar.

His scar.

His lovely, white scar that cut from eye to chin.

This Kiren had no scar.

## Six

## Earlier that Day

Kiren tucked both hands into his sleeves, kept his head down, and walked through the township as if he were on urgent business. He was, just not the kind he wanted anyone learning about.

"Arik, you cannot help people who do not want to be helped," Zeph said, keeping pace although he'd been dismissed more than once.

"Can I not?" Kiren retorted, thankful for the cover of night at this ridiculous hour—the thieving hour. Zeph had rushed after him without a cloak or head covering, and not only did his nub-sized horns catch the moonlight, but his wings strained obviously at the back of his tunic. Kiren even thought he caught a flick of his friend's tail.

"It is a stupid idea, and it is going to bring stupid trouble."

"Like someone mistaking you for a demon?" Kiren asked, smirking out the corner of his mouth. Zeph's gray-green wings didn't exactly appear angelic, even if they were made of feathers. "We can always play *the holy friar against the monster* scenario. *Again.*"

Zeph scoffed. "I only came to keep you from getting yourself killed."

Kiren scowled. He didn't want anyone feeling obligated to him that way, not anymore. No one's blood was going to be on his head.

"I do not need your help, Zeph."

"Good. I am not offering help."

No matter what he said, he was glad Zephaniah had chosen to stay by his side, not just tonight, but in the journey he'd been pursuing. The harpy's son was only a season older than Kiren, and though he preferred chilly cliff faces and brutal winds, he endured the ground for the truest friendship Kiren had known since his twin sister's disappearance. Zeph had whisked him out of danger enough times he'd lost count.

They stopped. The wattle and daub walls before them were framed by dark wood and dual balconies on the second floor—the sheriff's home, the only home in the hamlet with a slate roof.

"Do not expect me to follow you." Zeph crossed his arms.

"I never do."

Kiren tugged his monastic robes into his rope belt, gave Zeph a *watch-this* nod, and leapt, catching the underbeams of a balcony. He pulled himself up the side, dropping noiselessly over the rail. Who needed wings?

Zephaniah rolled his eyes from the ground below.

Shutters had been fastened, barring the window except for patterned slats that allowed for ventilation. Curtains obscured Kiren's view beyond. He stilled and listened: one set of lungs in the room, the heartbeat at a steady, slow pace. He stretched his senses. The next room over housed a snoring sleeper, someone of significantly larger proportions. He'd found the right room.

Kiren pulled the shutters back and pushed the curtain aside. Anyone else would have had a difficult time picking her out of the dark, but there she lay, the young woman with ochre hair. By all appearances, she was the picture of innocence. A perfect specimen...except for where one leg ended in a nub. He pulled himself through the opening, a tight fit, and grimaced as floorboards creaked beneath his feet.

She stirred.

He took the three steps between them and hovered over her. It felt wrong, being in her room, watching her sleep, but this was the only way this would work.

He'd be quick then.

Deep breath. He rubbed his hands together and placed one on her shoulder where the blanket and her chemise had slipped free.

The pulse beneath her skin called to him. Circulating blood took him down, through the chambers of her heart, lower, to the pinched spot in her thigh where a leg had never fully developed. A thin limb dangled off her knee, impossible to use. He could work with that. Her father had been carrying her down the street when Kiren met them. The man had brushed Kiren aside when asked to see the young woman's malady, and she had hooded her eyes with the shame that befell all with such physical imperfections. But when Kiren said he could heal her, her gaze had flashed up at him, a hopeful, begging thing, snuffed out by her father's gruff laughter. *"And what price would I have to pay for such a miracle?"* He had shoved Kiren into a wall and continued on.

Angry as he was at the cynical man, Kiren had compassion on the daughter. *Grow*, he told the leg.

Her blood flow increased. The cells in her withered limb bloomed and doubled. They thickened in muscle and tissue, stretching to match her other limb. Bone lengthened and broke off into the correct pieces, tied together by forming sinews. Strength drained through Kiren's fingers, his arms trembling as power pulled at his core. He breathed deeply, clenching his teeth.

The girl's mouth popped wide in a scream. He threw a hand over her mouth, muffling as much noise as possible.

Skin smoothed. Hairs grew. Toes stretched outward. Nails pressed through the flesh.

The girl jerked away from his touch.

Kiren released her, panting.

Eyes met his in the darkness, a gaze full of awe, full of gratitude, full of wonder. Her mouth opened and he pressed a finger to her lips, silencing her. He'd done what he came to do, now it was time to make a speedy escape before he was discovered.

Kiren backed away and the floor groaned. He cringed and glanced at the door.

The young woman sat up. She lifted her new limb, flexing the toes and flattening them. She opened her mouth.

"I was never here," he whispered urgently. "Go back to sleep. This is all but a strange dream."

"Are you an angel?" Her eyes danced, chest heaving like she was about to cry or scream. "However can I repay you?"

Kiren angled toward the window, suppressing a twinge of annoyance. *Do not get me caught?* "Sleep."

She slid her legs out of bed, rubbing her hands down them and breathing heavily. Her feet smacked the noisy floorboards.

He clenched his fists.

She shoved upward and teetered forward, stumbling, arms flailing. Kiren leapt forward and caught her. He opened his ears to the rest of the house, certain her clumsiness had awakened someone.

"You are too beautiful to be of the cloth." Her breath warmed his chin.

Kiren froze. Her lips curled in a demure smile, wide, insistent. It was not uncommon for women to like his appearance, but he'd never landed himself in this precarious a circumstance. He laughed uneasily and let her go, backing up a step.

Noise from the next room pulled his head up.

"I know how to reward you." She threw her arms around his neck and yanked him to her, slamming her mouth into his.

Whoa. How had that happened?

It took him all of three seconds to process how dangerous this was—not just to his physical health if someone should bust through the door, but to his deeper core. He was not going to be bound to a woman. No way. Never.

He tore himself free and stumbled backward, slamming into the wall next to the door. The floor moaned under his feet.

And the door flew open.

Zeph had been right. This was a really bad idea.

The sheriff's nightshirt caught the window light like a bulbous onion. He froze in the doorway, fixed on his daughter standing on two legs.

"With my fondest wishes." Kiren bowed and ducked under the man's arm out the door. Fingers scraped at his robe, but he twisted and dodged, smacking into the wall of a narrow hallway and bouncing off. Miraculously, his feet were still under him. He kept moving, sprinting down groaning floorboards.

Feet pounded the timber behind him. "Stop!"

Nope. That wasn't going to happen.

Kiren hurdled a stair rail and leapt for the floor. He landed hard, jarring his teeth and rattling his brain. The man above him growled and thundered down the stairs.

Kiren stumbled forward, focused on the gleam of moonlight between curtains. All he had to do was get to the other side, and Zeph would fly them both away to safety. Of course that would mean he could never come to this township again, but he couldn't change that now.

All for a leg.

"Stop him!"

Movement in the shadows. Kiren zagged, startled by the arms reaching for him.

Of course the sheriff had a servant. He should have known.

He twirled around the shadowy figure, rolled back to back, and dove for the window. Shutters burst open, scraping his shoulders as he laughed.

This was what he lived for—that pumping of the blood, the thrill, having gotten away with something that was entirely forbidden.

He braced to slam the ground.

And remained suspended in midair.

*What the—?*

Zephaniah crouched in the shrubbery, watching wide-eyed, his wings fully extended.

White clouded the corners of Kiren's vision. It wrapped around him, tightening like a vise.

"No, no-no-no-no-no!" he shouted, but he couldn't stop what was happening.

# Seven

# *Familiar Faces*

"Who are you?" Kiren's voice hit Alexia like an iceberg.

She opened her mouth to reply, but words escaped her. Winter filled his countenance. He lacked more than just a scar. His skin didn't possess the glow of their bond.

Alexia sucked in a shaky breath and turned her gaze away so he couldn't read thoughts in her eyes. This was not her Kiren, not the man whom she knew and loved. This was a Kiren from somewhere in the past, one who had never loved her. It was so clear—the hardness in the set of his jaw, the wariness of his stare, the way the air prickled about him.

She placed a hand over her mouth, tears building. The sunrise had been torn away from her, only to be plunged into an eternal pitch.

Given the strength of a full night's rest—absent the irrational emotions of being with child—she would have stood her ground, told him exactly who she was, demanded that he be gentle with his future wife. But the burning at the back of her eyes and tightening of her throat witnessed that she wouldn't get the words out. After five months, all she wanted was for him to hold her. To promise they would never again be parted. To speak excitedly about their child. About the life they would have together.

This man was a stranger. A phantom of her happily-ever-after.

Alexia turned and fled for the far end of camp.

The scuffling of feet brought her head up. Regin and Amos barred Kiren's attempt to follow her, Regin's bare hand outstretched as he watched her for a nod. A single nod and the shadow of the man she loved would be a slumbering heap. She shook her head.

Alexia loved them, all of them—her people. She had protected them, and they would protect her.

Mae appeared at her side, the scrolls Alexia had dropped piled in her arms. Neither said a word as they moved toward the outskirts of camp. Finally her friend spoke. "When a woman greets a man that way—"

"I was mistaken." Alexia's nails cut into her palm. "He is not who I believed he was."

Silence.

"The father of your child?"

Alexia turned to Mae. "My child has no father." Not in this time. Not in this existence. It was possible he would cease to exist if her actions here worked to his detriment.

"Alexia." Mae's tone was that of her mentor, a rebuke. She stepped forward and placed a hand on Alexia's cheek. Her memories flooded through Alexia:

*A cave, isolated from the world. Mae left only when she needed nourishment—which meant siphoning strength off something because food turned to ash in her mouth. An encampment of soldiers took up residence in the valley beneath her home. They erected a fort and she watched, fascinated as it came together. One soldier looked up and squinted her direction. Mae froze. He turned back to his work. A day later, she woke to the scrape of boots over dirt. The soldier stood at the cave's entrance, his head tilted. He was broad from hard labor and sun-bleached, a look fitting of the desert. A scabbard hung from his belt, fingers resting at his weapon's hilt.*

*She grabbed the iron charm dangling from her leather necklace and leapt to the back of the cave. She lifted her hand in warning. "Do not come closer!"*

*He leaned on the entry stones and scratched his nose, completely at ease. "Who are you?"*

*She wanted to tell him exactly what she was, but it was the first time anyone had spoken to her since she'd drained her hometown. Iron singed her palm, keeping her gift in check. "I am dangerous."*

*"To me? Surely not." He was golden, so full of life, so strong. He would fill her need easily…but she didn't want him, even as her inner demon screamed for his essence.*

*And what would happen when he never returned to camp and others came searching? The inner beast licked its lips.*

*She bowed her head, searching the radius of her hunger. He stood just outside the circle, but if he came closer…*

*"Why are you watching us?" The man placed a hand on his hip. "Are you a spy?"*

*Mae gripped the iron tighter, trembling. "I beg you to leave."*

*"You are frightened of me." He smirked. "Many are frightened of Bjorn the Mighty."*

*She lifted her eyes and met his, hers menacing. "I am frightened for you."*

*That was how it started. He came every day near sunset, sat at the cave's entrance and spoke with her. Bjorn had come from a family across the sea, consigned to the king's army at the age of ten to fill his father's place. The metal shield he owned had been his father's and would be his son's when and if he married and had a family. For the last twelve years he'd excelled in his service, and he hardly remembered the place of his birth.*

*Over the ensuing weeks, Mae came to love him, and he, her.*

*Upon her request, he gifted her with an iron fetter. It made the hunger lessen. He was able to sit by her side rather than lingering at the cave's opening. Then came the day he braved the distance and placed a hand against her cheek.*

*Nothing happened. Overjoyed, they both laughed. He leaned in, his gaze intent on her lips…and she felt it. Exhilaration. She opened her mouth to warn him as his lips touched hers. Mae pushed him away, but it was too late. His eyes were black as coal, his skin shriveling from the inside. She cried. She begged God not to take him, but strength flowed into her anyway as he collapsed, body writhing into dust.*

*Mae took up the shield and fled for the desert—where no one would ever suffer the same fate. She would join Bjorn in the afterlife and beg his forgiveness.*

Mae released her. "That is why you found me in the state you did."

Alexia recalled the shifting sands beneath her feet as she lifted the shield and found Mae, curled on the desert floor. Her lovely brown hair had been chopped unevenly and stood in frazzled clumps. She'd worn a dirty linen tunic, holes at her shoulder and knees, a shackle locked firmly about one wrist. Mae's skin had been ashen, the gray of someone near death. Alexia's heart had broken. Cornflower blue eyes had turned upward, so thinned by weariness they were like water in palm-deep pools. When Mae had rasped, "Stay back!" Alexia had rested a hand on Mae's arm. Tingling had crept up Alexia's fingers, hungry, invisible spiders crawling through her skin. Strength bled from Alexia into Mae, a trickle of power that instantly burst to a gushing river. The medallion had warmed beneath her dress, energy coursing through her chest and down the siphon into Mae.

"You saved me when I did not wish to be saved," Mae whispered, "because I would have given anything to have him back." She placed the scrolls in Alexia's custody. "Whatever this is, do not surrender to the pain."

Alexia gave Mae a weak smile and slipped into the trees.

*** 

Kiren watched her skirt swirl behind her, his mouth tingling. He touched his lips, bewildered by the tenderness that remained and the strange yearning to chase after her and kiss her again.

Hello, insanity.

Twice in one day. What were the chances? Was he wearing a sign that said, *Kiss me, I beg you. I am free to be bonded?* Still, he liked her shape, the curve of her back and swell of her hips…

He jerked himself out of that thought. Where had that come from, and more importantly, why was he dwelling on her? He wasn't going to be tied down. Especially to these people.

…Even if the glow of her skin resonated with his very frame. It had tickled the edges of his consciousness with a familiarity he'd only experienced in the family he'd lost. But she couldn't be of his blood, could she? He had only one living relative as far as he knew, and from the color of her hair to the contours of her cheeks, she presented no physical similarities. Plus, she'd kissed him. That would be wrong for a blood relative in so many ways. Too wrong. Especially since that was the most amazing kiss he'd ever experienced.

He shook the thought free.

No woman would bind him. Ever. And she was with child, so clearly the property of another man. Kissing him while belonging elsewhere? A lewd one at that.

He breathed deep, slowing his hummingbird heart. His hands still trembled from touching her.

She knew his name. She seemed to know him, but that was impossible. They'd never met. Perhaps she stole the information through their kiss, the physical contact. That must be her special talent, and Amos must have ordered her to ensnare him the instant he joined the company. They needed a healer.

Speak of the devil.

Two men barred his pathway. Amos and a black-haired man who reached toward him.

Kiren met the stranger's glare, reading his thoughts: *Anger my girl, and I'll make you sleep until solstice.* Kiren delved deeper. *Regin.* The man's name was Regin. He scoffed at the sleeper's bare hand. "I do not see how I can assist you if I am slumbering."

Both men stepped back.

*My girl.* Did that mean Regin was the father? If so, why had he stood by as she kissed another? This wasn't making sense. He'd noticed the ring on her finger—gold. Metal. She could wear metal without effect, or she wore it to diminish the consequences of her gifts. Or because she was married.

"You promised to let me be," Kiren shot at Amos, crossing his arms.

"I did, but we need you now." He waved at a row of injured people, with from cuts to burns to broken bones. Men and boys wore drab tunics, girded by sweat-doused bands he could smell from here, and the women? Their dresses blended with the woods about them. A dull, pitiful attempt to become invisible. The inhabitants looked as if they belonged in a beggars' colony, without a hint of the grandeur their bloodlines demanded. Where was their dignity? Their pride?

Gone. Just like everything else. They no longer knew what an incredible heritage might have been theirs, or that their ancestors had rejected it.

A glory he would never be able to give them. One he no longer wished for himself.

Kiren sighed. Just standing in their presence made him itch with guilt, but he knew most of the fallen and couldn't leave them like this. He pulled both hands through his hair and nodded. "I do this, and then I go my own way."

Regin shrugged and yanked a leather glove over his fingers. "Sounds borin' reasonable."

"And you have to get Zeph," Kiren added.

Amos patted him on the shoulder, turning him toward the injured. "I believe we can do that."

Kiren groaned. Just like that he was back.

*** 

Kiren healed one and then another, anxious to be gone. Anxious to escape the accusing stares that followed him from one victim to the next. Strength seeped free with each healing, and he wasn't running on full power to start. That girl's leg had taken more than he'd anticipated.

He moved on to the next injury while Regin hovered. Kiren rolled his eyes. Clearly the man believed he had to keep watch and stop Kiren from chasing after the mysterious young woman. It was for the best. He would do what they asked, then they would uphold their deal and take him far away. Back to the freedom of endlessly wandering and healing.

A flash of raven curls snatched his attention.

The kisser.

His head spun with the memory of her lips pressed to his and the overwhelming wholeness in her touch. It couldn't be as amazing as his brain insisted. If so, he suddenly understood that stupid, glaze-eyed bewitchment so many men fell under. But he wasn't like them. And it wasn't real. Couldn't be. It must have been an illusion she'd forced into his mind while stealing his secrets—part of her gift. For her sake at least, it had better be.

Everyone he cared about was doomed.

Kiren shook the senseless thoughts away, but he couldn't force his attention from her. She stood in the distance, speaking with another woman, one who reeked of death. A thin lock of white hairs interlaced the kisser's near-black ones, white far too stark to have been earned from age. She must have suffered a great loss, and recently. Perhaps she had lost a husband—unless Regin was her other half, but he didn't share her luminescence. She may be the victim of rape.

The kisser smiled, a sad thing that only touched her cheeks. Pain hunched her shoulders. It filled the very air with sorrow, and part of him—most of him—wanted to go to her, to take away her heartache.

But he couldn't do that. He could only take away physical injuries.

Kiren knelt over another of the wounded. A gaping laceration consumed his attention, but only for the matter of seconds it took for skin to knit back together. His thoughts snapped back to her, and a small part of him hoped she was watching, that she saw and appreciated what good he was doing for the camp.

Like a dog that wanted its belly scratched.

He huffed. The sooner he got away from here, the better.

Except...

She knew his name. That alone was dangerous, and he should discover how much more she knew from diving into his mind. It could be tricky getting the information out of her.

And reckless.

He found himself grinning. Zeph would call him a fool for entertaining the idea—which meant it was a good one.

Kiren glanced around at the people in camp. How long could he stay with these people and not drown under their accusing stares? Sarlic—the inflictor— glared as if he were ready to teach Kiren the true meaning of pain. The boy, Willem, glanced his way with hurt eyes. Near ten years now, the lad's pout said he hadn't understood Kiren's departure. The empath, Oriel, averted her stare, quite clearly feeling his discomfort. Surely she wished he would leave and put her at ease. Despite the guilt clawing at the back of his mind, there was a comfort in being here, almost like being home. A great, dysfunctional home.

Except he destroyed every home he inhabited.

The kisser moved away into the trees. Alone.

His heart leapt. She was alone. What would he do with her if he had her alone? He pushed that thought aside. Wrong direction. The opportunity to speak to her without observation had arrived, and he needed to discover how she knew his name. No one knew his name.

Kiren exhaled heavily and wiped his brow, standing.

Regin lifted an eyebrow.

"I need rest."

The sleeper waved him forward. Kiren moved away, keeping his gaze off the accusing faces turned his direction, blood pumping with the prospect of what he was going to do.

He could almost feel the woman's body pressed to his, their passions entwined and searing through his veins…but why was he thinking this way? Never in his twenty-two years had he desired a woman—not like this. A touch of charm, a smile to obtain information or simple favors, never a yearning to consume just for the joy of imbibing.

But oh, he wanted to imbibe.

*Stop. Get yourself under control.* Kiren cooled the crazed whispers at the back of his mind as the woman disappeared around the corner of a ruined wall. He slipped away to approach from another direction.

# Eight

# *Treachery*

Leofrik pulled the small wooden wolf from his pouch while waiting for his lord's order. He didn't much care for waiting. After all, he had witches and demons to hunt and a sword that ached to be used. He really would rather slay the necromancers, but his master preferred their imprisonment. He rubbed the rough edges of the wolf. It had been his gift to a pilgrim boy in the Holy Land, a child he found slain not a week later. He carried it now and always as a reminder that evil must be put down for the sake of the innocent. He straightened the tunic that declared him one of the most holy order of knights, the Knights Templar. Anxious to be on the move, he shifted his weight from foot to foot.

Words echoed inside the chamber while he waited for Lord Ulric to finish whatever conference was so important that the holy pope's servant had been commanded to wait. And who was so important that he should stand here wasting the day? He leaned against the doorframe and pressed his ear to the jamb.

"You are telling me the ships will return with nothing to show for this *costly* voyage?" Lord Ulric bellowed. "I acquiesced to voyaging to the far reaches of the world—just to maintain your secrecy, but no more. Where have they relocated?"

"They are beaten. Leave them be." The voice was nothing more than the rasp of wind through the shadows, a nearly indecipherable hiss.

"You will give me their location while they are weak, or so help me...!"

Silence.

Leofrik pressed his ear closer.

Feet scuffed across floorboards. "Their location?" Lord Ulric growled.

Quiet.

"The location!"

Leofrik pulled back from the wood, rubbing his ear. He knew Ulric's reputation for rage along with his devious business dealings. The fact that Leofrik himself had been summoned away from Jerusalem, torn from his sworn duties of protecting pilgrims, irked him to the ocean and back. It undoubtedly had to do with Lord Ulric's silver tongue.

He leaned back into the door.

"There now. That was not difficult. Back to your place, poppet."

A snap.

Quiet.

Leofrik wished he could see through the door. His impatience was getting the best of him. Feet thudded toward him, finally. He assumed his stance a respectable distance away.

The door creaked open. Ulric gave him a considering perusal and offered a parchment bearing his seal. "Take thirty men to the monastic ruins southwest of Bristol. And for God's sake, approach silently."

Leofrik bristled. He wasn't the one thundering about and bellowing orders. He took the paper and bowed.

Finally time to be moving again.

# Nine

# *Without Time*

Alexia's knees faltered. She landed against weathered stone, hidden by shadows as deep as her shock.

Kiren had lied to her.

Her Kiren.

She hugged herself, frozen in his loss anew. He'd said he wouldn't be here, and yet here he was...in a fashion. Unless they'd never met in his past. What if he hadn't known, because she was altering history for the first time? Except her daughter had been born into the past—that much she knew. What if Kiren simply didn't remember her from the past—if something had happened that claimed his memory, or one of the Passionate took it? She was stretching for a plausible excuse now. She recognized that, but she couldn't reconcile that he would keep this from her.

It didn't make sense.

She set the scrolls down and unrolled one but couldn't focus on the words. Her mind kept spinning reasons, but none of them added up.

Alexia stepped out of time, to its absence—the one place she could truly escape the world. Minutes didn't count against her here.

The breeze ceased. Silence reigned. She turned to find Grandfather watching her. She'd discovered him, a prisoner in the absence of time after she came to this timeline—taking the place of her long-dead mother in a realm only her family could occupy. He was the rightful guardian of time in this era, but he'd stepped into this abyss for the short duration she would occupy the thirteenth century. Many times she'd postulated what had become of his physical body, but she'd only anticipated being in the past a short time. Now she questioned if she'd overstayed her welcome.

He tucked his hands in the girdle of his tunic, shoulders rounded and relaxed, cocoa hair veiling his ears and coal-like eyes. Kind eyes. From the quirk in his cheek and the way skin creased in happy lines around his eyes, she felt certain she'd met him before—perhaps in the future—though she had yet to connect him to anyone.

His head bobbed in greeting, fingers tapping out a rhythm against his leg as if it were hard to stand still.

"He was not supposed to be here," she said.

"Mm." He nodded. "But he is, and like it or not, here he will stay."

She brushed a tear off her cheek and straightened up. This flustered state would not do. She had an important mission and she would accomplish it. "There is a traitor."

"Aye."

"Why did you not warn me?"

The man laughed. The chugging sound tugged at something in her memory, but it was too firmly buried. Laughter never was far from him. She wondered how he had weathered his decades and still found reason to be jovial. In her near twenty years she had seen so much sorrow.

"You know the rules well as me."

She did. Her mother, Dana, had refused to reveal anything to come while in the absence of time because of how it would alter her future. A traitor or not, there must have always been a traitor in this time. It meant nothing but that she had to be more careful and find this person out.

"I could speed through time to see what will happen," she warned. "Then return to this moment."

He nodded. "And imperil yer child."

Dana had warned her about that as well—the dangers of speeding time. She could hasten the moments, but that would mean placing herself at the mercy of whatever changed in the world around her. If a horse came barreling through the spot she occupied, she would die. And her child with her.

"I could dream the future."

"Always," he agreed. "But where be the fun in that?"

She gave him a look. Fun? How about survival? A new thought hit her: when she had this baby, Kiren's gift might be able to save her. And her baby. Perhaps his being here was a blessing.

"Do I dare trust him?" she asked.

"Why not ask him?" Grandfather pointed.

She squinted at him then turned. Outside of frozen time, Kiren was stationary in the trees, one foot lifted in approach.

He was so beautiful, the smooth quality of his skin, the sharp angle of his cheekbones, the perfect line of his nose. Her soul reached for his, wishing he was hers, needing as much of him as she could have in the little time that remained for her.

"I do believe I will. Goodbye, Grandfather." Alexia resumed her seat, the same spot she'd occupied before stepping out of time. She settled back into the ticking seconds.

A shadow draped over her. She straightened up, squaring her shoulders and suppressing the flutters in her stomach. He met her gaze, his as blue as midnight, a boundless sky promising terrifying storms as much as starlight. He stiffened, as though what he'd come to say could no longer be said.

She lifted a barrier over her thoughts and stared him straight in the eye.

"You know my name?" he asked.

Alexia closed her eyes and let the sound of his voice penetrate her, let it move her as it had in the past. The depth of her mistake struck her like a jackhammer. Kiren had guarded his identity with a zeal that put King George's palace guard to shame. If he did so in this time as well…

"Yes," she replied. How could she deny it? She had used his name to address him.

He cocked his head, stepping closer, his eyes both amused and wary. "How?"

Alexia struggled up off the ground. If he was asking, this must be an age after the loss of his family and kingdom. Otherwise, his name would be known among the dignitaries of the world as the arising prince. Her heart ached for him, the depth of his loss. How heavily it must weigh on him even now, bearing him to the ground with the force of ten men.

"You told it to me."

His foot slid back, his lips parted. He shook his head. "I would never—"

"I apologize for kissing you." She pulled in her emotions, grunting as she steadied on her feet.

He squinted at her. "Yet you do not claim to have mistaken me for another. We have met?"

She could see his mind working, stumbling back over the hundreds of faces he'd encountered and searching for hers. "Not yet."

He leaned back from her.

She curtsied. "I am Alexia, the Maiden of Time. If you have come to join our struggling band, we could certainly use your gifts."

His head turned back toward the camp and his mouth opened like he was about to protest.

*Keep talking. Keep him from asking questions*—at least until she'd figured out what to tell him. "Your gift for growth, for healing, your unique love for exotic flora, all are welcome. I pray you will not fear to let these people near your heart because of the danger it poses. They are worthy."

His fists locked, his brow twisted, shoulders turned inward. This was precisely how he'd stood the evening he'd given her up, locked in his own silent battle and broken by what he must do. He hissed in a breath. "You may know what I can do, but you do not know me."

Alexia stood to her full height, wondering if he would welcome her hand on his cheek, if she could soothe the ache in his stare. "Perhaps not yet, but I am most anxious to learn."

He stepped forward.

She should back away, but she didn't have enough willpower.

He snaked a finger forward and tipped her chin up. "Why did you kiss me?"

She averted her gaze. Her stomach clenched with the memory of that kiss, echoed by a hundred others. Kiren's lips on hers. The heat of his passion filling her so fully she had no need to eat, to sleep. "It was a mistake."

His finger pulled away. He shook out his hand like he'd been stung. "Tell me about this future. When shall we meet?"

Cerulean blue burned into her, drawing out her secrets like a searing prod thrust into water. Her struggle evaporated. She had no desire to stop him from her thoughts and every reason to welcome him in. His palm touched her cheek, and he drew everything in on a breath, her tortured existence for the last five months, her purpose here, the suffocating love that even now shattered her resistance.

Kiren released her. He stumbled backward, head shaking. "No. This, this is not…" He slid both hands into his hair, denial and fury twisting his lowered brows. "It is a lie."

Alexia's heart squeezed. She forged past her own pain to recognize his. Allowing him this glimpse proved that he would never recover his father's throne, that he would wander for centuries until finally finding a love he clearly didn't want. It was cruel. No person deserved to have their hopes dashed in an instant. Perhaps there was a reason Dana and Grandfather withheld what was to come from her.

Alexia reached back in time one minute, to before she lost control. Blackness. Steadying on her feet.

"Tell me about this future. When shall we meet?" he asked.

"Do not touch me." She backed away. *Do not melt my resistance.* "I know that trick too." She closed her eyes to keep him out. He'd warned her she'd never be able to fully block her thoughts from him, not while gazing into one another's eyes, but he was so magnetic. How could she succeed in keeping him out?

He sucked in a breath, startled. "Is there anything you do not know?"

*What comes next.* She hadn't expected him to be here, and that might change everything. One wrong move and she might condemn their fates. Alexia tentatively met his stare. She wanted to answer him, but how could she do that knowing it might ultimately destroy him? His necklace felt especially heavy around her neck.

Kiren's brows crunched down. She realized too late that he was reading her. He lunged and caught her bodice, his fingers crimping around the medallion hidden beneath the material. His necklace from the future.

His eyes widened.

Alexia jerked time to a stop. The impact of what might have come next slammed her with the force of an axe. Her last thought about his untimely destruction—which he must have intercepted—along with her possession of his necklace must look like irrefutable proof of a coming assassination.

The early dawn caressed his fingers, curled so intimately close to her heart. She wanted to linger, to allow this wishful closeness to permeate her being, but the terror in his eyes crushed the idea. His nose flared wide, teeth clenched. Here was a man to be feared, not loved.

He must not know that she had his necklace. Ever.

One more try. Alexia jumped back to the pivotal second. Pitch. Regaining balance.

"Tell me about this future. When shall we meet?" he asked.

She gave him a sad smile, meeting his gaze and solidifying a mental barrier that would keep even sunlight out.

He stared deep and flinched, deflected. "That kiss. Have you agreed with someone to ensnare me?"

The words stabbed. *Oh Kiren, you will wreck so many hearts, but now it is your turn.* "I am certain you are strong enough to resist."

"Ah, then I am correct."

"If that is what you choose to believe."

His jaw clenched and released. "You love me in this future?" It was a blind accusation, a fishing allegation. He was trying to get her to confess something or distract her enough to find the answers in her eyes.

"Every woman loves you in this future, as I am certain they do at present." Her cheeks flamed, both with jealousy and embarrassment.

His smirk said it all. "I have no time or appetite for women."

"That will simplify things for us some." She turned and gathered up her scrolls, gripping her heart with a tight fist. It was not a rejection. He didn't know her. He didn't realize that saying she bore no sway over him was nearly enough to crush her. She was just a woman like any other he'd met. "If you will excuse me, I have duties to attend."

"Who is your husband?" He was right behind her. "Or your lover?"

How dare he accuse her of being an unchaste woman! She steadied the shaking from her voice. "I hardly see how that is any business of yours." *Even if it is.* "You are welcomed in our company, but if you stay, do make yourself useful. I trust you can do that?"

"Wait."

The word harbored a modicum of desperation, and she could hear herself in it—the frantic plea in her father's garden ages ago when she had needed to know what she was. She couldn't deny him.

Alexia turned back. Her mouth instantly dried. He looked on her with an expression he had so often used, one where he peered to her very core. *Do not stand so proud. Do not look at me that way. Do not be my Kiren in all but reality.*

His shoulders relaxed, his head tilted inquisitively. "I am pleased to know you, Alexia. I hope we shall become…*friends.*"

The silent plea for more information in his posture too felt familiar, except this time they stood on opposite sides.

"I should like that." She inclined her head and turned to leave.

He grabbed her arm. "You will kindly keep my name a secret?"

Alexia recognized the same creases of pain that had always been around his eyes. "What happened to you?" she whispered.

Guilt crinkled his brow and his teeth clenched.

She pressed on. "I know how you lost your family and kingdom, but this is different. You fear these people?"

His mouth worked, but no other words escaped. He released her, backing away. He turned, halted and looked back, almost said something, then shook his head and sped into the trees.

# Ten

# *Warped*

When Kiren returned, Zeph mingled with the others, his wings fully visible, all attempt to hide his horns or tail abandoned. Relieved as he was to have his friend present, Kiren felt like he was stumbling across uneven terrain. He kept his gaze down and fought to get himself under control. His chest heaved. If he had wings like Zeph's, they'd be ruffled, feathers pointing all different directions, making it impossible to fly. She knew about his kingdom. About his parents. About his heritage. The fact she knew his name was the least of his concerns.

Her sorrow had been for him this time. For the death of his parents.

Yes, Amos knew of his family line, as did a couple others. They'd overheard him telling Zeph that he belonged to the family of Kir in the confidence of friendship, but the depth of Alexia's understanding outweighed them all. She knew about talents and interests he kept hidden. She'd addressed the silent battle he constantly fought.

He would tell her his name in a time to come. In the future... He couldn't quite make that concept settle. Would he tell her more than that, or did she know about him because she came from his home? That thought opened too many doors to even consider, but one predominant question must be answered: Was she a friend or foe? She played the friend, but he had mistaken others in the past.

Alexia was new to this group of Lost Ones, at least, newer than when he'd last been with them. He needed to discover how she'd come to join them and if her actions had been calculated—grabbing his attention in a way he couldn't ignore—or a simple accident.

How could anyone *accidentally* kiss someone like that?

He ran a hand through his hair, unable to smooth the way his pulse raced at the memory of her lips pressed to his.

"You look like you are going to lose your stomach." Zeph's voice was a grounding agent, bringing him back to reality.

"I might."

Wings flurried. "I am away from you moments, and you are as bad as before we left. You need to get away from here."

Kiren nodded, biting down. But first he had a line of injuries to mend—if he could calm himself enough to do any good. Even at full health, the number of injuries were more than he could heal in two days.

Alexia returned from the trees, four scrolls tucked under one arm. Her cheeks were rosy, her shoulders back as if nothing of importance had occurred. Perhaps nothing had. The initial kiss must have been a simple mistake as she'd suggested. Her vision might be bad. He shouldn't have followed her into the trees, but even now he needed to close the distance and uncover the mystery of her actions.

"That is a change."

Kiren ripped his eyes away and turned to his friend.

Zeph chuckled. "You were picturing her to the skin, were you not?"

"No," he scoffed. Although now that it had been suggested... He forced his gaze to the sky and centered his focus on cuts, bruises, and the exhausting night ahead. Zeph knew about some of his past and that the kingdom waited for him, but he didn't know everything—not Kiren's name, not his secret gifts, not how he came to be the sought after heir. No one knew it all. Except maybe Alexia. It was how he protected everyone.

His friend whistled. "We are going to be here a while."

Kiren shoved past him, returning for the injured.

"She is nice to look at, but did you notice her middle front region?"

"Hard to miss, and the fact she cannot be read."

Zeph froze in his tracks. "You cannot read her thoughts?"

Kiren turned back. "Not a single one."

His friend shivered. "Scary."

*And that is only the beginning of it.* If Zeph had any idea how hard he was fighting to stay on the opposite side of camp, he'd either laugh his gourd off or swoop Kiren to safety. That woman was danger.

Zephaniah's wings fluttered. "Is that Silivia over there?"

A smile tugged at Kiren's cheek. His friend was still obsessed with the island girl's dark hair and bronzed skin. Who cared that she'd thrown a boulder at his unmentionables—with her mind.

"Yes, terrifying."

Zeph waved him off and crossed the camp like a lovesick puppy.

Kiren knelt to mend a head wound, but when his friend crossed paths with Alexia, he couldn't pull his gaze away. Despite her girth, she moved with the grace of a queen, almost floating. She stopped in front of a gangly, tall man with long blonde hair and handed him the stack of scrolls. He was the kind whose skin had only seen the sun because he'd been forced into it. Not at all beautiful like the Lost Ones. An awkward smile and subdued speech made him look like a twitching weasel.

Alexia's laughter carried across the camp. Glittering specks of joy. They tugged at his heart, reminding him what it was to be so light. She was laughing at the strange man—no, with him. Her hand landed on his arm in a flirtatious gesture, and the weasel smiled at her as if she were the only woman in the world.

"Have ye come to heal me?" the man on the ground below Kiren asked.

Below him?

Kiren hadn't realized he'd stood back up, or that both fists were clenched. He shook his hands loose and forced himself to kneel, although it was like bending ironwood.

"Unless ye have somewhere else to be?" the man asked.

"Let me see your wound." Kiren turned the man's head. This was another unfamiliar face. In the five years he'd been away, the Lost Ones had doubled in number. "How long have you been with the group?" Small talk. Something to keep the wounded distracted through the pain of healing.

"Four days. Terrible timing, ay? I am Hammond. Glad to meet ye."

Kiren hesitated. It always gave him a twinge of guilt offering a false name, but to stay safe, he had little choice. "Arik. You were attacked?"

"Them crusaders. Knights. Like we are demons right out of hell."

He studied Hammond's eyes, sinking into the memory within:

*Flying debris. Children screaming. A ship on the horizon. Men dressed in red crosses charging across the beach with raised swords.*

Kiren pulled free. He closed his mind against equally horrific scenes that scarred his conscience and weighed every waking moment. "I am sorry."

"Why should you be, mate? You didn't send them monsters after us."

No, but he should be the one leading them to safety, protecting them under his family's banner. He shrugged the idea off.

"This is going to hurt."

# Eleven

# *Descent*

Leofrik signaled his men to stop and slid from his horse, landing in spongy moss. Smoke in the distance marked his destination like a lighthouse over troubled waters. He'd spent a few days gathering his force—reluctant men, grubby farmers, and fortune-hungry mercenaries. He didn't particularly care for this lot, but Ulric's directives didn't allow him to travel across the seas and retrieve the men he'd most prefer to have by his side.

His back ached from riding half the day, and his legs desperately needed stretching. He walked a circle, waving the men inward to hear him. If he were a more impulsive man, he'd charge now and get this over with, but experience had taught him the wisdom of being prepared. "If you need refreshment, take it now—but quietly and no fire. We march soon."

Men collapsed into heaps, drawing on waterskins or chewing dried fish.

Leofrik stopped two young men crossing his path. "Not you. I need you two to scout the camp and report back their numbers. Quietly. Give us away and I will have your heads."

# Twelve

# Slides

Alexia's head ached from deciphering the ridiculous print, and from poor sleep. In the last two days, she'd rested as needed and pored through the curly script, attempting to ignore the suspicious way Kiren stared at her or how he'd attempted to corner her regularly. Regin usually came to her aid. She had said too much again, and now he was even more curious. She couldn't crush him. The future hadn't happened and wouldn't necessarily play out as it had. She needed to stay away from him.

On to the traitor.

The only thing she knew for sure from the scrolls was that a Lord of Dorset had commissioned the knights to attack the island home she and the Passionate had inhabited. The men were instructed to capture, not kill, locking their enemies in irons, branding them with a special mark, and returning them to his prison. They were to attack at night, and the defector would alert them by means of light signals when the enemy was vulnerable. The missive further warned that the group possessed unique talents, wielding magic of a most terrifying nature. The men were to exercise extreme caution. Each scroll contained orders to visit a new location: a lush valley in France, the desert, the mountain caves, a remote island…

Whoever had been reporting on them had done so since before she'd joined the Passionate. She'd never seen any sign of a traitor. Figuring out this person's identity was going to prove difficult.

Alexia reported to Amos, and he assured her he would puzzle this out.

\*\*\*

Kiren had disappeared. Alexia had overheard chatter about him leaving. He specially requested to be removed as soon as he was finished healing people, according to Regin. As of this afternoon, all were healed. He was gone. She suppressed her disappointment—it was for the best—and focused on Amos who stood before their bonfire to give his usual end-of-the-day remarks. Tonight, he complimented them for holding up under hardship and expressed his pride in this brotherhood who'd banded together when the enemy attacked.

"But it is not enough," he said. "They come and they come again. It is determined we have a traitor in our midst."

Gasps rang through the crowd.

"We know you are among us," he continued, "but whatever the enemy holds over you, we are ready to fight for you. Come forward of your own, in private if you lack the courage, and we will go to war for you."

Silence reigned, broken only by the crackle of fire.

"You are all my brothers and sisters. I would bleed for any of you," Amos vowed.

"As would I." Remus stood.

"And I." Mae rose.

Alexia lifted an arm. "Me as well."

The pledge continued around the gathering. Tears and fierce determination mingled together in an oath of love so complete, Alexia knew for the first time in ages, she was home. Here was her family.

With or without Kiren.

She pressed a hand to her chest, missing him with all her soul.

Amos lifted both arms. "If you are afraid, do not be. We may have discovered a way to escape the enemy forever. Deamus?"

Her awkward friend scrambled to his feet, straightening his tunic with exaggerated tugs. He brushed the hair back from his face, turned to the crowd, and went snow white.

Alexia shifted onto her knees, grabbing his attention with her movement, and gave him an encouraging smile.

"Um, it is not a…there are some…" He took a deep breath, meeting her stare. His jaw clenched, shoulders squared. "Some of you have heard of the other world and um, a great gathering of our kind who left…this world…for that one."

A couple heads bobbed. Most watched him curiously.

He licked his lips and lifted both hands right in front of his chest, pulled them back as if rethinking what he was about to do, then extended them again.

A window of light appeared above the fire. Alexia gasped. Energy drained from her fingertips, a tingle of strength that bled into the projection. People backed away, startled by the manifestation and resultant sapping. The brilliance of the window dimmed, and a landmass appeared through the ring, lush and green against a sapphire ocean. The view zoomed inward on a shore, a forest, roads and merchant carts, great mountains, waterfalls, and finally the gates of a bustling city. Inside, people of various shapes and sizes meandered through the streets. One woman was bending wood into a spinning wheel with her bare hands for an eager customer. Children laughed at a puppet show presented in the streets—but no, not puppets. Flickers of light that took on a life of their own, pixie-like essences. A smithy pounded away with his hammer, only to present his customer with a bouquet of tulips that glittered when stroked.

Deamus lifted his arms, and the window faded like smoke.

Alexia reattached her jaw. If that was where he came from, it was little wonder he yearned to go back. She wanted to see it for herself.

"The other world," Deamus finished, turning as if to regain his seat.

Regin stood. "Beautiful though it be, what of the dark corners? The terrors? If the punches of life taught me anythin', it's that every light has a dark. Every joy has sadness."

Deamus halted with a lifted foot and twisted back around, stumbling off kilter and regaining his balance. "Um, yes. The bad…" His eyes flicked across his audience like a rabbit facing a pack of wolves. Alexia tapped her nose. His gaze snapped to her, his chest lifting with a measure of restored confidence. "There are places where terrifying…things…dwell, but they are behind a barrier, a fence of, of magic. It protects everyone." He tugged at the edge of his sleeve. "The terrifying and the benign."

The words settled over them.

"Is there a reason for showing us this other world?" Sarlic spoke up, a man Alexia hadn't spent much time coming to know. His arms were as wide around as his neck and he'd been branded upon the brow with a cross just over his left eye. She knew that his gift was to inflict pain on others, something that had saved many of the Passionate from capture.

Deamus's hands dropped to his sides. He closed his eyes and stilled. "Soon the stars will align…enough. I can maybe open the gateway, but I need your strength." His head lifted, and he looked each person directly in the eye.

Nervous gestures and hesitant whispers filled the assembly.

"Is there any chance it will not work?"

Heads turned. Kiren stood at the edge of the camp, arms crossed and jaw locked as he stared directly at Deamus.

Alexia's heart stuttered.

He hadn't gone after all. She closed her eyes briefly, so filled with gratitude she could cry, but he wasn't hers—and she needed to keep away from him.

Some of the crowd averted their gazes from Kiren, others glared, one or two covered their faces. Amos's grimace softened, and Regin scratched at the back of his head.

What had Kiren done to earn so strong a reaction from the Passionate?

"I am locating where the gateway will open, and I—" Deamus straightened up, cheeks lifting with the hopeful hint of a smile. "I am going."

Alexia gauged people's responses. The boy, Willem looked to be salivating. Amos stood back, nodding with an optimistic frown. Mae poised in the shadows, fingers cutting into her crossed arms. Alexia could almost hear her thoughts—no matter where she went, she'd be just as cursed. She would be one of those locked behind the barrier to protect the others.

What about herself? This world was where she'd discovered love. If she joined Deamus, she might never return to her Kiren in the future.

The babe kicked. Then again, she might die before she could enter that world, or shortly after reaching it, and Kiren would never know his daughter. Which might be better.

What came next? Would she find peace in the next life, or would she remain a captive outside of time until another heir of time took up the mantle? She hoped not.

Deamus's shoulders drooped, his gaze falling from people's faces to their feet.

"How do you know of this place?" she asked, encouraging him to continue.

His cheeks lifted in a grin that bordered on childlike. "It is my home."

Kiren's eyes narrowed. Alexia looked between the two, wondering what Kiren was thinking. She might be able to discover, but it would require playing the seductress and exposing her heart to discovery.

He cleared his throat. "It is my home as well. It cannot be done."

# Thirteen

# *Blocked*

His home. A different world, his home.

How many lies had Kiren fed her?

Breaths escaped her in rapid succession. She pounded the ground with a fist. How dare he rip hope away from everyone and humiliate Deamus in such a public manner? How dare he lie to her while professing the truest love?

She stood. "It can be done. Lucian saw this world in our future. It will be done." She turned to the crowd. "Deamus asks only for your permission to try. For those who dare, prepare yourselves for this new world, but if you choose to remain, that is your decision. We cannot help you further." She stormed away into the trees.

\*\*\*

Kiren wanted to lift his hands in surrender and shout, *What do you want from me?* It was the truth. They couldn't reach that world—he'd tried. Instead of voicing his frustration, he watched Alexia storm away and ignored the loud debate ensuing around the campfire.

He had done his best to discover her history the last two days. She had been in this company for nearly half a year. Men and women alike uttered her name with reverence, citing her goodness, her compassion, and the speed with which she moved when exercising her gift. She laughed easily and cried without shame. Her heart seemed pure, and other than the periodic touch or flirtation with this Deamus, she showed only appropriate affection.

So what was Kiren to her? They would meet in a time to come, true, but she'd kissed him. Was that how they greeted one another in a coming age? Was that how she greeted all the Lost Ones when they first entered camp? He doubted it. Perhaps they had been paramours, but that didn't make sense. He wouldn't initiate a relationship. He wouldn't. And he would never impregnate a woman or care for one who'd allow herself to enter that state. Not in this world. Not in any world to come. It was not that he didn't like children—they were grand and all that—but he would never father one only to make their life a potential bargaining piece in a political game. As had been the case with his parents.

Not that anyone would target him or his future child anymore. He had given up any claim to his father's throne and any pretense of becoming a leader. Still, there were enemies in the other world who didn't know that. Anyone attached to him was in danger if one of his foes were to somehow successfully cross over.

Could Alexia be such an enemy? Seeking something from him? Perhaps hoping to enthrall him so fully that he'd have to claim her child and proffer it all the protection his father's throne had to offer?

He had to know why she'd kissed him.

He stalked after Alexia into the darkness.

***

Alexia stomped through the underbrush, furious.

That was his home. Kiren's home. This other world. A hundred conversations they'd had finally clicked into place. He'd said he couldn't reach his home, that it was elsewhere, that it may not even exist anymore.

Kiren was not from Earth. His kingdom was on another planet, his family's duties in another land beyond the stars. How did that even make sense? How had he come to be here? And why hadn't he told her?

Her mind reeled another direction.

He'd never returned to the land of his birth. This gateway couldn't work because Kiren was still on Earth in her time—unless they'd never met in the past before. Or he'd chosen to remain. Perhaps even to find her again? But that was wishful thinking. Still, her child had been born in this age, but it was possible Kiren never knew the child was his until centuries later. All of this was new territory, and she could so easily destroy what should have been. Was she rewriting history?

Alexia collapsed against a tree.

She couldn't undo this, but perhaps she could fix it. Perhaps she could help Kiren return to his home, become the king as was foreordained, and lead the Passionate in the world of his birth.

It would mean they'd never meet in the future.

Perhaps that didn't matter. It had happened, and now she was here. Perhaps here and now was all that mattered.

***

Kiren halted several steps behind Alexia. "It is true." He crossed his arms. "It is cruel to give them false hope of this other world."

"I suppose that is something you know all about," she hissed back at him.

46

"It is, in fact." If only she knew how much. He'd sought a way back to the Neitherlands after his twin sister suddenly disappeared in the night, assuming she had been swept there. She never would have left him willingly. His search of the world since had solidified the belief that she'd been transported home miraculously. Upon her vanishing, he'd begged his medallion to open the portal between worlds, even given it all his strength, but he was convinced it could only be opened from the other side—a failsafe and protection instituted at that world's conception. Still, the hope had carried him for years, until that defining moment when he'd learned how terrible a leader he would be.

Kiren lifted his head and met her gaze. Her mouth pleated in compassion, shoulders leaning toward him as if she wished to approach. A chain around her neck caught the light, disappearing beneath her bodice in a *V*.

"Why are you still here?" she asked.

He snapped his thoughts away from her bosom. Why indeed. Because his mind had been on fire since the moment she pressed those pastel lips to his. He'd healed everyone that had been injured, and Zeph had been casually nudging him to go, around hazardous flirtations with Silivia. Kiren sensed his friend didn't really wish to leave, but he would without question.

Kiren had tried to go this morning. He'd walked as far as the spring where he saw Alexia filling her goatskin. Standing behind her, even out of sight, his heart warmed. He felt like he was standing in the sun, absorbing its rays. Then thoughts started in: the Lost Ones had been attacked. People had been injured, killed. Alexia and her baby could have been among them. This probably wouldn't be the last attack, and what if she was injured and he might have saved her, but he'd decided some sheriff's daughter in a human township was more deserving of his gifts?

*Why am I still here?* He waved her off. "How is it you know about my past and gifts, but I cannot access even your thoughts from your eyes?" It was always best to answer a question with a question—take control of the conversation.

She leaned back. "I shield my thoughts."

He advanced, fascinated. "There is a way to shield thoughts?"

She nodded.

"How?" This close to her, electricity buzzed, two opposites needing to touch, driven to be connected. He forced his hands to remain at his sides rather than cupping her face.

Her lashes lifted, slowly. "You block them."

"I have never attempted such a thing."

"Visualize a wall or barrier and keep it there."

It sounded so easy, but how to make sure it held? Had she been inside his head before? "That is how you know so much about me. You," he swallowed hard, "entered my mind."

She lowered her gaze.

"When?" It must have been when she kissed him. Perhaps she had been lying all long.

"If you wish to keep me out, you will have to practice."

Well, she knew most everything. There was no risk of her learning more—unlike anyone else in camp. He kicked at the ground. "Will you help me learn this *barricading*?"

She blew out a breath, her gaze bobbing to his lips and back to his eyes.

Every muscle tensed against grabbing her right that instant. Would another kiss be as intoxicating as the first? "After all," he tried to keep his tone light, "we know one another in the future. I must trust you to have given you my name."

She nodded once.

"Are we physically intimate?" he asked.

The color drained from her face.

That was a yes. Or embarrassment at his boldness. Curiouser and curiouser.

She stiffened. "If you wish to know, you must overcome my barriers and obtain the information for yourself."

"And so I shall." Kiren closed his eyes and built a wall of vines in his mind, growing them up in front of his treasured secrets. He kept that mental picture as he returned to gazing upon the woman who made his heart feel like a leaf in the wind. He would manipulate her, fluster her in order to weaken her fortifications. Then he would enter her mind rather than the other way around. This may be easier than he'd thought.

She stepped back and lifted her palm to his. "Resist a sharing." The distance did little to diminish the fluttering in his chest, and hopefully hers. She attacked.

A battering ram slammed into his wall. The vines shifted and tore. Kiren grew new mental creepers, wrapping them around the ram and trapping it. It shifted, melting into a snake that slithered through the openings. No matter how fast he reacted, she found a way through. He threw brick up behind the vines, and her attack turned to mist, seeping through the miniscule holes of the mortar.

Kiren pulled away. "You cheat."

She stepped after him. "There is no cheating when you face an enemy. If you cannot keep me out, you are doomed."

Had she just admitted to being his enemy? Again he wondered what she knew of his fate…but the thought fled when he inhaled. Ambrosia: golden pomegranate. His fingers trembled as he lifted them to her neck. "Again," he demanded, and this time he blanketed his mind in darkness. She entered and burst into light, illuminating all around her. He tried ice, she brought fire. He attempted water, she infiltrated with an air bubble. Steel, she tossed the contents of a blazing kiln at him.

Sweat dripped down his brow as he stared, panting, beaten.

Alexia brushed the hair back from his face, fingers grazing his skin. He quivered, and not from the effort of blocking her.

"Try fog," she whispered. "It is fluid, it reflects light, and distance is swallowed up by its presence."

He pulled the thickest fog over his thoughts and pressed his fingers to her cheek. She seeped into his mind but could find no direction. Up, down, forward, back, she couldn't claim solid ground.

Kiren grinned.

Her lips touched his.

All thought of fighting ceased. Sunlight was pouring into him, all the happiness he couldn't have. He greedily inhaled it. The fog dropped. He wrapped her in his embrace, marveling at the rise and fall of her chest in time with his. He pulled her closer, delving into her so fully there was no him or her. There was only bliss. Completeness. One.

And then she was in his thoughts, filtering through whatever she wanted, but he didn't care. He wanted her there. She belonged inside.

Alexia shoved away, scowling. "You let me in."

"Yes, I did."

The anger dropped, replaced by shock. "You cannot do that. There are things I am not meant to know, things you are not meant to show me."

He blinked quickly but couldn't wrap his brain entirely around what she was telling him. Things she wasn't supposed to see now, or things from when they would meet in a distant day? If they were close then, why wouldn't he allow her in?

"I am sorry, Kiren." She withdrew a pace. "Your future should not be decided by this past. You must keep away from me."

Now his head ached for an entirely different reason. Did she want him or want nothing to do with him? "Am I not entitled to make that decision?"

"No." She stepped around him. "Unless you wish to die."

He felt like he'd been punched. Was she saying she'd seen his death or knew how it would happen? Is that why she'd kissed him—because she was so relieved he was alive? "You are going to have to clarify that statement for me."

"When you can beat me, you will have your answer, but this"—she touched her lips—"this cannot happen."

That sounded like a challenge. He'd always liked a challenge. "You kissed me."

"To weaken your resistance." Her jaw clenched. "I should not have."

"How can that make sense? You kiss me to weaken me, but then insist being attached will bring my death? Why would you do that unless you wish me dead?" Kiren followed after, ready to defy her will and take another shot at breaking through her barrier.

His ears perked.

In the distance, multiple feet, heavy—meaning they were large men or men clad with armor and weapons...near a hundred of them at least.

He grabbed Alexia's hand. She twisted on him. He silenced her by covering her mouth and leading her back to the heart of camp. He opened his thoughts to her and showed her what he'd heard.

"Amos!" She sped away.

***

Children huddled within a ring of adults, everyone in camp packed into a small circle. A small party hurried away, creating a false trail led by Velia. She would mist them away once they'd finished their work. Dead coals smoldered at Alexia's feet. She held her skirt over the smoke to trap it while Amos built a bubble of darkness over them, a murky, ethereal substance that barely reached beyond the last trembling person. No one moved a muscle or made a noise as knights and soldiers filtered past, scanning the trees as if expecting monsters to burst through them any second. They passed within a breath of the barrier.

One man stopped. His flaxen hair caught the moonlight, the holy crest emblazoned across his chest. He signaled the others on, scanning the ruins with great focus. His gaze pierced into the darkness. Alexia swore he was looking right at her through the barrier. She stopped breathing.

He shook his head and pressed forward.

One of the Passionate sneezed.

*Fourteen*

*Breathe*

The knight turned back, searching the blankness. He stepped closer to the barrier, sliding his sword from its sheath.

Alexia tensed. If he crossed through the barrier, their subterfuge would be lost. They would be forced to attack. She gripped her dagger.

The man stood within a fingertip of the murk, searching the black with a piercing stare.

She reached for time, ready to stop it.

"Sir!" a soldier hissed.

The man turned.

"We found a trail. They have fled."

The man returned his sword to its sheath. "We will follow them."

Men filtered through the trees, disappearing.

Alexia slumped with relief, and a hand touched her shoulder. Deamus smiled down at her. She patted his fingers. Long moments passed in the bubble before Velia materialized at its center. Amos nodded, and the child of mist burst into a haze, taking two of them with her. The move had begun.

\*\*\*

The air was impossibly thin. Alexia pushed her lungs harder as she trudged across the mountaintop. Vegetation covered the highland peaks surrounding them, sharp inclines framed in late afternoon rays. It had been afternoon when they first arrived, although they'd left the woods in the middle of the night. That was one aspect of traveling from landmass to landmass that never ceased to amaze her—the difference in time of day.

A portion of the mountain had been leveled off and terraced, as if someone intended to build a home and farm in this remote, airless location. Still, she had to appreciate the open sky above her. Willem used his gift to shift the earth, tumbling stones into place about them to block the wind. Others were erecting roofs or were out scavenging for food. They would complete more huts each day, and all things considered, this unreachable spot could be a steady home for her people, if she could just catch her breath.

Zephaniah, the winged man, landed in front of her.

Alexia gasped and placed a hand on her chest, slowing her heart.

"It is your turn," he offered a hand. He had been flying the children and other women in the company around the mountain to "*strengthen his wings*." She recognized his efforts to familiarize them with their surroundings so they understood their limits.

"I am far too great a burden." She touched her belly and turned away.

He laughed. Arms slipped through hers from behind, elbows locking around her shoulders.

"Zephaniah—"

"My friends call me Zeph." And he leapt off a cliff, taking her with him.

She screamed. The ground rushed at her, wind tearing at her eyes until tears trailed her cheeks. Large wings swooped above her. His arms jerked tight against her, yanking them to a halt midair.

Her scream cut off. She sucked in a breath before he dove. They swooped steadily down. She grabbed his arms, fingers cutting into him. "Drop me, and I swear Mae will burn you from the inside out!"

He laughed and caught an updraft, carrying them toward the sky.

The mountain range bloomed beneath her. Green. Rocky. Remote. The Passionate dotted the cliffs, ants from this distance. It was breathtaking and so peaceful.

She was still angry with him.

"I have never seen Arik like this."

Alexia attempted to twist his direction, but it was impossible. She'd heard Kiren addressed by that name in camp. As in the future, even his close friends didn't know him. "Like what?" she asked.

"Hungry."

She laughed.

"I am not talking about his near-nonexistent need to eat. I mean how he disappears mentally when you walk by. How he stares. He is mesmerized. What did you do to him?"

*I kissed him.* Had that been enough to initiate a bond? Certainly not.

His grip on her tightened. "A word of warning—if you do not care for him, you need to send him away."

That was a clear threat. She was glad Kiren had such a loyal and protective friend. "What happened to make him this way?"

He flinched. Silence. She'd decided he wasn't going to answer her when he spoke. "He was fifteen when they asked him to lead."

"To lead what?"

"Us."

Alexia stilled. She could hardly imagine so immense a weight on someone that young. Zeph flew them over a ridge, out of sight of camp. Scrub brush passed below and he flapped his wings, slowing. Her feet touched down.

He folded his wings and landed next to her. "There were more then, so many more—at least eighty of us. He did his best for two years, but no one could have known what was coming." Bronze eyes turned to the setting sun.

"The crusaders?"

"They surprised us. We fought back, but we were not organized to clear out and defend like they are now." His voice softened. "We lost a third. Some were taken. Most died."

Alexia absorbed it, heartbroken for her friends.

"He could not heal them all. He could not save them. Many of them blamed him for not taking precautions. Some left. A few even threatened his life."

She could imagine Sarlic being one of those, and who wouldn't fear his ability to inflict the deepest pain? Her poor, dear Kiren.

"He tried to put them back together, but he was beaten. Something in him died the day we were massacred."

Alexia touched his arm.

He met her gaze. "He abdicated and took up friar's robes. I went with him, obviously, and we have been wandering, healing people while he heals. Being here is hard on him. They remember. Some still blame him. He still blames himself."

She nodded.

His head bowed. "Some have even said things. It tore him to pieces, being with them after it happened. He feels it every day, and I worry it will be enough to destroy him. If you do not care for him, you need to tell him to go."

She smiled sadly.

"He would kill me if he knew I told you."

"Then I suppose we will not tell him."

A smile tugged at his cheek. "We should return." He looped his arms through hers again. "Break his heart—I promise you will regret knowing me."

## Fifteen

## Open, I Say

Deamus stopped in the open field and scoured the stars. They weren't aligned as they needed to be, nor did he occupy the grounds where the gate originally opened, but if he waited any longer, the gifted ones might be dead or captured. This would have to be close enough. He had to see if he could make it work, for everyone's sake. He'd been guiltily siphoning trace amounts of strength off the Passionate for almost half a year, and that should be enough to power his experiment. All he had to do was command the elements and release the force caged in his chest.

He shook out his arms, placed both feet firmly on the ground and gazed into the heavens.

The Neitherlands.

Home.

It wasn't that far away.

Lifting both arms, he opened his mouth. The right words spilled out—a language even the stars had to obey. The language of his father.

Night air stirred.

He loosened the power from his core, unraveling it like a ball of yarn.

Pollens popped from their blooms. More energy. The heavens rumbled and swirled. More! A bolt of lightning flashed out of a clear sky. MORE!

He freed the trickle to a stream.

Light burst overhead, a crack of sunlight in the darkened firmament.

It was working!

A yank at his chest jolted him upward. He'd come to the end of the string, the riverbed run dry. It wasn't enough.

He needed more.

The universe demanded more!

Life eked out of his limbs. The gateway would take everything, all he couldn't give it. His life!

His skin wrinkled and shrank.

"NO!" He severed the incantation, ripping the wild spell free. Light swirled in the sky like a whirlpool and blinked out.

He collapsed.

Wind died. Pollens dropped to the ground. They landed on his trembling limbs, dusting him like the snows of failure as he lay, unable to wriggle free from the fatigue.

# Sixteen

# Vanished

Leofrik stood before Ulric's war room, waiting again—only this time he was in no hurry for the confrontation. He didn't understand what had happened. Every detail played out again in his mind:

*The spies returned to the hill where he waited, anxious to have this done.*

*"There's at least two score of them, but they do not have many weapons," the boy reported. "Many are children or women."*

*Leofrik's gut twisted at the idea, but he would follow orders and then voice his concerns with the king before returning to his usual post. If these people, these creatures, could access the devil's power, even children and women were a threat. "Where are they stationed?"*

*The spy cleared the moss, baring a spot of soil. He drew a finger through the dirt, making a circle and plotting out where the majority of the creatures rested. Unsuspecting. That would make things easier.*

*Leofrik gave assignments—one deployment to approach from the west, one from the east. They would surround the group silently and have them captured before anyone could react. It was perfect.*

*But what should he expect when going up against peasants?*

*They marched on the camp, silent as death. Only moments before he and his men entered the site, the fire disappeared. Like someone had blanketed the sun. It was there one instant, gone the next. They found nothing but trees and bushes. Not even the remnants of a fire.*

*They followed a set of footprints, only three escapees unless they'd all been careful enough to step in the footprints of the previous fugitive. The trail died a league away. Boot marks ended in nothing—like they'd been carried into the sky or disappeared.*

*He made the men search the area all night, but come dawn, there was still no hint of life. In the full light of day he discovered the scorched pit where a fire had burned, but they'd been over that land again and again, and no one was there. Either his spies had been deceived, or these creatures were an unholy foe who could channel the very powers of Satan.*

The door groaned open. Leofrik held steady.

"Come," his lord demanded.

***

The verbal reaming he received trumped all others. Leofrik was ready to be done with this man. Far too ready. He spread a map in his bedchamber and scratched a charcoal dot on the location of the camp he'd infiltrated. He placed another dot on the island the creatures had inhabited. Another in France. Another in the desert oasis. One in the mountainous caverns. What did all these locations have in common?

Water.

All of them had a water supply.

Too many water supplies in the world to take that approach. He'd been right on top of them. He wasn't going to overtake an entire camp of witches while they had many powers to pull on. He had to come at them a different way.

Leofrik had to think like the enemy. They could travel in the blink of an eye. If he had that resource at hand, he would pick a spot to settle and travel for crops or other supplies when necessary. No need to keep a garden in the desert sand or rock cliffs—not when you could blink or fly yourself to the most fertile lands in existence. So where were they getting their supplies?

His finger landed on the dot in the countryside of France, their original home.

Ulric had been going about this wrong. He'd assumed that once the group abandoned a home, they never returned.

He may be wrong, but Leofrik finally had a plan.

# Seventeen

# *Seeds of Torture*

Amos held interviews with every member of the company, searching for the traitor. Each person spent hours to an entire day in his hut under interrogation, with Lucian listening in for any premonitions or hint of lies. Alexia's interview lasted less than a minute.

"Is it you?"

She shook her head.

"Clearly. Who do you suspect it might be?"

"Oh that I knew! Any member of our company has been away at various seasons, gathering supplies or running errands. Whoever it is, they must not wish for us to be captured that terribly."

He smiled. "Nor is it likely we can be touched in this unsettled part of the world. This may be the place for us."

"And what of this gateway to another world?"

He shrugged. "If it comes to be a necessity, we will make the sacrifice, but upon further thought, I find Regin's reasoning sound. We know nothing of this new world. It could be worse for us there than here."

She leaned in. "Do you truly believe that?"

"No." He rose, directing her toward the door, but he stopped her at the exit. "Alexia, if something should happen to me because of this traitor, I wish you to lead."

"A woman?"

He grinned. "You will make them believe in you, for you are a power to be reckoned with."

\*\*\*

Alexia rounded a hedge of shrubs to where a pool of water glistened, reflecting the clouds above.

She stopped. Kiren knelt before the water wearing only leggings, his tunic laid carefully on the ground as he sponged himself with a cloth. He'd abandoned his monastic robes in favor of more practical wear after joining them, and he filled the attire quite nicely, when he wore it. She didn't mind him not wearing it.

Water glistened on his back, skin she would so often draw her fingers across while he slept, a spine that would bear immense weight his entire existence and remain upright. She recalled the comfort of cuddling in his embrace through the night.

Her throat constricted. All things she was giving up—things she would never have again.

A smirk tugged at his cheek. She had been detected.

Alexia whirled away and hurried back toward camp. "I am sorry. I did not realize this area would be in use."

Fingers rounded her arm, pulling her to a stop. Golden warmth spread from his touch, calling to the aching core of her heart. A siren song. She swallowed hard, unwilling to look at him and see the ghost of all she was giving up. His honey-oak musk left her feeling hollow.

"There is room for more than one." His words caressed her ears, not so much a suggestive intonation, but a hopeful, breathless one. "Unless you would prefer to have it to yourself."

She was going to lose all resolve to keep him at a distance if she didn't run far away this instant. "I would not hurry you. I shall return later."

He didn't move. She glanced up at him, across his chest that was still excruciatingly bare except for his necklace. Blood pumped to her cheeks.

The muscles in his jaw twitched. "I daresay this is the first time you have looked at me in days." His brow tweaked. The openness of his ocean sky startled her. Had she hurt his feelings? He grinned. "If all it takes is baring my chest, I shall have to do it more often."

She closed her eyes, tugging free from his grip. "Respectfully, I am keeping my distance."

"Which means you are not allowed to look at me? To speak with me?"

She bit the inside of her cheek. This was a mess, one big mess. She'd never have kissed him in the first place if she'd known the truth. Unfortunately, it was too late to jump back and fix it without trauma.

He rested a hand on his hip, his tone teasing. "You challenged me to take the knowledge of my future from you and have given me no opportunity to try. Must I tie you down to gain access to your mind?"

She forced herself to breathe, her heart to slow. He was so much the man he would be, and so different. Could she face him?

Her babe lurched. She placed a hand on her womb, thinking only of the child within. The very idea of speaking with Kiren was torture, but he would remain if she perished in childbirth. If she didn't wish her babe to end up an orphan, she must enlist Kiren's allegiance. He must raise this little girl.

He extended a hand. "I call a truce. Can we start again?"

She studied his fingers, wondering if she dared touch him ever again. She opened her mouth to accept, and hesitated.

"Allow me to finish my mind training"—he shrugged adorably—"which I hear is terribly important to my survival, and I shall keep a respectable distance."

A smile escaped. Treacherous thing, but she rather liked the view. She tucked that thought away before he intercepted it, she hoped. He really needed to attire himself appropriately.

He was grinning along with her. "Let us begin again, the proper way, shall we—since you know most everything about me?" He bowed shallowly. "My name is Kiren de Kir. It is an honor to meet you—"

She crossed her arms. "You expect me to greet a half-naked man?"

His cheeks reddened. Reddened! Alexia couldn't restrain her grin as he ducked his head and slipped the tunic back over his shoulders.

De Kir. She had never heard his full name. Did that make her Alexia de Kir? She couldn't possibly introduce herself that way. What would he think?

A glow still warmed his cheeks as he straightened up.

She curtsied as low as she dared. "Well met, Kiren de Kir. I am Alexia Dumont."

His head tilted. "That is not a family name I have heard before."

"Careful, one might think you have been attentive to your abandoned kin." She brushed past him, aimed for the pool.

He followed after her. "Despite what you may have heard, I am aware of my kind."

Alexia lowered herself next to the pool. He caught her elbow and assisted her into a sitting position, halting with his face mere inches from hers. The universe twinkled back at her in his eyes, the possibility of new beginnings and glimmering hope.

"Too aware of my kind." His whisper warmed her face.

She turned to the water, focusing on the steady in and out of air.

"I know nothing about you, Alexia, except what others have told me. Who are you—besides the Maiden of Time?"

She didn't answer.

He leaned around her and met her gaze in the glassy ripples. It was a portrait of a woman, her husband, and the new life they were creating. Her dream.

She dashed the water, dispelling their joined reflection.

He settled on the ground beside her. "Perhaps if I tell you my story, you will wish to tell me yours?"

She didn't answer him.

He continued on anyway. "I was abducted and brought to this camp because my once-allies had injuries they feared would claim lives. But before I could begin to think about this forced servitude, a woman kissed me. It was not the first time, even that day—"

She scowled.

"—but it was unlike anything I have felt."

*Unlike anything he'd felt...* She shivered. Alexia expected him to continue on, but he watched her in the ripples, waiting. "What did it feel like?"

"Coming home."

Alexia clutched her hands together, awed by his description.

"Which is terrifying, because I had never seen this woman before." He glanced at her sideways and squirmed. "Yet she knew me, far too intimately."

"And that frightened you?"

"Should it shame me to admit the truth?"

She couldn't hold in a laugh. "I believe that an appropriately terrifying circumstance."

He turned toward her, cupping a hand around her cheek. "In kindness, Alexia, give me the opportunity to know you better."

She pushed off the ground, rising to her feet, barely able to breathe around her pounding heart. "Why would I do that?"

He stood beside her, clutching her arms to steady her. "Because in exchange, I will stay until your child is born, and I will ensure that both of you survive."

Alexia closed her eyes against him. He was her Kiren, every bit of him. She yearned to wrap her arms around him and sink into the warmth of his promise, but she loved him too much to risk his life. His future.

"I am not asking for secret kisses in the dark, although I will likely not refuse those either." The teasing tone was a stab to her heart.

"Likely?"

He smirked. "I only wish to know you."

Could there be any harm in that? "It is a dangerous game you propose."

He cleared his throat. "And it terrifies me, but I cannot help but wonder how it would feel to kiss you every time you are near."

She barely uttered, "Even now?"

He lifted her chin. "Especially now."

The flaming blue of his eyes melted her, a fierceness she had never known him without. This was not some illusion. Here stood Kiren in the flesh—even if he lacked the memory of their time together. His fingers trailed goosebumps down her arms and came free, lifting to cup her face. Like he couldn't get enough of touching her.

He licked his lips. "Where do you come from, Alexia?"

"The future. I told you that."

"But where?"

Tell him the truth and he would go into denial again. She wouldn't do that to him. Alexia locked down and stepped back, but he moved with her, keeping her face tenderly clasped.

His breath curled over her cheek and traveled down her neck, a tendril of wishful touch.

She swallowed, hard. What was he doing?

*I am asking myself the same thing,* the thought rang through their connection, an involuntary sharing. His eyes burned over her skin, the simmering blue of a star's flame. They consumed her careful chill. They ate away the determination to forget. They filled her with an ocean of fiery longing. His fingers stole around her back, trembling.

She trembled too. He leaned closer. Alexia stayed perfectly still, entranced by his parted lips, both terrified and hungry for them. He breathed her in. His eyes closed and he shuddered.

She inhaled: oak. A hint of sweetness. The slightest tang of fear. She placed both hands on his chest, that solid surface that heaved with something primal, ready to push him away.

His lips touched hers.

Alexia froze.

He was kissing her.

Kiren was kissing her.

The tenderest of kisses. Like he was afraid of even so light a touch.

Tears slipped down Alexia's cheek as she asked silently, *Why are you kissing me? Why are you torturing us both?* Did he feel a connection despite the fear stiffening his body? If his pledge to save her after childbirth held true, she might not have to die in this time, which meant neither would he. They could both survive this, together. She could have this.

As much as she wanted more, wanted him, he could not intercept the memories locked in her head. She blocked the doorway to her mind with a dark cloud and prepared to push away. Just in time.

His lips parted hers.

Strength drained from her arms. She wanted to swim into the velvety darkness caressing her soul, to live within him so fully that life possessed only one meaning. She needed him as she'd always needed him. From the way he pulled her closer, deepening the kiss, he needed her too.

His mind opened to hers, no barriers, no fences. It was like stepping into an open field with a clear view of the world. Briars tore across the ground—ripping open the wounds of having lost his family each time they healed. His earth was raw, shredded, and trembling. The need to be restored to his family's throne loomed above her, a crumbling iron pinnacle, a once-firm structure that had been brought to ruin. He had picked up stones and attempted to build something new with them, but each effort had been torn down. The tower, his family, his throne, they had been the only things that mattered. Now the icon of his purpose threatened to collapse, leaving naught but waste in his world—no hope, no tender relationships to ease his suffering, no soft hand to guide him toward something better. No home.

He was broken. So young and so broken.

Alexia pulled back, staring up into his eyes. It was one thing when she kissed him, when mistakenly she'd initiated the contact her soul alone craved. His kiss was different. Sincere. An opening of the heart. An offering.

"You know everything about me," he whispered. "Now, I plead in all fairness, tell me where you come from."

"Oh, Kiren…" She traced the skin from cheekbone to chin where he would one day bear a scar. "You should not have done that."

His Adam's apple bobbed and nostrils flared. She watched the reality dawn over him—that he had willingly opened himself to her, that he had started something neither of them may be able to end. His kiss might be enough to initiate the cycle that had granted Kiren only a couple months of bliss after centuries of loneliness. She didn't want that for him.

"You do not want to be bonded to me," she said quietly.

When they first touched intimately in the future, he had claimed she would be the death of him. It had been said jokingly, but he never rescinded the statement. If she allowed him in, allowed the bond to form, then died in childbirth, he would die along with her. That could not happen.

"Have it out then. Did you ensnare me when I first entered the camp because of my healing gift?" His chest puffed and he waved at her womb. "I would have helped you if you asked."

There was the anger she'd expected. He wouldn't be Kiren without that righteous indignation. "No." *You were my husband. Will be.* She stopped the confession before it left her tongue. "I believed you were someone else."

His single eyebrow peaked. "Someone with the same name?"

This was sounding less and less plausible with every question, even if it was true. "Yes."

He gazed over her head, jaw clenched. He exhaled and turned away.

She watched him go, uncertain what more she could say. He didn't believe her. He would never believe her.

She didn't need him to. It was better if he left it at that, left her for good.

***

Kiren punched a tree branch as he veered through the brush. He'd been right. She had been attempting to bond him in order to save her baby, and now she'd developed a conscience and backed away. Rage consumed him. To be used for one's gift was the greatest insult. Not only had she violated his mind, she'd violated his budding trust. He should have left the instant he finished healing the others. Perhaps it was time.

***

On her way back to the camp, Alexia stumbled over Deamus's body, prostrate on the ground. She knelt and patted his cheek. His eyelids fluttered and a mumble escaped his lips, something about a seal and revenge. Had someone attacked him?

Kiren had come this way not much earlier, but he wouldn't harm Deamus. That was absurd.

She found Regin and Sarlic to carry Deamus back into camp, but Kiren refused to heal him.

Perhaps it wasn't as laughable as she first thought.

# Eighteen

## *An Echo of Chaos*

Kiren knew he was being petty, but he didn't like Deamus. It wasn't anything the man had done other than imagining Alexia would become the love of his life. But this was something more. Something unseen. Maybe it was the guilt over abandoning his responsibilities, made fresh by the presence of someone from his home. He felt terrible about this unsubstantiated dislike, but not enough to actually lay hands on the man—even to revive him. Call it a fear of being siphoned? Instinct was strong among the Lost Ones, and should Deamus wake to a near infinite supply of strength, who knew what would happen. Kiren had more to lose in a draining than most. More than any man should possess.

And he was tired of being used.

Alexia gave him a deep scowl when he refused, but he wouldn't change his mind. She was only using him anyway.

He returned her disapproval with an air of indifference and escaped to the woods for solitude.

Kiren began questioning if Alexia did know someone else with his name from another time—perhaps his son or grandson—not that he was ever going to have children. Still, it would explain why she could mistake him for another who bore the same name, why she would be terrified of caring too intimately for him, and how she could know so much about him. How awkward would that be if the same woman loved both a man and his grandfather? It might also explain why she felt like family to him. But it didn't explain why she believed him caring for her would lead to his death—unless she had some insight about that as well.

Had she seen his death? Merely heard stories?

A prickling sensation started at the back of his neck.

He froze. Kiren turned slowly, eyeing the night sky behind him. There was nowhere to hide, and therefore no one watching him, in theory, but he hurried back to camp a little faster anyway.

\*\*\*

From its perch in the night, inky intelligence hovered, waiting for the last of them to slip into slumber. The gateway had been cracked, allowing just the faintest wisps of itself through. Throw that barrier open and *it* would reign on this earth, wreaking the same self-destruction that it had inspired in society after society. Soon. Very soon its hour would come.

## Nineteen

## *Perspective*

Leofrik stopped at the edge of the field, impressed by the variety of colors and leaves—a blooming garden able to feed at least fifty souls. The farmhouse nearby had been burned down years ago, but portions of it remained—a single stone wall, charred eaves now covered in creeping ivy, and most startling, a sun-bleached tunic hanging to dry.

The horizon showed no other residence.

He knelt and brushed a hand through the leaves of a berry bush. Fruit had been plucked from the plant—not merely nibbled off by pests or rodents. If he didn't know the truth, he'd question if ghosts harvested and maintained this place.

He would watch. If these necromancers were using this space, he'd observe their patterns and decide the best way to trap them. Know thy enemy.

# Twenty

## *Mischief*

A scream.

Alexia dropped her stitching and threw back the curtain door of her hut.

Deamus squealed again. He brushed grubby worms off his head and shoulders, stumbling over a bucket that still contained a number of grubs. She glanced at the roof of his hut where the bucket had been perched.

Kiren and Zephaniah stood in the distance, chuckling.

Deamus had been mending the last week, slowly recovering what would have taken Kiren mere seconds to restore. Tensions had increased between the two, and she'd been struck with a growing animosity toward Kiren for his unkind words, and now actions.

She gave him an incredulous glare and went to aid her friend. She understood that Deamus and Kiren had disagreed, but this was childish and demeaning. If Deamus hadn't insisted Kiren was innocent of knocking him out, she would have taken steps to banish her once and future husband.

Since he'd kissed her, they'd hardly spoken two words to one another. Something she'd said must have sunken in, but she didn't understand why he stayed.

\*\*\*

Kiren threw his hands up at her glare. Just because he thought a man being doused in wigglers was funny didn't mean he'd made it happen. She truly didn't know him if she believed him the cause.

Thank the heavens she didn't know about the incident earlier today when Willem couldn't find his whittled knight. Kiren had discovered it wrapped in his bedroll. He'd snuck it away and placed it on a rock near the center of camp. Zeph caught him, but thankfully his friend believed his innocence. There was also Mae's shield which found its way to his prayer spot in the trees. He hadn't been so lucky there. Amos had needed his assistance with one of the children who'd consumed poison berries and found him holding the shield.

Someone was trying to make him look like a villain.

68

\*\*\*

Another scream. Alexia and Amos exchanged looks and hurried through the underbrush, pushing through other people who had gathered. Little Filia crouched near the pool, trembling. Regin knelt next to the girl, speaking softly.

"I-it was a monster." The little one tucked into Regin's chest, and he lifted his hands and chin away, avoiding the contact that would put her to sleep. Her voice was muffled, "Black like midnight. Hiding."

Alexia sighed. Wonderful. Now they had a bear to watch for.

Someone whispered behind her, "Beware the Soul Eater."

Another person chuckled. "He will come for you at night, whilst you sleep in your bed."

"He will steal away your soul and plant stories in your head."

She turned on the group, scowling at their rhyme. "The Soul Eater?"

Amos waved them off. "It is a silly story, passed down through generations to scare children."

"I have never heard it."

He smirked and shook his head. "They say a monster was created out of people's hate long ago. It was a beast that could not be contained by any physical element. The thing roamed free, stealing people's souls until it was trapped in a great cage."

"A cage in the sky," Regin shook a fist at the heavens as he arrived at her other side. Filia now resided safely in Oriel's embrace. Regin cupped his mouth conspiratorially. "But it sneaks out to steal the souls of naughty lads and lassies."

"I know this story," Deamus said, surprising them not only by speaking up, but with the youthful bounce in his step. "They tell it in my home as well, but they say the man who created this other world sealed the monster in the between, to guard one sphere from the other. It eats the souls of naughty children to keep itself strong."

Although they jested, Alexia couldn't silence the warning bell in her head. "These children who have their souls eaten, what becomes of them?"

The three men looked at one another, tipped off by her tone.

"They are silly stories." Amos dropped a hand on her shoulder. "But we should be more careful. Any kind of creature could inhabit this mountain."

She nodded, still uneasy. "We could erect walls?"

"Is that how long we plan to stay here?"

She shrugged.

"Let us bring it before the council. But for now, we should keep constant to the young ones."

She agreed.

\*\*\*

Amos approached, and Kiren didn't like the sober look in the man's eye. Without a word, he signaled Kiren to follow.

They entered a hut where Alexia stood, arms crossed in one corner, Regin and Lucian bent over Sarlic on the floor, his branded face white. Mae clutched a bloodied cloth.

Kiren knelt to search for a wound. "What happened?"

"He attacked Mae," Regin supplied.

"He was not in his right mind," she whispered.

Kiren found the wound on the back of Sarlic's head and brushed his fingers over it, telling the fibers to mend. Still, the man's mind was silent—more so than merely being unconscious.

Kiren lifted his gaze to Mae. "What did you do to him?"

Her grip tightened on the bloodied rag. "He came at me, inflicting pain, his eyes all wrong." She twisted the cloth. She lifted her golden cuff, the metal clasp bent out of sorts and nearly broken. She met his stare. "He tried to force my bracelet free while muttering about the gateway. How he would stop us all…" Her shoulders hunched inward.

"And you touched him?"

She nodded. "The forehead, just a fingertip."

Kiren placed his palm over the man's brow, closing his eyes and seeking deeper. He found a glimmer of consciousness, suppressed, but there.

Amos spoke. "We could not go to this other world if Mae sucked everyone dry."

They were all watching Kiren, even Alexia, although she averted her gaze when he met her stare. He lifted his hands in surrender. "What do you believe that has to do with me?"

"Did ye put him to it?" Regin asked directly.

Kiren turned on the man. Grinding his teeth together, he asked, "Why would I do that? Why would I care in the least if any of you were stupid enough to try and reach the other world? It cannot be done."

Lucian stood. "I said it was not him."

"But he is the only one who can alter the body and mind," Amos argued.

"It was not him," Alexia finally came to his defense. "He cannot alter minds."

How convenient that her intimate knowledge of his skills should finally come to his aid. Even if she was revealing things he'd rather they not know. Kiren rolled his eyes in disgust and surged into Sarlic's mind, reaching for that flicker of consciousness. He focused on expanding it, opening it wider, feeding it into the rest of the brain.

The inflictor startled. His arms flew out either direction, and his head jerked around to take everyone in. "Where am I? How did I get here?"

Kiren didn't waste any time. "Did I ask you to attack Mae?"

The branded man scowled at him. "No. We have not spoken in days."

Kiren stood. "Search my memories if you like." He turned directly on Alexia. "You will see the truth."

No one moved. No one said a word. He shook his head and exited the hut, appalled.

\*\*\*

Darkness fell over the camp, the sun taking its warmth with it. The usual evening fires had burned down, and Alexia shivered in her bedroll, comforting herself with memories of her husband's arms wrapped around her on chilly nights. She remembered how, without fail, his hand always found its place over her heart. It was nights like these when his loss became unbearable.

She tugged the blanket tightly around herself and rose. The makeshift hut housed three women and two girls. The girls, sisters, huddled together for warmth next to their mother. She stepped over Mae and Ravia, reaching the doorway.

The song of insects filled the night, and the most amazing view of stars littered the sky as she wandered, like pulsating specks of sand, thousands upon thousands—so many she would never be able to count them all. They reminded her of souls. Thousands upon thousands of people who had lived upon this Earth, each a shining beacon at some point, eventually fading into old age and finally death. But not the Passionate. Or at least, not most of them. They went on. While lights burned out around them, they survived the centuries, brightening or festering as they refined in character.

Kiren was like one of those stars—a light that had only begun to shine. By the time she would meet him again, he'd be as brilliant as the North Star, and just as fixed in character. She questioned if she would be the same after centuries of existence. Although, she wouldn't get centuries.

Kiren sat in the darkness near the edge of camp, alone. Moonlight caressed the planes of his high cheekbones, too perfect without the defining scar. His soul bore all the scars in this age. Alexia couldn't decide if she should approach or turn and walk another direction. She hated what they'd put him through earlier, but no one would listen to her. Something unspeakable had happened and they all wanted someone to blame. She'd insisted Kiren would never harm another living soul, and Lucian had vaguely mumbled his assent, but the evidence stacked too greatly against the one member of their band. Pranks and other troubles had started after he'd appeared.

She'd been standing too long, indecisive about changing course when he muttered, "Have you come to gloat?"

"Gloat?"

His ultra-blue eyes turned on her. "About having turned everyone against me."

She huffed. As cruel as the comment was, she knew it came from a place of pain. Indeed, they had turned against him, and she had been terribly slow in coming to his defense. But she had. He must believe she'd encouraged their attack with how she'd pushed him away.

"Why are you still here if you feel so ostracized?"

His head fell into his hands. "That is the answer then. Flee. Run away again."

Heat burned in her cheeks. She understood why he'd left the first time, and it stabbed her to the core knowing he felt entirely homeless, even among his own people. The accusations tonight hadn't merely been because of recent events. There had been plenty of animosity toward him before.

She maneuvered into a seat next to him, loosened her blanket from around her shoulders, and placed a hand on his back. "No one is asking you to flee." Firm muscles beneath the wool belied the aching soul they shrouded.

"I should have let Zeph take me away."

"See now, then you would not have learned how to guard your mind from attacks." It was a weak attempt at levity, and not enough. She slid her fingers over top of his, pulling his hand away from his hair.

He met her gaze. The desperation and hurt was too much. Alexia touched his cheek, opening her memories just the slightest. A glimpse of Miles slipped through, the lonely, sad child Kiren had reared and saved from the fate of becoming Soulless or losing himself to the self-gratification of his gift. She allowed him a snatch of Nelly, the earth shaker he'd saved from both the Soulless and Breeders, how he'd housed her and asked nothing of her until she learned what it meant to be loved.

"You are not a man who runs." She slid her fingers up into his hair, loving the feathery softness. "You are a man who embraces and shields those who need it most, those who have no one else."

His brow met hers. "Like you?" he whispered.

She bit her lip, certain of what was coming. "I was different, but you saved me nonetheless."

His mouth reached for hers. She knew she should resist, but she let him have it. His heart was torn enough. He needed something and she could be that thing. She could be so much more than that thing. She ached to be more.

He pulled her closer, one hand traveling to the back of her head, locking her in place, and the other rounding her back—as if responding to her unvoiced wish.

*Whoa.*

A whisper at the back of her mind warned against relenting. She half-pulled away, but he tugged her closer, delving deeper. Her body erupted in tingles, an aching to have him more fully, to have him completely.

*More,* his mind begged. It was a wild vortex, swallowed completely in sensations. No rational thought remained, no tender feeling toward the woman he was quickly consuming. She was his ale, his escape, his distraction of choice. Alexia burst into his torn landscape, startled to find a bust of herself shaped atop the crumbling tower. He'd begun to rebuild by molding everything around her likeness.

*I cannot save you,* she whispered to his mind.

*I do not need to be saved,* he answered. *Not tonight.* No indeed. He only wanted to expend all his pain by exploiting her.

Alexia shoved out of his arms, hard.

They watched one another. He panted. She trembled with the need to return to his embrace, but he was not her husband, no matter how much he felt like the man.

"I am here because of you, Alexia." He pushed up onto his knees. "I do not know what you were showing me with these people who are...who will be so desperate for help. I am not that man. I have never been that man."

"But you could be." She struggled to her feet, taking her blanket with her. "You will be."

He laughed and turned away. "Whatever you say."

She hugged herself. He was aching. She knew that, but she didn't need to stand for his abuse. More importantly, she was suddenly feeling tired, so much more tired than a physical weariness. She couldn't carry them both. All three of them. He had to stand on his own, to at least strive for something better than this.

"Goodnight, Kiren."

***

Kiren listened to her go, instantly regretting that he'd been so hostile toward one of the two people who valued him. He was doing everything wrong. All of it. So much so that they had blamed him for an attack.

He ripped both hands through his hair.

He was to blame—not for this attack, but for those they'd lost. For their animosity. It was deserved. If a ruler couldn't rule, he should step down, and Kiren had, but it wasn't enough. Years away hadn't been enough either.

It never would be.

Alexia was right. She'd stopped him from going down a physical path he'd regret, but she'd also turned him from a mental road. He could sit here, feeling sorry for himself, or he could be that man—maybe not the one she envisioned, but a man of confidence, good feeling, and service. He wouldn't let anyone's glares or unkind words determine who he became. From this moment on, he was his own. Let them think what they might.

***

Alexia dismissed Kiren's lack of chivalry when he didn't follow her or offer to escort her to safety, but it hurt. Sometimes he was so much the man she'd known, and sometimes he was a boy pounding his fists against the glass. Kiren had warned her: *"You will see many whom you recognize, but be patient… Recall that they still have five hundred years to become who they are now."*

He'd been warning her about himself.

Alexia gasped. Kiren had carefully concealed the details about when he'd first met her, because it was in this time. She'd assumed it was when she was born. Ah, the dangers of assuming. Still, he'd attempted to prepare her for this. Why? What forbade him from telling her everything? The same reasons she kept his fate from him?

Tonight had been a mistake. It was one stitch deeper into the bond, the unbreakable ropes that Alexia didn't want choking her future husband. She stilled and felt for the timeline. Only a few minutes back and she could erase the moment from existing, except for in her mind. Her mental fingers stumbled over a blank wall. Ebony. She shoved against it, but it held firm. She reached harder. The barrier softened but remained.

Alexia withdrew.

Strange. It had never happened before. Perhaps it was a consequence of her late pregnancy, or the shield of her own subconscious against pushing too hard and fast.

Peculiar.

Coolness settled over her skin, a sadness weighing her heart. Was it even worth fighting? If he wanted to be a wretch, let him be a wretch.

No, that wasn't right. She didn't feel that way and didn't want to feel that way. Why was she suddenly so down? The sorrow hung on her like a London haze in the dead of winter.

She halted. While consumed in thought, she'd wandered further from her hut, not toward it. Twisted branches reached from the ground to her waist, scattered trees behind them stretching to just above her head.

The air had stilled like it was holding its breath.

There was always wind here. She shivered. No insects hummed. Hairs on her arms bristled.

Movement.

She jumped and twisted.

Nothing.

But something hid in the darkness, something she could only see out of the corner of her eye. Probably a llama or bear. Nothing she wished to stumble into after dark.

Still, goosebumps ran up her arms.

She wasn't alone.

Another being occupied the stillness, one she couldn't see. An animal—whose heart must be pounding as quickly as hers. It was silly to stand here, allowing her mind to build horrific fantasies.

Resolved, Alexia turned to go home.

An inky haze sucked away, disappearing behind jagged branches.

Twenty-One

# Disappointment

Ulric pushed the shutters open to spill daylight on his little prisoner. The mini captive. His progeny and most profitable venture to date, even if the child was somewhat repulsive.

She lifted a tiny, grayed hand to shield her eyes, jingling her chains with the movement. "Mommy?" she asked.

He ground his teeth. The voice was the epitome of innocence and childhood, but its source didn't reflect any such beauty. "Is it not enough that I have come?"

She lowered her gaze—a good little girl who knew when to hold her tongue. Her shoulders shook once, twice. "I want Mommy."

"As do I, poppet." He smiled. He'd been told his smile was more menacing than comforting, but his little doll seemed to find comfort in it. At least she rubbed at her eyes and sat very, very still. It was unnatural the way she held herself, unflinching even at the loudness of his steps in the stone tower. That unnaturalness kept her from being loved or embraced as she clearly desired. It made his skin crawl. He sat next to her on the thin mattress. "I had rather hoped opening this window would encourage Mommy's appearance, but it looks like she will not see you today."

The child sniffled. Her blonde tresses bobbed and she curled inward. It wasn't that he enjoyed injuring the child, but there was a slight sense of satisfaction in watching her cringe. Pain was a part of life. It was the best education. If her frail body could withstand the lash, he'd teach her by other means (and had on occasion), but for now, words would do. Only after her mother arrived would he break this child's little body to teach both mother and child the consequence of disobedience. For now, listening to the imp sniffle and stifle her emotions would have to suffice.

He waited until she calmed. Until she held unnaturally still once more.

Finally, he rose. "Mommy is not coming today. Maybe she will come tomorrow."

The child huddled in on herself.

"Well, until tomorrow, poppet."

"Bye-bye, Papa."

75

# Twenty-Two

# Decided

All night long Alexia relived the moment, the feeling, the silence brought on by…whatever it was. She'd glimpsed darkness—a cloud of darkness. Like the murk Amos created.

"Did you have any strange or restless dreams last night?" she asked their leader. It was possible he could use his gift while slumbering, even without knowing.

Amos waved Alexia off. "None for me."

She explained her experience, asking again if it was possible he might have brought the haze.

He rubbed his chin. "I suppose it might be possible, but I have never done anything like that before."

They left it at that.

But Alexia wasn't alone. Others started reporting the strange feeling, the stillness, and when they turned at the movement, they blacked out. She asked Amos again if it might be a result of his dreams, and he suggested, "Perhaps this is another of the Passionate reaching out to us."

Twelve. There had been twelve reports now. In the last sighting, little Filia had been found screaming, cringing against a boulder. Alexia thought that warranted some kind of action, though she had no idea what.

"What would you have us do?" Amos waved a hand at his hut's new, wooden door. "Hunt this thing? It harms no one."

"It scares children."

He nodded and clasped a hand over his forehead. "We are building something here. In three weeks no one has been injured, so we leave it alone, it leaves us alone. Perhaps it is even a protection. Keeps others away."

She drew a finger across the wooden table in his hut. He wasn't the only one who'd begun filling his space with permanent furniture. People had started believing this could be a home—that running away to a new land wasn't necessary. Routines had begun to manifest—harvest twice a week, duties fulfilled, new clothing produced and mended… Even Velia enjoyed time away. Alexia didn't want to take that from them any more than Amos did, so perhaps it was a benign thing that prowled the night. Considering how settled they were, birthing a child in this environment might be ideal.

At least Kiren was still present.

She left Amos and went about her duties, delivering mended clothing and gathering the torn, or taking orders for necessities. She was grateful Ethel had taught her the important skill of sewing. Especially since she could contribute without risking her child.

Mist curled across the ground. Velia stepped out of the fog with two others, having just returned from the lush fields they farmed on the other side of the world. Alexia waved, grateful for their buckets full of berries, greens, wheat, and turnips. They would be eating well tonight.

She pulled a curtain door aside and stepped into a hut to return Ilberd's mended tunic. They were slowly replacing curtains with doors, children and women first.

She froze.

Kiren knelt beside Ilberd on his mattress. The mattress was Oriel's handiwork. Oriel and little Filia had been gathering straw, down, wool, and whatever else they could to fill the mattresses while Alexia and Silivia sewed.

Kiren gently squeezed Ilberd's forearm. "And the weakness continues?"

"It was better yesterday, but I swear it don't heal right."

Kiren grinned. "It would if you'd keep it in the sling I made for you."

"How's an able bodied man to chop lumber if he's got use of but one arm?" He leaned around his medic. "Ho there, Alexia. Thank ye much for the mending!"

"Glad to assist." She set his tunic on the single stool in the room. When she looked up, Kiren was watching her, a blank expression on his face. Her cheeks burned.

Every time she caught a glimpse of him her heart leapt into her throat, her belly filling with longing so potent it drowned out even the need to eat. The torture was divine. Each morning he crossed paths with her by the pool, and she looked forward to it. They would speak, sometimes briefly, but once for half the morning. He'd always inquire after her health, then subtly dig for more information about his future. She liked making him dig. She'd let little bits of truth drop: her father's dislike of Kiren, aspects of the house he'd built that she admired, how much she missed Sarah. He lapped every confession up like a thirsting dog.

She didn't know if he stayed because he wanted to, or because she insisted that they needed him. He had healed so many ailments and saved lives. The others saw it too. Despite a rocky start in this mountain, attitudes were changing. She saw in him a determination to make it so and that pleased her. He had become a favorite with the children.

And with her.

Still, no matter how amiably they talked, every morning their discussions devolved into a fight. This morning it had been a disagreement about the permanence of this community. Kiren didn't think it would last. She insisted it was an attitude like that which would end up costing them their peaceful abode.

"Alexia," he greeted and got quickly to his feet. He snatched up her basket of repaired clothing. "Where are you off to next?"

"Oh, um, Mae's new hut."

"Oye! What about me?" Ilberd asked.

"Sling," Kiren commanded and pushed a curtain aside for Alexia. "One arm until I say otherwise."

The curtain dropped behind them, and she waddled self-consciously in front of him. He leveled next to her, eyes fixed ahead. "Seen any monsters in the night recently?"

She prickled. "Tease all you like, but you will not when you see it."

He chuckled.

They arrived at the center of their budding township. Huts formed a circle around the well Willem had tunneled the first week. Each building had begun to take on a unique look thanks to Oluchi's brilliant paints. Crimsons, vibrant blues, yellows, greens, and oranges. The variety filled Alexia with joy. It was like spring every time she walked by.

"I can take that." She reached for her basket.

Kiren lifted it away. "You should not be carrying heavy things, not at this late stage."

"I have been carrying heavy things every day of my life. Doing so now will not change my fate. My basket?" She swiped for it, and he lifted it away again, laughing. "You are being ridiculous."

"I am sorry. That is a woman's job, is it not?"

She gasped indignantly and jabbed a finger at his ribs. He dodged most of the blow, backing up a step, as she lunged for her basket. Alexia's balance was off. She landed against his chest, struck by the scent of his honeyed-oak and the firmness of his body. His smile faded as he studied her face.

The stars shifted in his all-encompassing sea, not merely a projection from a distant sky, but an embracing light that reached for her own. Something clicked into place. He was no longer looking at her like a challenge, but a part of himself he couldn't lose.

His gaze bounced quickly away and back, and he leaned in. His lips pressed to her cheek in a tender caress.

This was what she'd been waiting for. At last a touch that said, *I adore you with all my heart. Please be mine.*

He pulled back, and Alexia remembered where they stood. In the center of the township. With several people watching. He may as well have just declared his feelings for all to see.

She backed away.

They were supposed to keep a distance. She could not endanger her husband's life. Her cheeks warmed. "What are you doing?"

"I thought that was clear." His gaze lingered on her, filled with such warmth that she may never need the sun again. He lifted her basket. "I am taking care of you."

A flurry of movement caught her periphery. She turned as Deamus hurried away.

Kiren threaded her arm through his and smiled at her, just for her. In her heart, she felt as though a great battle had come to an end, one she didn't wish to fight anyway. Perhaps they had finally reached that magical place: not enemies, not allies, but something dear.

***

Kiren stared into her eyes and it hit him. He cared about her. Too much. Every morning he looked forward to verbally sparring with her near the pond. It was the best part of his day. The part that kept him fighting. If she could care for him, it didn't matter how many of his people held grudges. She was the heart of the Lost Ones. She represented all that was good about them, and he could thrive no matter what came, so long as he had her.

But he didn't have her. Not really.

Kiren caught a glimpse of Deamus over her shoulder. The lanky giant lifted a hand and approached, as if to whisk Alexia from him.

There would be no whisking. Not now, not ever. He leaned in and pressed a kiss to her cheek. Not just a kiss, a declaration. He had been dancing around it long enough. If he adored her, and he did, it was time to make his claim.

She'd said she wouldn't live through her child's birth. He was determined that she would. He would make sure of it. And then he would take her delicate, determined hand into his own and never let go.

Kiren pulled back and she blushed. He loved watching the flush of realization and embarrassment stain her cheeks. It made him want to kiss her again, more intimately, enough to make everyone else blush. Would she let him?

Perhaps being bonded might not be so awful. It may actually prove to be the most amazing experience of his life.

Deep breath.

Yes, he'd thought it, and he believed it. No backing down now.

She put space between them.

"What are you doing?" she hissed.

"I thought that was clear." He lifted her basket, filled with a sudden warmth that exhilarated and terrified. "I am taking care of you."

Deamus fled, and Kiren grinned. *That's right. She is mine.*

***

Deamus burst into the clearing, flexing and loosening his hands. She was slipping away from him. The one thing he thought he had, and here an enemy poached his prize. She would be his if he could just open that gateway!

He plowed through a depressed haze, dropping to his knees.

So be it. There was only one course of action to take. He lifted both hands above his head and recited the incantation from memory. Wind swirled around him. It tore at his cloak and funneled into the sky. He focused on the energy stored within, the energy stored without, the passion of the community only a short distance away. All this he directed upward into the gathering storm.

A seam ripped through the clouds, revealing midnight pitch beyond. A crack. Just enough for someone to slip through. Already the draw of power was too much. It would kill them all.

He grated his teeth and pounded his fists into the earth, severing the connection.

The sky healed. Birds cawed in the distance.

It was no use. He was never going home.

# Twenty-Three

# *The Traitor*

A trap for someone who could turn to mist?

Leofrik straightened the chainmail net and backed away. He'd been observant and invisible, and now his efforts would pay out. Metal links spanned the spot she always appeared, suspended between a tree and the burned out house.

A chilly breeze washed over him. He grinned, poised to pounce. Success was about to be delivered.

Wind rattled the chainmail and a shriek rent the air. Nothing but mist one second, woman the next. She hit the metal links with the force of a horse-drawn carriage, and the mail caught around her, torn loose from the tree and building. It tangled over her. Leofrik rushed in as she ripped at the metal. He hugged it tightly about her, securing it like a blanket around her torso and knocking her to the ground.

She jerked, arms secured in the web. She kicked at him, but he crushed her legs beneath his own. Her teeth snapped at him. He leaned away, one arm pressed against her collarbone.

Silver eyes glared death at him through a mess of snowy-blonde hair with a hint of sunshine. Cautiously, he brushed the strands back from her face. Thin brows crushed down over upturned eyes. The pink of rose petals warmed her cheeks, and berry wine lips pursed, twitching in rage. She smelled of lilac and a hint of rain—such an intriguing mixture.

Lovely. Beyond lovely. She belonged in men's dreams, not the light of day.

Her chest heaved beneath him, and he became aware of her form, a shape quite pleasingly proportioned from what he could feel.

*Head out of the bedsheets. To your duty, man.*

She twisted again, a futile attempt to break free. She slammed the back of her head into the ground with a growl. The sound startled him. Had it come from a wolf or lion it wouldn't have surprised him, but from a young woman who fit the image of an angel? He couldn't reconcile the two. Except that she was a witch. And dangerous.

"Hello, lovely," he greeted.

She twitched beneath him, attempting to shake him off again, grunting with the effort.

"I am twice your heft." He pressed down harder. "Save your strength for a battle you can win."

Her head tilted, bottom eyelids squeezing upward. The silver of her stare cut through him like a blade, and he swore it sliced into his very soul. She exhaled and turned her head away.

Good. The fight was gone. Now he could get down to business.

"*How is it he trapped me?*" he mimicked what he thought her voice might sound like. After a week of plotting, he needed to explain his genius. "Every morning she comes with first light—like a feather on the breeze. I hide in the burned out house, watching as she takes her turns about the field, checking crops and tasting them for ripeness. Cannot see her face. It is like fog. Most of her is. I wonder if she is actually here, somewhere else, or both."

He snatched the rope dangling off the metal net and looped it around her chest, tugging it tight.

She grunted, nose flaring.

He gave the rope a single knot and looped it around her waist. "Nothin' can catch the wind, but I have it from good authority that metal can trap her kind. So I reconstruct my chainmail, turning it into a net, and stretch it out in the night—right at the spot she appears every sunrise. And here she is." He finished securing the rope around her knees. Peculiar that she wore no shoes. Not much by way of clothing either—only a flimsy shift, as if the weather didn't affect her. Curious. The thin fabric did little to hide her enticing curves. "And now she is wondering what it is I want with her?"

Her chin lifted stubbornly away, mouth clamped tight.

"Well, *lady,*" he said mockingly, "it is probably not what you expect." He sat back and examined his handiwork. The rope cut deep, securing the metal right against her skin. The tiniest bit of him twinged against what he'd done. His mother would roll in her grave if she could see this, but he reminded himself that this woman would just as happily kill him as listen to his request. "I want you to take me to your people."

She choked and shook with silent laughter.

As expected. "And why should you do that?" He rose to his feet, adjusting the sword at his hip. "Because I can be terribly persuasive when I choose."

She closed her eyes and her face relaxed as if to say, *Do anything to me you want.*

"My lord has bid me capture and enslave the demons who plague his land. Are you demons then?"

The woman scoffed.

"You have my ear, maiden, but my patience thins, and with it my empathy."

She glared at him.

He exhaled. This wasn't going as well as he'd hoped. He had to find the right trigger.

# Twenty-Four

# *Love and Blood*

Zeph threw an empty coconut shell at Kiren. He ducked, and it hit his shoulder before bouncing off the stone wall of their hut.

"Brain boiled," Zeph laughed. "I thought I was too close to the rift, but you, you jumped over the edge, head first."

Kiren grinned, regardless of his friend's teasing. "Says the king of cliff diving."

"Yeah, the one of us with wings. You are really willing to give up everything for this, this girl?"

Kiren lifted his hands in surrender. "One kiss on the cheek. People greet one another that way in several countries we have visited. I am not offering my heart on a platter."

Zeph huffed. "And how many women have *you* greeted with a kiss?"

One. Exactly one, and they both knew it.

"You said you were never going to be bonded." Zeph sat, crossing his arms. "You said it was a bad idea."

"I know what I said, but she knows me, Zeph. From the future." Kiren sat across from his friend, giving him a moment for the words to settle. "What am I giving up by choosing her?"

Zeph ticked off his fingers. "Your father's throne."

"Already gave that up."

"Your kingdom."

"Do not want it." Kiren shrugged.

"Your freedom."

"What is freedom without a reason to appreciate it?"

Zeph paused on the fourth finger. "A virgin."

Kiren rubbed at his eyes. Yes, that aspect bothered him some, but he'd made it clear to everyone he intended to pursue her, and it wasn't a decision he came to lightly. He cared for her, regardless of her history. "Next?"

"Marital bliss." Zeph knocked that finger a couple times. "The baby is not just going to disappear because you are busy with its mama."

Marriage. He hadn't thought that far. Pursue her, yes. Enjoy the heat of each kiss, absolutely. But marriage? He scratched the back of his neck, fingers stumbling over his necklace. His parents had been happy. Until they died because of their children. Promising a woman forever when his forever might be riddled with danger—especially when she had a child—what would she have to say about this?

He should go ask her. Right now.

Zeph crossed his arms triumphantly. "I just think maybe you are jumping into this without exploring all the possibilities."

Kiren laughed. "I thought you would appreciate me leaving the *possibilities* for you."

"Not me. I am not sealing my fate for a long, long time."

He opened the door. "While you are ruminating about these possibilities I am missing, I am going to find my reality and enjoy how warm and solid she is."

***

Alexia clipped the thread between her teeth and set the needle aside. Ravia's cloak was finished. It had been chilly enough at night that she'd promised to return it today…although today had worn into tonight. She knew only because Regin had insisted she start a fire when he entered and forced dinner upon her. He was right. The single window had dimmed until she was squinting to see her stitches.

She tottered to her feet and wrapped the cloak in her arms. Mae had moved to her own hut this morning or else she would have been present to accompany Alexia. She'd also have told her to quit stitching long ago, which meant the job wouldn't be done yet. They'd have spent the last hours of the day exercising Mae's gift and helping her refine her control as they did every night, but this evening Mae had been settling into her new home. It was going to be strange, not sharing the space with her dear friend, but Mae felt it safer to occupy her own space, especially once the child was born.

Alexia slipped out the door.

And slammed into someone. Warm hands wrapped around her.

She gasped and stared up into the heavenly sea of possibility, the man who had made his intentions toward her public this morning. The man she could barely breathe without. She recalled how he'd escorted her through her deliveries and then back to her hut, carrying her basket the entire way. It was such a sweet gesture. And then he'd dipped down and placed a timid kiss on her lips before returning to his duties.

Looking up at him now, the starlight painting his lips in soft light, her heart sped. "You could not wait until morning to speak?"

He shrugged, rubbing his hands up and down her back. "I missed you."

Her face flamed. He missed her? This was not good. From the intimate touch to the glimmer in his eyes, she was in trouble. Had he meant *take care of her* as in guard her health until after this baby, or *take care of her* as in husbandly-type duties? She craved the latter, but no. It would destroy him.

84

"You had only to wait until daybreak to speak." She smiled up at him, questioning if her misgivings were leaking through.

His hands stilled, head quirked to one side. "You were going somewhere."

She slipped free from his grip—not wishing to be free, but dreading how vulnerable his touch made her. Alexia lifted the finished cloak. "Delivery."

"In the middle of the night?" He leaned in and grazed his lips across her ear. "You must take care of yourself at this late stage, adequate rest and all. It can wait until morning."

She shivered, melting into the heat of his breath on her skin. Why couldn't he be her Kiren? She was stranded on the shore, able to see and touch the ocean, but fearing its unfathomable depths. She could dive so easily and never return for a snatch of air or daylight. Just let it swallow her up.

Alexia stopped herself, lips an inch away from his neck. This was bad. So terribly bad. His desires were now quite clear, and she didn't know if she had the willpower to resist.

"Perhaps we should wait until morning to speak." Her voice trembled.

"I like that idea." Kiren shoved her door inward and pulled her inside, locking his mouth to hers as he kicked the door closed behind him.

Her heart jumped into her throat. What did he think he was doing? Did he believe a simple kiss in public was a declaration of eternal love and that he now deserved to have all of her?

She tore her mouth from his. "Kiren."

"Hm?" He reengaged her lips, stopping any protest she might utter. And indeed her protests were melting away one by one under the heat of his passion.

*What are you doing?*

*Let me show you.* His fingers pulled through her hair as he deepened his kiss, filling her core with molten lava. She was done resisting. Alexia strengthened her mental barrier and attacked him as if he were her husband. For a few brief moments that's all he was. The man she loved. The man she'd left. The man she'd never see again.

He kissed her harder and lowered her to her mattress. His lips ran over her cheeks, her jaw, her chin, her neck. She rose with each nip, aching for more.

He pulled back, breathing hard as he stared into her eyes. Ocean swells tossed with vexing frustration. He dropped onto the mattress next to her, facing her. She rolled toward him, disappointed, but careful to make sure her necklace remained hidden.

"I still cannot break through your barrier," he said.

"Is that what you were attempting?"

He grinned.

She wanted to follow up by asking, *is that all you were attempting to do?* Goodness, he needed a leash. Or she did. She couldn't be in this close proximity and not expect to fall.

He leaned in but stopped short. "Why? Why do you keep me out?"

Her pulse sped. "You are not ready for the secrets I protect."

His fingers trailed down the side of her face. "If I am such a white knight in the future, you should not need to protect them from me."

"Perhaps I am protecting *you* from *them*." She trapped his hand against her jaw. "Is that it then? You came merely to interrogate me?"

He leaned up over her, his eyes blazing once more. "Oh yes. Interrogate." He kissed her. "Tease." He kissed her harder. "Enjoy."

*Please.* She lost herself in the length of his kiss, her mind wandering to Father's garden so long ago when Kiren had asked for her hand and kissed her this same way—with joy, with contentment, with his heart. He didn't know how to give less, and she didn't want less.

He opened to her, and she stumbled into his mental landscape. The grounds looked as though they had been tilled, new growth springing up. She turned and found the tower of family purpose still in ruin, topped by a very shiny sculpture of a pregnant woman in white stone. Flattered though she was, she scowled at a demigoddess, an untouchable woman whose entirety was as cold as stone, no matter how she lit the space. The goddess stood triumphantly over the crumbled tower, as if she had toppled it.

That wasn't Alexia's purpose at all. She wanted him to rebuild the tower. To construct the crystal palace that had been his mental prison. To frame the majesty that would take five hundred years to complete.

"Kiren." She pulled free, looping her fingers around the laces of his tunic and holding him away. "Why have you given up your family?"

He curled his fingers around hers and pressed his lips to her thumb. His words were timid. "Making room for a new family, I suppose."

She sat up, scowling. "And what of your sister? The throne your parents left to you?"

He knelt across from her and shrugged. "What about them? They are gone. I thought you would be pleased with the idea of a *new* family."

His meaning smacked her and she pressed a hand to her chest, reminding herself to breathe. This was exactly what she'd feared. It wasn't a game, no ill-hatched attempt to get at her memories, but an expression of desire that she could never give into. He wanted her entirely.

"Alexia?" He leaned in, searching for her gaze.

Her heart sank. How could she refuse him and not hurt him? How could she tell him 'no' without crushing the confidence and strides he'd made the last weeks?

Hurting him was better than costing him his life.

In a gentle censure, she said, "No new family can replace the old. Would you give up on them that easily?"

He frowned, his tone abrasive. "I did not give up easily."

"Of course not." She studied her hands. He'd heard her rejection loudly— the reason for the venom behind his words. She was crushing him. "But nor are you fighting for them any longer."

"There is nothing to fight for," he insisted, nostrils flaring.

She cupped his cheek. "You cannot know that."

He tore his face free, staring into the shadows, away from her. Alexia could almost feel the fissure in his heart, his constant battle and loneliness seeping into her.

He shoved to his feet.

"I believe your kingdom awaits," she continued. "I believe your sister needs you. And most of all, I believe you need them."

His head shook. "I am no king, Alexia."

She struggled up onto her feet. "Not yet, but you will be."

Angry blue pierced right into her, a shard of ice. "I. *Will*. Not."

Fury fueled his glare. His shoulders bunched and his fists trembled.

*Will not.* He hadn't said cannot or should not. Will not. He had decided.

"You cannot change your blood," she insisted. His heritage was bound to his bloodline, and if he didn't step up and fill the role that belonged solely to him, either his sister or his daughter would be forced to. Likely his daughter. She would not place that burden on her child. "You may run from your responsibilities, but they will still be yours."

A humorless laugh escaped him. "You think I do not know that?" He turned on her. "No one asked me if I wanted this heritage. No one even questioned if I would be adequate to fill my father's throne. Do you know why?" He leaned toward her. "Because I am not. No one is. I cannot lead our people."

She slid her fingers through his. "But you can."

He pulled his hand away. "I will not."

Alexia couldn't contain her disappointment. Perhaps he hadn't healed as much as she'd believed. She turned away and picked up Ravia's cloak, feeling heavier than she had all night. "I have a commitment to fulfill. When I return, it will be to sleep."

Quiet.

He exhaled. "It is dark out. Allow me to escort you."

"I need no escort."

"But one is here nonetheless."

She scowled and exited the hut. He followed behind, the silence so heavy between them she wished he hadn't come. Just when she believed she'd discovered her truest friend, that things between them might finally ease, he showed another face. One she recognized. A man who cared deeper than he dared admit.

*He is not my husband,* she reminded herself. If she didn't keep her guard, he never would be.

The pathway between huts was abandoned, snores filling the air as a growling lullaby. Willem stumbled tiredly past, slipping into the hut he shared with Lucian.

She didn't turn, didn't stop until she reached Ravia's door. Light danced across the draped window, so perhaps her friend was still awake? She knocked on the stone.

No response.

Kiren skidded his boot back and forth across the dirt, the sound grating on her nerves.

Ravia must have fallen asleep, but she would be pleased to find her cloak waiting for her in the morning. Alexia pushed the curtain aside, hoping not to wake her friend.

She froze.

Dark liquid stained the corner of the mattress, a glint of metal protruding from the woman's body. Alexia inhaled a familiar metallic scent and her fists tightened.

Blood.

# Twenty-Five

# Captive

One whole day. Leofrik sliced off a piece of a turnip and offered it. The mist woman turned her head. She hadn't eaten anything or said a word since he'd tied her up. Worse than that, she had lain there struggling when she didn't think he was watching, sniffling in the night and pulling herself under control before he opened his eyes this morning. No answer to his questions. No response but to glare or grind her teeth. Her skin had taken on a gray pallor, sickening.

But what was that?

He squinted and leaned in. She inhaled, her neck tensing. He brushed the metal back from where it rested against her clavicle and tensed. The links had left black stains across the skin—like soot. He licked a thumb and brushed it across the skin.

Her eyes snapped up at him, but he ignored her.

The flesh remained blackened, burned. A knot twisted inside him. What was he doing to her? Could this imprisonment be more cruel than a cell? More importantly, what kind of *creature* burned at the touch of chainmail? His fingers found the wooden wolf hidden in his tunic pocket.

"What are you?" he hissed.

Her head turned away.

"The metal," he asked. "It hurts. Can it also kill your kind?"

Her mouth tightened.

Perhaps he was going about this the wrong way. If he offered some compassion, perhaps she would respond in kind. It might work better than forcing answers out of her.

"Forgive me, I did not know." He rubbed the toy wolf's smooth surface. Now what to do with that knowledge? If he released her she'd likely kill him. If he kept her like this, guilt and shame would eat him alive until the chains drained her of life. Perhaps if only a small point of metal were touching her it would not be so unbearable?

He tugged at the links on the end of the mail, using his dagger to pry between them. He freed a string of metal. It took half the day and a blazing hot fire, but he reshaped a bracelet of metal and fastened it about her wrist. Her glare flashed at him as he worked, but he didn't apologize or even lift his gaze to hers. At last it was complete, a skin-tight fetter of links.

"Now I will untie you, but I warn you, I am most capable with a sword, as well as my hands."

Her eyebrows lifted at him in a sarcastic challenge.

These two days she'd given him angry looks, despairing when he turned away, but never once had she complained. She'd grunted. Growled. Hissed, but never a vocalization. Was it possible? "Are you mute, my lady?"

She spat at him.

That would certainly make their communication more challenging. He untied the ropes and lifted the metal away from her. She inhaled deeply, unable to hide her relief, but her skin remained ashen.

The woman sat up tentatively and he leaned back, giving her room. She rubbed at her limbs, warming the blood back into them and frowning the entire time. That pout could stop men in their tracks. It held the power to turn them on one another for the honor of her favor.

Her head lifted. She smiled at him through her lashes and leaned forward. His heart thudded. To be in such close proximity to such breathtaking beauty, he couldn't stop it.

But she was a creature, something unholy that defied even nature.

She tilted her head as if considering him for the first time, her silver eyes washing over him in a hail of glitter. Tingles rained through him like fresh snow on a sunny day, or sparks of fire while chill hung in the air. She grazed a finger across his cheek, fire and ice all in a single touch. Leofrik imagined what it would be like to possess such a tantalizing blossom, being on constant guard to protect his prize, always hoping her affections were for him alone…

It was a foolish prospect. Why was he considering the notion when he had a brotherhood to return to—men true and selfless who would give limb and life to protect the less fortunate?

Her fingertip stopped at his chin, tilting his face to hers. Waking every morning to her lilac-rain, running the softness of her hair through his fingers, knowing the welcoming embrace of a woman who lit the fire within his chest…

Her eyes hardened to steel.

Light flashed in his periphery. He twisted, but not fast enough.

Smack!

Pain exploded through his temple. Leofrik hit the ground. His head throbbed like a volcano. He blinked through the agony as a skirt whipped across his face. He reached out, caught an ankle, and yanked.

A gasp.

She slammed into the earth.

He crawled forward on his elbows, fumbling over the sword she'd slipped from his hip while distracting him and bashed into his head. He trundled over the rope he'd used to bind her and leapt on top of her, trapping her to the ground with his weight.

"I was doing you a kindness," he ground out, looping the rope around her legs first. She kicked and wriggled, but he shoved her shoulders into the ground with such force that her head slammed down and she ceased struggling. He tied her wrists and ankles quickly, but as he finished, his gaze landed on her face, so innocent and sweet in slumber. Too bad the thing was a little vixen. Or demon.

Yet in all his travels, he'd never encountered something like her. Not in the Holy Land, nor France, nor all of the German lands. If he took news of her to the holy pope, he questioned what would happen. Had the Church any idea things such as this existed?

His gaze touched on the blackened flesh at her neckline. Could she be one of the Nephilim, here to try his heart and prove him worthy or not of God's allegiance?

He slipped his sword home. She could have turned the blade on him in his distraction, but she hadn't. It had only been her intention to escape, not to slay him. Heaven knew how prone he'd made himself in her grasp.

Then she wasn't a murderer. A witch. Vicious. Not a killer.

Studying her serene face, he questioned what her life was like. Who had she been? A vagabond child or the offspring of a loving family? Some mythical creature who fought battles in Heaven and now on Earth? Were the men in her childhood villains or heroes?

She stirred and he shifted back a safe distance. Her eyes fluttered open, and he tossed a turnip at her.

"Let us not do that again, shall we? Eat and regain your health. If you are going to best me, you will need all of your strength."

# Twenty-Six

## Angels and Demons

Alexia's scream wasn't an expression of horror. It was an expression of sorrow.

A dagger protruded through dark skin, spearing the woman to the heart. Alexia's dagger.

She patted her hip and found an empty sheath. Had she misplaced the weapon some time throughout the day? Had someone taken it? Who would do this?

Voices crowded her thoughts, startled voices, cries and shouts, but she was fixated on that weapon, an accusation. Someone was framing her.

Hands latched around her arms, strong hands. They drew her away and she lifted her eyes through a daze.

Kiren cradled her cheeks, his mouth moving.

She pulled out of his hold and stumbled away.

Six months. Six months they'd been building this company, and while mild disagreements had occurred, no one would have slain another. An enemy could not possibly have entered their village. Not in the middle of the night with Amos's shrouding darkness up. Not while friends slept close. Not after their jump across landmasses.

Yet her nose told her the same thing as her eyes.

One of their own, a soul she had diligently cared for and shouldered hardships beside, was dead. And it looked like it had happened at her hand.

She dreamed of death so regularly, terrible nightmares where she woke gasping for air after drowning in the pool of the Soulless's blackened blood. It couldn't be happening again. It wasn't possible.

Amos grabbed Alexia's shoulder. The tension in his jaw said he recognized the dagger, but didn't believe she was capable of using it. She knew exactly what he was thinking, that she should use her gifts to investigate.

And keep it from happening.

"Go," he encouraged.

She reached into the void, and the sands of time shifted through her fingers, ready to be altered. Alexia snatched onto a moment in the late afternoon, an hour at which she was certain Ravia lived.

She jumped.

And slammed into a black wall. Pitch slid across her limbs, swallowing her fists and ankles like cooling tar. It enveloped her skirt, her skin, sliding its way up her neck and over her chin. It fought to ooze its way through her nose and mouth. She ripped herself out of the darkness and landed hard on the ground.

Pain seized her midsection. Alexia curled in on herself. Dirt scraped into her cheek and arms as she lifted her head to search for help. She lay in the pathway between huts, womb contracting with a fury.

*Calm. It will not be tonight.*

The tension eased, her muscles limp like noodles.

Since when had time become her enemy?

She breathed in night air. She *had* traveled through time, just not as far as she'd wished. Perhaps Regin was correct when he insisted she was too far along to demand so much of herself, but that pitch substance…

Another contraction seized her. She breathed through it, squeezed into a ball.

"Grandfather," she whispered. She wasn't ready for this, not ready to die. The world around her melted away to the absence of time. Her pain eased. She pressed up onto her elbows and Grandfather sat next to her.

"It's dark out here," he said.

She caught her breath, muscles relaxing.

"Too dark."

She turned to him. His profile reminded her of another, if the nose were slightly larger, the chin a little less firm and the hair gray…

"Lester!"

He glanced at her. "You grant me a new name?"

"Oh no, not unless you wish for one." It had to be him. The realization settled something within her, like finding her favorite book in a time before books. A warm corner in a frozen wasteland. She wasn't alone. She'd never been alone. Somehow Grandfather Time had always been part of her life. Watching over her. So close.

She blinked through her memories of him, the gruff old man in the Wilhamshire prison, a steady and kind fellow, the man who ran faster than anyone had ever run…because he could alter time.

How was it possible? Her mother had insisted there could only be one to govern the flow of time. Had Grandfather given up that role when her mother was born?

"There can only be one," she whispered. "In the future, how can we both exist if both of us can alter time?"

He grinned and ruffled her hair. "Aye, she's figured it out. Knew ye'd come to it soon. Bright, this one."

"Grandfather."

"Meh. There be two worlds what need us. Two worlds, two of us."

"But my mother died when I was born so that I could become the Maiden of Time."

"There be *only* two worlds." He looked pointedly at her, then at himself. "I were in the absence of time when it happened, and young Dana chose to give her life so you could be."

Sadness passed through her, for her mother's fate, for the sacrifice she'd made.

Lester glanced back at the murk. "Too dark."

She studied the gloom. "Is that a riddle? You know what has happened in the village this evening, and who did it."

He climbed to his feet. "Have you dreamed of chaos recently?"

What a strange question. She rose to join him. "Death, perhaps. Not chaos. I tried to jump through time and hit a wall."

His lip twitched. Kind eyes turned on her. "We have an enemy in our midst."

She was confused. "An enemy within time?"

The corner of his mouth pulled upward. "An enemy what has no bounds. An enemy what was sealed away long, long ago. Stay away from the darkness."

"The darkness inside of time?"

He gave a nod, his mouth set in a way that she knew she would not get more out of him. There was something larger at play here.

"We already have a traitor, and you are telling me we have another enemy?"

"Those what govern time have many enemies."

She exhaled a heavy breath. In her own era it had been the factions of the Passionate, the Soulless, and men who collected the Passionate for their own gain. This felt like a simpler age, but perhaps she'd dismissed the complexities too readily. Alexia squared her shoulders, willing to face the challenges. Her babe lurched. She stumbled.

Grandfather/Lester caught her arm, helping her straighten.

She smiled at him. Here was a piece of her world, restored to balance, and to think he'd been with her all along, watching over her. She patted a hand over his. "You are so careful with me. I am not a fragile creature."

"What, like a sparrow?" He returned a knowing wink. It was his nickname for her in her own time. "Even them what take wing can fall."

"Not when they have so apt a protector watching over them."

His head tilted. "You have a baby to stop from birthin' and someone what can help you do it. Go."

She blushed and nodded.

***

"Kiren," she whimpered through the pain. Surviving childbirth was difficult for the Passionate, but Kiren had…or would save many women in the coming years. Perhaps his arrival had been an intervention of whatever greater force governed life. He would insist it was God. She called it luck. Maybe Grandfather had even orchestrated his arrival. Alexia squeezed a hand around her necklace, begging for strength. "Kiren."

A shadow dropped over her.

"Be calm. Relax." The words were clipped.

She obeyed him, slowing her heart in time with her breaths. Fingers landed on her forehead, individual points of light as brilliant as a summer day, summoning her peace, her joy, the happiness of cuddling with him while watching clouds drift by. The only thing that existed was this frozen memory where no evil, no sorrow could ever touch it.

*Never let go,* she begged.

But his fingers pulled away.

Her eyes fluttered open and she met his stare, his lips pressed tight. Moonlight caught the edges of his frown, brightening the trouble in his stare.

"What just happened?" he asked. "You were leaving the hut, and then you were gone."

Alexia groaned. She had only made it seconds. It must have appeared she'd run off on him after their war of words. She pushed onto her hands and knees getting one foot, then the other, below her. Kiren caught her elbow and lifted her. A tenderness filled his gaze, despite the flexing jaw muscles.

Willem stumbled by.

Kiren's nostrils flared. His mouth dropped open, and he turned the direction of Ravia's hut. He took off running. She followed and arrived as he shoved the curtain door of Ravia's hut aside.

Alexia's heart sank. She couldn't be too late. Not again.

She patted her hip. No dagger.

Kiren knelt over Ravia, the dagger pinned through her chest, dark blood seeping down her sides. He pressed two fingers to her neck and groaned. He bowed his head. "She's warm."

# Twenty-Seven

# *Death*

Alexia stared at the corpse. Four years ago the sight would have terrified her. Now it only saddened her. How had she come to this point? More importantly, who had stolen her dagger and done this?

"You still believe this is a safe haven?"

She bit down at Kiren's jab and pulled her dagger free from the woman's chest. She expected blood to gush from the wound, but it stagnated like a well of midnight tar.

Blood stained her blade. A blade that was meant to kill the Soulless. She wiped the weapon on the mattress and tugged a blanket over the woman's wounds. Alexia slipped the dagger home and dropped her head into her hands. Ravia was dead. Her friend.

"Seems you have a problem," Kiren said.

She met his stare. His accusation softened to an aching compassion, such a familiar look that Alexia couldn't breathe. She was standing next to a time traveler, the man she'd left in the future—except that he possessed no scar.

She looked away. "It could have been anyone."

His shoulder nudged hers. "Including me?"

"No. Not you."

"Well, that is a relief. Where were you?"

Silence. "I went back to stop it. I failed."

He wrapped an arm around her, and as much as she longed to remain within its comforting fold, she took a deep breath and shrugged it off.

Alexia wiped away the tears. "We should call Amos."

\*\*\*

Amos decided to keep the cause of Ravia's death among council members in order to investigate silently, and he claimed it was a suicide to the others. They held a firelight farewell for her, complete with Willem shaking open the earth to accept Ravia's body. It was tradition that a seedling be planted over the deceased, but people gasped in awe when Kiren knelt over the planted seed, one hand to the soil, and hummed a farewell song. Green limbs sprang up between his fingers and grew to a young sapling. Alexia loved seeing him finally appreciated for the wonder he was.

The instant the ceremony ended, Amos employed the council to search out the murderer.

Alexia found nothing. No reason. No one with a motive.

Air hung thick with humidity. Heavy clouds dangled above, threatening to drop their stock as she stepped into the trees. Her joints ached, and her body weighed like the stone that protected their home, dragging her toward collapse.

She hadn't slept the rest of the night. She'd sat, envisioning the dead woman and wondering if she might have somehow prevented this outcome, but failed.

She was only supposed to be here to stop the Soulless from existing.

Alexia had no idea when it would happen or how to recognize the time. She'd been told that thirteen of the purest Passionate would give themselves to a madman, that they would be drained and become eternally hungry, unable to die. She had yet to meet a madman, especially one who was demanding Passionate loyalty. Unless Kiren was the one. But he hadn't asked for anyone's allegiance. Not yet. So long as she kept vigil, that outcome could be prevented. Of that she was certain.

Unless she died first.

She slowed. It was entirely possible her time would come before the Soulless were born and she had merely given up half a year—or a lifetime—of joy in her husband's embrace. Should she have stayed with her Kiren?

Alexia lifted his medallion about her neck and pressed it to her lips. Energy surged into her bones. She missed him. More desperately than the earth needed the rain, she craved the man who had taken her heart and loved her enough to let her go.

She arrived at the pool and her weariness washed away. There he stood, watching her with a mix of dejection and a desire to comfort. His arms opened to embrace her.

Perhaps he wasn't the man who sacrificed and adored, but for this moment, he was enough.

# Twenty-Eight

# *Coup*

Leofrik stoked a fire. She sat next to him, arms tucked as tightly across her chest as possible with bound wrists, her knees drawn up to preserve body heat.

He had taken to speaking when she would not or could not, believing that if he formed a bond or found some aspect of life to which she responded, he might crack her exterior and begin the true negotiation. "We fought together and bled together, placing ourselves as a shield between pilgrims to the Holy Land and the infidels who sought to end their righteous lives." He chewed a piece of salted pork. "They are my brothers, and yet I am forced away from them and my sworn duties to hunt creatures whose faces countenance the very angels. But you are not an angel, are you? A demon perhaps? Something not of this Earth."

Her mouth scrunched, and she shivered.

"Are you now feeling the cold, my lady? Your vesture would suggest you take no heed of the weather's power."

The flames lit her face like flares of gold across gray marble.

He rose and shook out his bedroll, removing the blanket. He dropped it around her shoulders and returned to his place, poking the flames higher in order to roast the rabbit he'd caught. The nobles would have his head for poaching, but it was not like his companion could betray his trespass.

"But you know about that—the bond of brotherhood or family, I daresay. It shows through your silence, which I admire." He sighed, placing a hand to the bandage over his right temple. "I pray thee understand, I wish you no ill, whatever you are. I only desire to return to my fellows. Fulfilling this assignment is the way to bring that about. I could hunt your kind and make this a bloody endeavor, but I have chosen the path of diplomacy. If you choose not to cooperate with me, others will come. They will slaughter your loved ones. I, at least, offer the alternative of a peaceful surrender and continued life."

She scowled as if he'd insulted her sensibilities.

An emotional response. Perhaps that was the way to breech her voice. "I had hoped you might see reason, but perhaps women are too daft for reason."

She bristled, eyes flaming.

"These are things she has heard before! Well, as they say—once is a laugh, twice is a gaffe, but three times is a truth."

She leapt at him. Chilled fingers locked around his jaw before he could lift a weapon. Thoughts slammed into his brain with the force of a full mounted regiment.

*Flames ate through roofs, women and children fleeing amidst screams, men on horses slicing through all who dared escape into the night. He, no, she—the little girl he was seeing through—ducked behind a barrel and held her breath. "Velia!" her mother screamed as the roof of her home collapsed in. And then Mother was silent. Velia remained hidden until flames ate their way down the side of the house and she had to run. By then the soldiers had vacated. She stumbled into the arms of a man with copper skin and chestnut hair. He created a veil of darkness around them and led her away.*

*Time passed. Much. She flitted happily through the French garden on a breeze, loving the freedom and at peace—even with the others mulling about, planting, or gabbing. She solidified on the rise, taking in the view of her happy home...when pain sliced through her shoulder. She gasped and reached to find a metal crossbow bolt burning through her flesh. Men crawled up the rise behind her, so many in armor, wearing white colours with red crosses.*

*Velia opened her mouth to scream, to warn the others. A fist slammed into her throat. She choked and dropped to one knee, unable to summon a voice. Soldiers rushed in on all sides. Her people fought back, but they were caught by surprise. They fled, the strongest holding back the tide until they were crushed by the enemy. She pulled at the bolt in her flesh.*

*"Oh no, poppet. You are mine."*

*She twisted, but she couldn't escape the nearing boot. It slammed into her brow. All went dark.*

*She woke in bonds, the air around her damp. Pain sizzled into her neck, through her arms and up her back from the metal locked around her collar and wrists. Stone walls encompassed her. She opened her mouth to call for help, but no voice came. He did, however: a man with thinning hair and a lewd grin. Ulric. He came again and again and again, claiming her every time. At last, when the roundness of her womb demanded it, he had her removed to a tower. Her child was born, but he wouldn't let her see it. "Not unless you help me find your friends."*

*And she did. Time after time—playing the part of an escapee while reporting her activities to the nobleman who kept her child. She had tried to kill him but couldn't. It was the bond. Once he was dead, she would be free. Perhaps she would die with him, perhaps not, but at least she would no longer be his slave. He'd taken her against her will, and still she couldn't put a blade through his heart.*

*"There is only one thing you can offer me."* Her voice echoed inside his head. *"Kill this man."*

She released him.

Leofrik stared at her in horror. What had she done to him? How could she share her history with a touch?

She pantomimed a stab to the heart and extended a hand to him.

"I do that, and I am a dead man."

She sat back, jaw clenched tight as if to say their negotiations were over.

# Twenty-Nine

# *Death Bringer*

Kiren watched from across camp as Alexia stepped into Amos's hut with the rest of the council. He'd tried his best to comfort her this morning, but her mind was harrowed with more guilt and anxiety than he could ease. The effort resulted in a session of kissing so heated he was still on fire. And then she'd dismissed him with tears in her eyes. Said goodbye. Walked the other way.

Before Ravia was killed, Alexia had kissed him with a fervor that said she wanted all of him as much as he craved her. Since his suggestion of a future for them—something any woman would be giddy over—she'd changed. Even her kisses this morning, post funeral, had possessed a distance, like she was dreaming of kissing someone else. Someone who wasn't him. Which drove him crazy with jealousy *and* stoked the fire.

He didn't like being this vulnerable and confused over a woman.

"You are completely besotted." Zeph slapped him on the back. "Do not think I missed how you snuck out this morning *again* after hovering over her all night at the ceremony. And afterward."

Kiren grimaced. Perhaps his motives were rather obvious, but he felt peace in her presence—whether arguing or locked in another form of passion…when she wasn't imagining he was someone else.

"With what happened, I understand. Have to protect your investment. Your life is literally at risk."

"What?" He turned on his friend.

Zeph rubbed the back of his neck. "You never came back from *visiting* two nights ago. I assumed you…"

He scowled. "I am not stupid."

Being bonded to her would mean trussing his life to hers. He could easily leap that boundary if things got too heated, and her life hung precariously upon the birthing of a child. Which would mean his life as well.

Was that why she'd been pushing him away?

Zeph nodded. "I know you are not stupid, but sometimes you do not think before, say, diving through a sheriff's window. You have been, well, not yourself. I figured…"

Not himself? Maybe because Alexia had filled his head with strange thoughts—like how she expected, *expected* him to take up his father's mantle. He couldn't be king. The first three years among the Lost Ones taught him that much. He didn't have the foresight and good judgment to protect his people, say nothing of leading them to glory. He didn't possess the eloquence, the restraint, or the strength to bear that burden.

Their cries echoed in his ears, the injured and suffering who begged for mercy when the only mercy he could give them was a quick death.

And Kiri was out there—the only family he had, an orphan and lonely soul, his twin sister. She would be fighting for their family heritage, which he'd abandoned with such ease. She'd never give up on him.

But he could do nothing to reach her. To stop her suffering.

So of course he wasn't acting like himself, because he was acting like a prince who'd been running from his responsibilities.

"It is not what it seems." He thumped his friend in the chest. "Alexia is teaching me something."

"Seduction?" Zeph lifted a hand. "Oh wait, how to be a woman's pin cushion? Do not lie to me about lip clapping. This is serious business."

Kiren chuckled and nodded toward Silivia. "At least she has never aimed something at my vulnerables."

Zeph grunted.

A metallic scent hit Kiren's nose. Hairs on his arms prickled, and his senses came fully alive. He was accustomed to smelling blood, but this was more than a nose bleed or minor injury. The tang of danger.

He waved Zeph off with, "I know what I am doing," though he had no clue, and hurried away, following the scent. He swerved to the trees that bordered the village limits.

A body slumped against a tree, sun haloing a head kinked awkwardly to one side. Cedric. One of the members of camp. Kiren strained his ears for a heartbeat.

Nothing.

Twigs crunched underfoot as he approached. He knelt next to the body and placed a hand to Cedric's neck. The skin was still warm. He closed his eyes and focused, searching for the spirit belonging to this cadaver.

Silence.

He was gone.

A year ago Kiren had come across a child with a head wound, one who had been brutally beaten by his father. The lad took his last breath as Kiren laid a hand to his neck, and it wasn't too late. He pulled the child back. Barely.

But he couldn't heal *dead*.

The tree behind the body was slick with blood, the back of the head smashed in. Cedric must have died from slamming into the tree with great force. No one among the Lost Ones could throw someone with that power. There was the shadow creature…

Leaves crinkled under his knee, too much sunlight spilling across the ground. He twisted to view the canopy. Branches above dangled where they'd snapped.

Thrown from above?

Zeph or Velia were the only ones who could pull that off, but they wouldn't. Zeph was the most likeable, friendly member of their band, and Velia was loved by all. She'd been gone for days anyway—likely dipping her toes in the ocean and enjoying the freedom. Like he should be.

This had just happened. His friend couldn't have done this without anyone seeing, or more importantly, being in terrible humor afterwards.

First it looked like Alexia murdered someone, now Zeph? This didn't make sense. Yet someone had framed him for several pranks. Whatever was going on, he didn't like it.

Kiren backed away. After all the blame he'd received, it was likely he'd be accused for the murder if he made this scene known.

He crossed the village square for Amos's cottage. Mae answered the door, but Alexia appeared when she heard his voice.

"Come with me." He grabbed her hand. Warmth crawled up his skin from the connection, seeping into his chest like liquid gold. His heart sped. She was worse than a draught of the finest wine. He clenched his teeth against the desire to whirl her about and claim her mouth for his own. If not for the uneasiness of his stomach, he might act on that impulse.

She filled the doorframe blocking out the council. "Will there now be mid-day sessions?" she hissed. "I have important matters to attend."

And she was back to being frigid. He cleared his throat. "It would be prudent if we spoke alone."

"We will. Later."

He ground his teeth and took a deep breath. Stubborn woman. He opened his mouth to tell her exactly what he'd found, and she blurred—fuzzy like his eyes weren't adjusted correctly. She shoved a hand against his lips.

Her palm was rougher than he'd anticipated but smelled of ambrosia, delicious ambrosia. He wanted to nip it with his teeth, just to see her yelp.

Her eyes widened. She pulled her hand away and dismissed herself from the meeting, following him toward his gruesome discovery.

"How did he die?" she asked quietly.

Kiren almost missed a step. "I cannot say—did you read my mind just now?"

"No."

"See my memories?"

"No."

"Observe me in my discovery?"

"No."

"I am confused." He pulled a hand through his hair.

"Yes, you are." Her grin said she liked him that way. "No matter, this must have occurred in daylight and no one witnessed it. What is happening to us?"

He watched the pebbles passing underfoot, wishing he had an answer for her. Someone was killing the Lost Ones.

***

Fires had been lit for the funeral rites at the peak right outside the village. People trudged silently forward. The second death in three days… It was enough to make Alexia nervous.

Men and women had begun talking, examining the manner of the deaths and turning wary looks on one another. Thankfully none of them knew the part her dagger had played in Ravia's death, but many watched Kiren and Zephaniah suspiciously. She'd even heard one or two low mumbles about a Soul Eater.

A shriek broke the quiet. Alexia shoved through the crowd, catching Mae's eye as they both hurried.

The crowd parted and Alexia stopped dead in her tracks.

The funeral pyre roared heartily, like a great mocking mouth. Posts stood to either side of the flames, erected in case of rain and the need for a canopy.

Now they were bloody totems.

A body dangled from each of the pikes: Perrin and Murial—the two who had been sent to prepare the funeral site. Their heads twisted the wrong direction like mangled marionettes.

Cold hung in the air, the winds stilled, despair clamping Alexia's windpipe shut.

Her fists trembled. Why? Who was doing this? How could they—?

Her breath caught.

Between the two drooping bodies hung a great inky haze, the blackness that had haunted their village. It swelled outward, an enveloping cloud of anguish.

She glared at it, teeth grinding.

In the murk, crimson eyes flashed.

Ice sliced through Alexia.

This was no longer a game of scaring people. This was the beginning of the Soulless.

# Thirty

## *The Soul Eater*

Alexia backed away.

The black cloud faded and wind cut through her dress. Kiren slid an arm around her as she shivered, and she met his eyes. She pushed him away and turned for Amos, dread weighting her veins and fueling her brain. This was happening. It was here—whatever nightmare would birth her greatest fear.

Regin, Mae, and Deamus followed her.

Amos nodded at her, Lucian at his side, and they all disappeared into his hut.

"I should have recognized the signs." She paced out her rage. "Can you not feel the entity's malevolence? It has been watching us and waiting for us to feel safe, all while feeding on our unease and ill feeling. Now it is...is..."

Regin's fists balled. "We all saw it, but there be nothin' there. Nothin' what we can cage or fight. Leastwise we know we still have a traitor in our midst. Mayhaps—"

"This was no traitor."

Mae cleared her throat. "If I say something will I be laughed to scorn?" They all looked at her. "The Soul Eater."

No one let out a single chuckle.

Alexia stopped moving. "We need to leave this mountain. Now."

Silence.

Amos stepped forward, his hands pressed together in supplication. "Tell us why, Alexia. How will it happen?"

She looked right at Lucian. "Can you see what is coming?"

The monk tucked his hands into his robe. "We should leave this place."

They all turned on Lucian.

"What have you seen?" Amos asked.

"Trouble."

No need for a vote. They would relocate and hope the thing could not follow. Decision made, people began packing, but no matter how thoroughly they searched the village, Velia could not be found.

# Thirty-One

# *Sealed*

"I bear no love for this man," Leofrik admitted over the morning meal. All night he'd mulled on what he'd seen and the bargain Velia had demanded.

She ignored him.

"But he is a lord and my superior. If I slay him, my life is ended."

She picked at her food. There would be no compromise, and he understood. She wanted one thing and one thing only.

He ground his teeth. "Lady, I believe your kind are dangerous—far more than this world can withstand. It is best they be kept under the guard of the Holy Church for everyone's safety. This is a cause I would stake my life on."

She glanced at him.

"I could make his death look the accident, but in exchange you must give me your people."

Her gaze flitted across the dewy greens, the pulse ticking in her neck as her fingers twitched.

"Do we have an agreement?"

No reply.

Leofrik didn't waste time waiting. He went about his morning routine, gathering food and wood for another fire. He returned to a solemn-faced woman. She met his eyes and offered her hand. He took it.

*"How can I know you are a man of your word?"*

He tugged at her bracelet prison. "I believe you want this man dead with everything inside you but have not the power or means. Give me your vow, and I will set you free. We work on trust from this moment forward."

Her silver eyes flashed. They had an agreement.

\*\*\*

Leofrik worried that the demand he'd placed upon Velia was too great, transporting himself and an entire force of men—which she did, one at a time—but though she wearied, she did not shrink from their agreement. The instant she had delivered the last of his fighters, she disappeared. For good.

Why should that sadden him?

# Thirty-Two

# Tides of War

Early morning mist curled off the mountain peaks and obscured the rising sun. Alexia faced the dawn, wishing it could warm away her dream: the clashing steel and fire in her veins. Sickness at the spilling blood. Shouts and the jarring of bones. It had been far too vivid, one of her prophetic dreams.

She gripped and loosened her hold on the dagger as she watched the fog. She hadn't meant to sleep, but fell into it while packing. The dream was a blessing. A terrible blessing.

Let it be a lie.

Regin sidled up next to her, along with Mae, Sarlic, and Amos. She nodded at each. Speed, sleep, death, pain, and darkness. They made a formidable force. A force she hoped would not be needed, but the nightmare felt too real not to heed.

Willem dropped into a crouch next to them, ready to shake the earth. Beatrice, who would wreak fear and confusion on the enemy, hung in his shadow. Ilberd, Hammond, and Silivia arrived, broadening their defensive line. Wind swirled around them and Zephaniah swooped into position. Lucian and Deamus would be leading the young and helpless to the safety of the next rise, and she hoped Kiren would remain in the background to heal wounds. Velia had more work than she could handle—if she ever appeared.

Shadows reared in the mist, silhouettes of men.

Alexia exhaled a pent up breath. It *was* reality. So be it.

She froze time and stepped into the fog, drawing on the necklace for strength.

Men. Weapons. Armor. A whole force. Sixty souls with drawn blades or taut bows. Just like in her dream.

Frustration bubbled through her. Why could they not be left alone?

Darkness slithered through the vegetation and disembodied crimson eyes cut through the gloom.

Alexia stopped. This battle was hopeless. Their enemy was too numerous, too strong…

She gritted her teeth and glared at the cloud entity, fighting the imposed despair. The thing swirled into a cyclone of movement and dove into the open mouth of a man wearing a white tunic with the red cross. The man's eyes glowed red.

She swallowed.

The thing didn't yield to time. It traveled without boundaries. And it could inhabit bodies.

Her memory flashed back to the night Ravia died—how Regin had entered her hut because of Mae's move. Or that was what she'd assumed. He could have taken her dagger. And then she'd passed Willem on the way to Ravia's hut. If this creature could possess men to do its bidding, it would not have been difficult to enter Regin and pass her dagger to the boy. Anyone could become an enemy.

Had this monster brought the enemy here?

Her blood pumped with a need to protect her people, to defeat the thing, to escape this enemy and keep her people from becoming Soulless. What had Grandfather called the darkness outside of time? Chaos?

She resumed her place in the line of allies, stilling her heart for battle. Only the ice of control remained.

Alexia released time.

Not a word escaped them as they waited. She wanted to see the enemies' faces, see their surprise at the force waiting for them. Mist cleared and their foe halted.

Alexia lifted her eyes to the sky, readying for the hiss of arrows. "Amos, now!"

Pitch hurled before them, a blinding wall of black.

"Beatrice!" she commanded.

Shrieks of terror broke from the warriors on the other side of night.

"Regin and Sarlic!" The two men swept into the fray.

Swords swooped through the murk. Alexia lifted her dagger and slowed time. She pressed her blade against the weapon nearest to her with enough force that it would fly from the man's grip the second she freed time. The next one she pressed downward forcing it into the ground. The third she simply tore from the man's hand. She turned her head up and forced herself to breathe. There it was—the slow hiss of arrows.

She released time. "Amos, drop the veil!"

Darkness disappeared. She yanked time slower as silent death rained down. Men shielded their eyes, suddenly blinded. Alexia pulled through time, knocking each deadly projectile away from vulnerable bodies.

First wave cleared, she released time. "Willem, Zephaniah, the archers!"

Zeph grabbed the boy and launched into the air.

"All to war!" Alexia called—the signal for free battle. This was where things got complicated for her—especially being unable to reverse time. Regin had already put three men to sleep, and Sarlic had one man on his knees in agony. The ground shuddered. That would be Willem with the archers. Amos threw darkness like a shield, blinding people as they neared and allowing himself the advantage. Silivia launched rocks at the enemy while Hammond and Ilberd swung clubs. Mae loosened her band, stealing life from the enemy as they came close—not enough to kill, but enough to drop them before her. Beatrice crippled them with fear.

*Thump.* Alexia gasped. Her pulse sped, her womb tightening. She dropped to one knee, startled by the surge. Her hold on time slipped.

"Not today. Not now." She shoved back onto her feet, pushing through the stiffness. It wasn't painful, just uncomfortable.

Beatrice was down. A man stood over her swinging a blade for her throat. Alexia yanked the minutes to a halt and shoved the man aside in stilled time. The enemy flew to the ground. Zephaniah dropped out of the sky and lifted Beatrice to safety.

The battle thickened. Dust clung to the air, rattled free by Willem's attacks. Pitch swirled through the breeze. Shouts filled Alexia's ears, eternal, forever-long battle cries and the suspended clash of weapons. They were the backdrop to periodic contractions as she stopped time and waited for them to pass.

Only the sun gave time meaning. It felt like hours to Alexia, sweat pouring down her brow, but that brilliant orb barely crept upward.

She blocked a sword from slicing into Hammond and whirled around at the same instant Ilberd screamed from across the field. Alexia raced to his side through stopped time.

His attacker grinned in triumph, weapon held high to finish the job. Alexia slammed a shoulder into him. The man went down, hitting his head.

Ilberd struggled and spat blood. Crimson bled into the fibers of his tunic. She shouted for Zeph, but the noise was too great.

Ilberd clasped her hand, his eyes focused on her. "Stay with me."

She couldn't deny the request. He struggled through two more breaths and fell limp.

The fool. He shouldn't have gone into battle with a weak arm! Alexia held in a sob, knowing the more distracted she became, the more likely she was to lose another friend.

*\*\*\**

*Kiren the coward.* The title fit. Even while calming terrified children, even while attempting to heal Beatrice, he was a whiteliver. He should be fighting side by side with the others. His ability to grow things could be used to alter the battlefield as well as heal. Alexia was out there, and with child no less, fighting the enemy. Who considered that a good idea?

Oriel skidded to a stop with the bandage he'd requested.

He snatched it and wrapped a wound. "What could you see of the fighting?" he asked. "Are any others injured?"

"They all look whole."

"And Alexia? Why is a woman in her condition on the battlefield?"

"Why, she is the commander—from before anyone knew she was with child. Have you never seen her in battle?"

Shamed to admit it, he hadn't. "The commander?"

"You can see for yourself from the rise."

He left instructions with Oriel and slipped away, crouching between huts to take in a view from between buildings. There were so many of them. Five to every one of the Lost Ones.

He counted his friends and found all but Alexia. But what was that? A flash of movement snatched his attention on one side of the battle. Just as quickly, it was gone. Black curls appeared on the other side of the field. He squinted, and she came into focus for an instant, disarming a man and then disappearing again. *Magnificent.*

Truly, she belonged to the fight. Were he fighting on the other side, he'd be well and truly terrified.

\*\*\*

The line held, barely. Alexia deflected an arrow from hitting Amos square in the chest and panted for breath as her womb seized. Her friends had been battling hours. She had fought the equivalent of two days. She didn't know how much longer she could keep this up—especially with the contractions intensifying. They were down two champions and weakening. The entity pressed his soldiers forward. Regin's touch hadn't worked on him, and her friend had nearly lost an eye in the attempt. Mae couldn't get close enough.

"We cannot keep this up!" Alexia shouted.

Amos grunted. "A headless snake is a dead snake." He dodged a blade and obscured the presence of a boulder in the attacker's path. The man tripped forward over the invisible impediment.

Take out the leader and victory was theirs.

She slowed time and punched a man in the stomach, knocking his helmet off when he bent forward and smacking the back of his head. "He is guarded by the strongest."

Amos scoffed. "Then we must attack in a way they will not see coming."

They met eyes briefly.

A way he wouldn't see coming. "Gather the others to you and full veil the line. I will need you shortly."

He glanced at her. "And what will you do?"

She hurried away in slowed time.

Zeph whirled away from a javelin in slow motion as Alexia stopped next to him and knocked the projectile off course. She turned on his attacker and reached out to push him when her breath caught. Another surge.

She shouted her agony and barreled into the javelin thrower. The man toppled as she lost her grip on time and landed on top of him, curled into her pain.

# Crystal Collier

Hands wrapped around her shoulders from behind and pulled her away, into the sky. "And I thought I was having a rough go," Zeph teased.

She exhaled a single laugh as wind embraced her, the battlefield falling away under the swoop of wings. She caught her breath and twisted her head toward him. "We will distract the others, but I need you to take the leader. The man in white."

"And what do you want me to do with him?"

"Knock him out and bind him on the next rise for interrogation. Then return."

"What about you?"

Alexia gritted her teeth and drew on the medallion. "I will fight until I can no longer."

Zeph set her next to Amos. She gave their leader a signal, and he shot darkness over the warriors protecting the knight.

Zephaniah dove into the pitch. A shout and startled voices followed flapping, and Zeph shot out of the murk and into the sky so quickly that the man in his arms must have passed out. The enemy surged forward.

"Fall back!" Alexia called. She didn't attempt to halt time any longer. She couldn't do it. Her friends ringed her in, protecting her, but it was time for a full escape. The battle was ending. Regin fought around multiple injuries, and Silivia tottered from a head wound, but they wouldn't leave the fight.

The Passionate were losing.

Her eyes snapped to Mae. The woman could end the conflict, but her hunger would attack the Passionate as well. She'd gained so much control, but not enough.

Willem shouted and shook the earth beneath a man's foot, throwing him off balance.

Shaking earth.

She remembered walls of earth and stone collapsing around her as she fled the Soulless's caves. Nelly had brought the caves down. If Nelly could collapse caves, what was Willem capable of?

She slowed time and grabbed the boy's arm, forcing her plan into his mind. Could he save them?

He nodded, cheek twitching.

Zeph returned, and she shouted at him to evacuate everyone to the next rise where the women and children had fled. He took the fighters one at a time. She drew on the necklace once more, defending the few that remained. She was trembling, every limb ready to fail before Zeph came for her, leaving Willem alone.

Her feet had barely touched down on the neighboring peak when Zephaniah dropped her and zipped through the sky, shaded by Amos's darkness. Passionate crowded around her. Kiren pushed through them, halting next to her, his eyes filled with worry.

They were all accounted for, except for the dead. And Willem.

110

The mount, their home for the last many weeks, shook. Stones tumbled free. Trees crashed down the peaks. Dirt rolled in voluminous breakers like the waves of the sea, shooting dust into the sky and blocking the sun.

"Fly faster, fly faster!" Alexia chanted, both fists clenched tight.

Wings flapped out of the haze, a boy clasped in the flyer's arms.

\*\*\*

They lit fires on the peak, but it did little to warm the homeless band. Leastwise their battle commander.

Kiren watched her, perched near a fire alone at the edge of the mountain, head resting in her arms. She'd done it. She'd saved them, but at what cost?

"It were a brilliant move," Regin muttered.

Heads bowed in agreement.

The enemy had been demolished. An enemy who didn't even know what they fought. The opposing force's leader lay unconscious under Regin's care, although no one had decided what they would do with him. An interrogation at the least. Kiren didn't want to think what the worst scenario entailed. The man belonged to the holy order of knights who had been chasing them—that much he knew.

He pressed off the ground, aimed for Alexia, but Regin caught his arm with a gloved hand. "Leave her be, lad. She needs this. Every battle, she needs this."

Kiren shook him off. "I go to assess her health."

Regin's eyebrows lowered, but he gave a tight-mouthed nod.

Alexia didn't move as he approached. Hair spilled loosely down her hunched shoulders, long and dark, her breathing uneven as if caught between sobs.

He perched next to her, ready to flee if needed. The last real conversation they'd had was when she refused his indirect offer to espouse her. He didn't know how to cut through the barrier between them, and so perhaps it was best that he remained on his side until she brought it down. "You do not seem pleased by our victory."

Her shoulders heaved. "There is no victory in war."

"Nay, but war is part of life. As is death." He choked on that last word. No number of words would ever convince him the death of his parents was acceptable. How was he to persuade her otherwise? "You saved many of the innocent today."

"Are our lives any better than theirs?"

Since she didn't glare or shove him away, he settled next to her, mulling that one over. "Did we go into battle to win a prize, or merely to protect our home and lives?"

She dragged a sleeve across her face, the hollows beneath her eyes deep. "I am so tired. Tired of the war and fighting. Tired of the constant battle. Tired of…" She placed a hand on her hardening womb.

He leaned forward and touched her brow, focusing inward. "You are dehydrated." He slid his waterskin free and offered it to her. "You need to drink and rest."

She slumped forward. "Who can rest when all I see are the faces of the dead? Again and again. Their anger. Their steel. Them dying."

His heart ached for her. He too knew this burden, the weight of deciding who would live and who would die, although he had failed to save so many.

"You are a worthy commander." He wrapped her fingers around the waterskin and let go. It fell into her lap, clasped in both hands. He slid a hand over hers and guided it to her mouth.

Her body trembled against his with the effort of staying upright as she drank. She was beyond exhausted, physically and emotionally. Kiren brushed the hair from her cheek, halting the labor-inducing hormones with a touch and calling for relaxants in her brain. It wasn't her time. At least, he wasn't ready for it to be her time. He could give her a few more days, weeks even.

He wrapped an arm around her. "You feel the loss of your enemies vehemently, the sign of a good leader. You are exactly what this people needs." *Not me.*

She leaned into him and yawned. "I learned from watching you."

He stiffened.

She laid her head against his shoulder, and he stroked the white strands of hair away from her face, dosing her with more calm. Her skin was drawn and gray. Tight lines eased across her brow, smoothing into sleep, and her lips parted in steady breaths. For tonight he could watch over her and grant her peace.

# Thirty-Three

# *Trapped*

The open window shed only enough sunlight to touch the girl's toes. Just a hint of warmth. Not nearly enough to fill the little girl's need.

Velia halted in the middle of the floor, throat tightening. Ulric sat beside her child with an arm wrapped around her neck.

"I was beginning to question if you loved this little thing," he spat.

She glared.

"More than you care for her father or your own life, clearly." His grip tightened around the girl's neck.

Velia surged forward, catching the child's fingers between hers and begging the little one for forgiveness with her eyes. Irons burned dark circles into her baby's wrists, turning the skin more sickly than even normal children of her bloodline. If Velia could free her precious one from the fetters, she would sweep her away to safety, far, far from this man and his dark intents.

Ulric tugged at the child's blonde locks. "I was beginning to grow impatient." He yanked the hair and the girl cried out. "You know how I get when I'm impatient."

Velia tensed. Wind gusted into the tower, answering her distress. It rattled the single stool and the refuse bucket.

Ulric grinned. "You will bring them to me."

She collapsed to her knees. Wind hissed her reply: "Never."

"Oh, I think you will. I would hate to see how your offspring handles the rack at such a tender age."

Velia exhaled a breath of rage.

"If you are afraid of revealing your traitorous identity, then bring them close enough and I will do the rest." He got to his feet. "I will let you say hello now." His eyes darkened. "And then you will join me below." He tilted his head. "Do not anger me by disobeying again. You know what happens when I am angry." He angled a menacing snarl at the child and departed, sending two guards to take his place.

Too dry and used for tears, she clasped her child to her bosom. She would have whispered an apology to her little one, but the girl knew how powerless she was to stop Ulric. Instead she held her baby, infusing all the love she could into their precious few moments.

# Thirty-Four

# *Return*

Alexia couldn't voice her relief when Velia arrived with the sunrise. Burn marks crisscrossed the woman's neck and arms, her skin sallow but recovering. Amos reported that she'd been captured while gathering food and held prisoner the last five days, escaping only last night in a moment of luck.

They remained on the mountain another four days, slowly moving elsewhere as Velia recovered. Regin allowed the leader of the opposing force, a knight from the order of the Knights Templar, to wake, and Sarlic questioned him, but the man refused to speak. The inflictor kept watch on the man, rotating with Regin.

Alexia struggled through her guilt, knowing it had been a desperate choice. But had it been the only way? She replayed a hundred different scenarios and found no better solution. Still, their faces haunted her. How many wives had been made widows by her? Women like herself. How many children had become fatherless? Children like her own.

Most everyone had cleared out, but she waited until last—searching the mountain ruins for enemy survivors. There were none.

Kiren stayed with her until the end, quietly offering what comfort he could. Making sure she drank enough water. Insisting she rest.

He sat beside her, the breeze sweeping past them as he brushed his fingers over her arm. "I am going to miss this place, for the good memories made here especially."

"Good and bad." Ravia's and Cedric's deaths, Perrin and Murial, Ilberd... "So many dead."

"But so many saved." He clasped her hand.

She looked at him. Had he forgiven her for accusing him of abandoning his family? Did it make a difference? Her mortality hung in the very near future, and she couldn't take him with her. Soon she would join her friends and enemies in the afterlife.

"Kiren." She slipped her fingers free. "We must end this. I have a baby to birth, and you have centuries yet to live."

"Centuries..." he repeated.

"Of which I have no part." She gave him a pointed look.

"I will save you."

Except she knew he wouldn't. Somehow.

His voice lowered and he leaned in. "Alexia, I will not fail." His lips opened to confess more, but he snapped them shut.

She covered her face with her hands.

"I understand the reason for your distance." His breath tickled a trail down her neck. "And when it is over, when I have saved your life, I hope you will open your heart to me." He turned her to face him. His eyes were a calm summer sea. "Why else would God have brought you into this time?"

"It was not God who brought me here."

His brows lowered.

# Thirty-Five

# *Capture*

Leofrik licked his dry lips. A stone wall cooled his back except where his wrists were bound behind him, his legs likewise bound, and Velia sat, eyes wide, watching him.

She had betrayed him.

When she had transported his men to the remote mountain, one small group at a time, wearying herself until she'd collapsed, he was impressed by her determination. He had even been saddened by her departure. Something of her sultry teasing had aroused a long-abandoned want inside him. Now he saw her for what she truly was: a snake in the grass.

Her eyelids drooped. In the shade, her skin was so ashen he questioned if she would begin to crumble.

"Set me free."

She snapped awake and glared.

"We had an agreement."

She rose, sunlight revealing the shape of her legs through the thin skirt—no doubt her intention that he be distracted by the view. She knelt in front of him and touched his cheek.

*If I free you now, they will know what part I played, since I am charged with guarding you. I have orchestrated a coming conflict where you will be able to fulfill your vow. Patience.*

He groaned and lunged forward, knocking her onto her back beneath him. "Treacherous woman, you will see me tortured and imprisoned and love every moment of it."

Her chest heaved below him, but she didn't melt away. Instead, she leaned up and placed a kiss on the corner of his mouth.

Leofrik stiffened.

She smirked and rubbed a finger across his brow. *They will enter your mind to learn of our accord. Not to worry.* Mist melted off her little finger and sank into his skull. *Your secrets are safe.*

# Thirty-Six

# Torture

The trees reminded Alexia of Wilhamshire. Of Sarah. Of Kiren's secret home in the woods. A stone wall cut through the forest, rising just above her shoulder.

Already they had erected tents and established sleeping, eating, and washing areas. They were resilient.

A scream ripped through camp.

People cringed but went about their routines. Alexia hurried to the other side of the crumbling wall. Mae, Sarlic, and Lucian stood over the captive knight, bound in ropes on the ground. His white tunic was bloodied over leather armor and chainmail, a trail of blood trickling down his lip. He was not a particularly attractive man. The lines on his face said he was no stranger to harsh weather, long nights, and battle.

Alexia stiffened. He had led the charge against the Passionate.

Sarlic lifted a hand toward the knight, a wicked sneer tweaking his cheeks. "You will tell us how you found us."

The man bowed his head, breathing hard. Sarlic's fist clenched. The knight's back arched. A vein bulged in his forehead, and his mouth burst open in another shriek.

"Stop!" she commanded.

Sarlic turned, his fist loosening. The knight collapsed to the ground.

"We do not torture information out of people." She met each of their stares. Mae averted hers. Sarlic's mouth popped open to protest, but Lucian beat him.

"Amos insisted."

Alexia backed away, confused, then she rushed off to find Amos.

His head was bowed over a tree-stump/makeshift table where he examined the scrolls they'd intercepted. Deamus leaned over his shoulder, pointing to the words as he read them to their leader.

"This is not what we do." Alexia slammed a palm on the stump.

Amos glanced up at her and wearily back at the text before him.

"Amos, you must tell them to stop."

"We have a traitor, and he will make them known."

She pointed back at the wall. "Why has his mind not been infiltrated?"

He met her stare, lips cutting a hard line. "We tried. Something is blocking it."

She straightened. "There must be another way."

"How many more will we lose, Alexia?" He rose. "I will not see them suffer. I will not see them die. This ends."

Her fingers bit into her palms. She glanced at Deamus who shrugged.

"There is still this other world," she said.

Amos met her gaze once more. He turned on Deamus. "Do you have a way?"

"I…"

"As I thought. Alexia, find this gate and I will follow you through. Until then, I have enough to worry about."

She took her assignment with a heavy sigh. They would figure it out together.

***

Deamus rubbed at his arm so incessantly it might fall off, spectacles sitting askew as they paced away into the woods.

"You said you know how to open this gateway if we can provide enough energy." She lifted her eyes to his face.

He opened his mouth and drew in breath, then closed it, gaze downcast.

Alexia stopped and placed a hand on his arm.

He groaned. "I tried to open the gateway, twice."

She stared at him, dumbfounded. "But the power needed to do so—?"

"It cracked, but I think…"

"Cracked?" Her mind flashed to Deamus's story of the Soul Eater, the barrier between worlds. They all insisted it was a children's story, but what if it wasn't? What if that was what had been attacking them?

He paced forward. "It did not work. I think the gateway may only be opened at a specific location, the place it was created. The place I entered this world."

She shook the idea away. "Is that where I first found you?"

He nodded.

She recalled the isolated grove that was now missing one of its willow trees, the tree that was a man, but that had been right after her arrival in this time. She had traveled so many places since. No matter how she strained to remember, she couldn't envision its location. Perhaps Velia could help them. "Do you know where that is?"

"I…no. I am sorry. I thought maybe…" He shook his head. "I was wrong. And then there are the stars."

"What about them?"

"When they align, the bridge naturally appears, but they will not be in alignment for many hundred years."

Alexia stopped him with a hand on the arm. "Can the gate be opened without an alignment?"

His head shook, shoulders lifting. He backed away, putting more space between them.

"There is something more, something you're not telling me."

His eyebrows lifted, lips pressed tight. They burst open. "I wanted to confess this to you before, but..."

She squeezed his arm. Let this not be something related to the entity.

He twitched and looked away, opening his mouth several times and closing it. Finally, his shoulders straightened. "I am not like you, Alexia. Not like any of you." He glanced back through the trees, the direction of the camp. "I am human."

She blinked at him several times. That wasn't what she'd been expecting. She laughed.

He wasn't laughing.

"But I have seen you use powers. You cannot possibly be human, at least not entirely. I myself am half human. There is no shame in it."

His shoulders drooped. "It is true. Not a drop of Passionate blood in me. There are very few humans who can feel the world around them, and even fewer who can reshape the energy."

"So you borrow our strength, so to speak, having none of your own? But you have participated in sharings. How is that possible?"

He shrugged timidly. "Borrowing. Only a little."

She stood back. "But you have intimate knowledge of the gateway and this other world."

"I am from there. My father was like me, and he was present when the gateway first opened."

Her brain hurt. "How many years back was that?"

He scuffed the heel of his boot into the ground. "Time is not the same here. It had been centuries here since the great departure and a handful of years to my world."

Her head spun. Different times on each world? She turned the conversation back to the subject at hand. "Your heritage changes nothing." She touched his shoulder. "You are my friend. We will find the gateway. Together." And perhaps it would lead her to the source of this enemy, this Soul Eater.

\*\*\*

Alexia left camp, not far, unwilling to return and listen to the torture. It was difficult enough knowing it was happening from the spring she'd located. Amos would be angry with her for wandering off alone, but she needed the silence, the isolation. The thing that would become the Soulless hadn't manifested here, and she hoped it had well and truly been left behind. Regardless, her dagger remained strapped to her hip.

She splashed water over her face as the stream gurgled past. Thumps pounded her womb, the baby ready to join the world. She pressed a hand over the kicks, smiling to herself. This beautiful little girl was the greatest comfort she found in the dark world she inhabited. And yet the child's future was so uncertain.

"Why is it I always find you near water? Are you part selkie?"

Alexia jumped, hand flying to her weapon. Kiren leaned on a hip, eyeing her up and down.

She turned back to the water, flutters curling through her chest. Her mind spun with the memory of him sneaking up on her under her favorite rowan tree or on the roof. So much of her Kiren was in him.

She rose and turned to leave.

He stepped in her path, arms crossed. The set of his shoulders was one she'd deflated many a time with a well-stated argument. Here stood the proud man who believed he could heal the world.

She sidestepped him, and his arm curled around her center.

"Avoid me to your heart's fulfillment after this, but you accused me of abandoning my family. Allow me to enlighten you."

She pried his arm free, stood back, and waited.

He wouldn't meet her stare. "I am terrified of what has become of my sister, that everything my father worked for is gone, that no matter how it pains me, I will never be able to take up his mantle." He lifted a brilliant purple flower and slid it into her hair, just above her ear. "I am frightened by what I feel for you."

She blushed and touched the bloom. A foreign blossom. She'd seen its like only once before, in Kiren's forested haven.

He brushed her hand away from the petals. "It reminds me of home."

Her stomach fluttered. "The place your family lived, in this other world?"

Kiren let out a painful breath and nodded. Sadness filled his eyes, an entire sea of it. He cleared his throat. "Certainly you are missing your home and family." He waved at her womb.

She gave a half-smile. "Indeed." Her husband most of all. "Though many of the people I most wish for are dead—my sister, my mother, my surrogate mother."

"Is there no one else?"

Alexia closed her eyes.

"There was someone. The father?"

She sighed.

Fingers landed on her shoulder. "It is strange to me that a man could have or would have abandoned you in this state—unless he was a villain. Methinks you have suffered some great tragedy."

She smiled sadly. "Tragedy is part of us. An intimate part."

"This is true." His head tilted, fingers tightening on her shoulder. "But I wish to understand yours."

Alexia placed her fingers over his, ready to remove his hand.

His ocean swells pulled her into their undertow. "You do not trust me, so whatever is going happen, I must deserve it." He grabbed her wrist and pulled her through the trees to a clearing. "Let me earn your trust."

Frosty wind tickled her neck, lifting her hair toward the horizon, a bare line that disappeared over the crest of a hill, disrupted by a small building and a single, tall willow tree. The stream they'd left glistened in the morning light, as wide as she was tall, originating from a formation of stones she recognized. The stone bench from Kiren's forested sanctum.

Nausea curdled her belly.

Purple blooms mixed with red and yellow across the meadow, all the way up to the nearby building. Wooden slats framed the small structure with a steeple, three steps leading up to the door. The lack of windows surprised her, but she recognized the rudimentary structure of its architecture. She had seen a much further advancement of these same skills.

He'd built a church? In his sanctuary? And how had they landed so close to this haven—not that she'd complain. He was much more relaxed when surrounded by the familiar. Perhaps he had suggested a location to Velia before leaving the mountains.

Kiren slipped a key out of his pocket and placed it to the building's lock.

"Why a church?" she asked. "Why not a house?"

He paused in the doorway and exhaled, then stepped into the building. If it had ever been used for worship, it wasn't by a populace. The roof was riddled with windows, ones she could only know existed from being inside. Beveled glass poured light like waves on the ocean. The largest one occupied the center, casting oscillations of luminescence on a woven mat, the only furniture in the entire building. Resting across the mat was a friar's robe. He stooped and slipped it over his head.

Squares of light circled the outer edges of the room, illuminating multiple murals that covered the white-washed walls. The paint strokes were wide, as if painted by fingers. The art wasn't particularly refined, but it possessed an emotional quality that moved her—extremes of light and darkness, vivid colors, harrowing scenes.

Kiren stood in the center of the room, dressed in his priestly attire, head bowed. He lifted his eyes. "Here I am."

She turned back to the walls, fascinated.

Nearest the door, lightning zipped from a clear sky, exploding against the ground and illuminating the crouched silhouette of a boy. The next image was a knight, riding atop a horse, dragging a tether that looped a terrified boy's neck— a boy dressed in a fine white jacket and decorated breeches.

Alexia stepped toward the poor child.

"The knight was Sir Godwin." Kiren's voice carried from the middle of the room. "At first he hoped I might win him a reward, but over time I became an annoyance, and then a slave."

She traced the next image, a building under construction, the slightly older boy dragging timber toward it.

Alexia's breath caught. The following scene depicted a priest offering a hand to the boy who knelt on the ground in rags.

Kiren's voice lowered. "But God is good to those who need him."

She glanced back at him, his head bowed.

In the fifth depiction, two silhouettes fled in the night, bright stars overhead. A church appeared next, the knight and a number of men standing out front, fists raised as they spoke with the priest, and the boy huddled beneath the floorboards of the building, gripping the pendant around his neck.

The lad and priest sat in candlelight, the priest pointing to words in a book, mouth open in speech, the boy holding a quill to a parchment, letters trailing behind his pen.

She moved to a stormy sea, Viking ships breaking the waves. On a hill overlooking the ocean, fire consumed the little church, the priest's face pressed to the window in terror.

"Everything I love is doomed." Kiren's words startled her.

She drew her fingers across the next scene, an adolescent boy sitting in the ash, face hidden in his hands. And then there was a crowd of silhouettes encircling the boy, a crown hovering over his head. The massacre had been captured as well, a tortured young man crouched over the prostrate bodies, frantically searching for a way to revive the dead.

She had reached the back of the building, a giant cross painted from ceiling to floor in white. On the other side was a teenage girl with fiery red hair and striking green eyes, both beautiful and terrifying. Behind her, a white palace with seven spires brightened the sky. The rest of the walls were blank.

"I have been searching for a way to her, Alexia. My sister. She found me briefly, and suddenly, she was gone." He lifted both hands. "I am not here to lead these people. I am here by mistake and must return to my home."

"But these are your people."

He huffed and pointed to the castle. "My kingdom is elsewhere."

She turned to him. "So you have a right to not care about these suffering souls? Your kin?"

He shook his head. "It is safer for them if I do not." He brought both hands together in front of him. "I did once. Do you know what happened?"

"Yes." The small admission drew him up short. His eyes flashed and he swallowed, gaze dropping.

He continued in a smaller voice. "I travel the continents, searching for a way back while performing *miracles* for the poor, despondent souls of this world. In time, God will provide me a way home."

She snorted. No he wouldn't.

Kiren's eyes burned into her, warning against her light response.

"Have you considered that God is not part of this debacle and you are here because life is cruel?"

He advanced toward her. "There is a higher reason."

In his righteous anger, he looked so much like the man she'd met while imprisoned at Haunted House of Stark, the hour she'd lost her heart and head completely to him. She averted her gaze and held her breath, determined not to take in his oaken musk.

"Everything we pass through is to prepare us for what will come." He stopped right before her. "Except perhaps you." His hand lifted, fingers outstretched. They grazed over her womb and she sucked in a breath. His palm flattened, warming her skin through the fabric. His voice softened, slightly breathless. "I have not yet discovered what part you play in my destiny."

The baby pressed against his touch. Alexia gasped.

His eyes flickered up. "Perhaps I am to save your child and that is why God brought us together."

She stared at him, saddened. If only he knew the truth.

"Why do I think of you always?" he whispered, placing his other hand at the base of her jaw. "Why can I not stop? And do not tell me it is because of a few mistaken kisses."

She wished with her whole soul that he could be her Kiren, the tender man who sacrificed everything for others. This glimpse hurt too much.

She backed away, lowering her eyes. A tear slipped down her cheek. "I thank you for sharing this with me."

Kiren reached her in a single step. The earnest waves of his all-encompassing sea dragged her under, swallowing her whole. She couldn't breathe, and she never wanted to again. Here was her eternity, waiting for her to seize it, to say just the right thing and lay claim.

The words hovered on her tongue. *I love you, Kiren. I've always loved you. You were the man I dreamed of all my life, the man I thought was impossible until you claimed me for your own.*

"Tell me who the father is." His brows lowered. "And I will make him suffer for his sins."

Her face burned.

He studied her. "Even if it is not for centuries that I meet him, I will bring you justice. Are you frightened of him?"

"Nothing frightens me."

His fingers slid over top hers, and he lifted her hand to his lips. "Not even me?"

She knew she should withdraw her hand, but the tender way he held it left her knees weak and heart thudding.

His head lowered, nose grazing across her neck like he was breathing her in. "Stay with me, Alexia. Believe in me. Be mine."

She shook herself free. "Kiren."

He growled. "You kissed me and started…whatever this is. Tell me what you want. I will do anything for you. You only have to ask."

"I want you to live." She faced him with tears in her eyes. Extending her hands to him, she whispered, "I need you to live. To lead. To become."

He stood back and hissed, "And yet you kissed me—knowing you might die and I would be drawn to you." His face scrunched up and his jaw muscles flexed, teeth clenched. "Why would you do that?"

Was that the only reason he pursued her? No words could adequately explain her actions, not without revealing her past. His future. Even that explanation felt too weak.

"Alexia, answer me." He spoke like a king. She snapped to attention as she had when Father used that tone. Kiren was past patiently waiting for her to volunteer information. Anger burned in his eyes.

She had no words for him.

"Or will you not speak because the only answer you have is a shameful one?"

She felt like she'd swallowed a frog. It was struggling down her throat, choking the truth within her.

"That is why you will not let me into your thoughts," he continued. "You are afraid I will discover the lie you told the others. You had no husband. You wear that ring as a farce and protection. It is convenient that he is gone and you can claim he existed, so now you can have whomever you want. Why not me?"

The frog hit her stomach and hopped around, pounding her further and further into the ground. He truly thought she had given herself to someone at random?

"I do not believe you are from the future. You kissed me to gain access to my memories so you might manipulate me."

Tears prickled through, blurring her vision. "Coward."

His nostrils flared, jaw clenching. "I would not call it *cowardice* to willingly embrace a woman who has conceived through shame."

Her jaw unhinged. Tears welled, but she held the dam, wouldn't let him know how deeply his words stung. Was that truly what he thought? That he was doing her a service by caring for an otherwise unsalvageable and undesirable woman? He was shamed by her. His attraction to her.

And she thought perhaps he just cared for her. Loved her even.

She twisted the hurt into anger. It was the only way to keep him from ripping her heart out. "You are a coward—a man who runs from his responsibilities after a single failure. A man who hides from the people who need him. A man who throws the blame for his failures at those who suffer because of him."

"You kissed me!"

"I wish I had not!"

He scoffed. "I am a fool for not taking my leave of you, as you continually insist. I deserve better than a harlot."

125

Rage seethed up from her toes. He was not the man she'd believed, but a scoundrel and reprobate.

Alexia smacked him, hard.

His head whipped to the side, and he gasped. Her palm stung. It was wet. Had she been sweating? Alexia turned her hand over and sucked in a breath. Crimson liquid stained her skin. Red. Manifesting like the many murders these hands had induced. Her pronged wedding ring faced upward, sharp edges glistening scarlet. She trembled and dropped her hand.

Kiren turned back to her, blood seeping between the fingers he clasped over his cheek, from the corner of his eye to just above his chin.

His scar.

Alexia fell back several steps.

She was the one who had done that to him. All this time she had wondered, and he'd never answered her questions.

But this Kiren had deserved it.

"You have less nobility than a swine," she whispered, shocked by her own words. But they kept coming, the only thing that stopped her from breaking into tears for what she'd done. "A man so selfish he cares only for himself has no business becoming a king. I am glad that you have given up the pursuit." Alexia spun and threw the door open. "I am going to save the Passionate, Kiren, and then I will torture you no more." Because she would exist no more.

She sped out into the chill of night. Tears coursed down her cheeks the instant she was free. He'd hurt her. She'd scarred him. Forever.

Kiren was right to keep this part of their history from her. She wished she'd never known it.

# Thirty-Seven

# *Timing*

Kiren watched her go, completely stunned. It wasn't the blood seeping from his face so much as her words: *Less nobility than a swine... Selfish...*

Wind snuffed the warmth of his sanctuary, his treasured prison of memories. His personal torture chamber. The past was filled with shame and misery, and his suffering was worthy of it, but how could he have said that to Alexia? Accused her of fornication?

The flower he'd place in her hair lay in the entry, petals flickering in the wind.

He didn't believe she was unchaste. Not for an instant. She was the embodiment of all that was good, and every mention of her child had brought an intense sorrow to her eyes, one he'd just aggravated. She was either a victim or had lost the love of her life and somehow survived.

She was right. He ran away because he was selfish. Gave up leading the Lost Ones because he was selfish. Turned his back on any hope of returning home to the Neitherlands because of that selfishness. Lashed out at her because of selfishness.

He tore at his hair, willing himself to cease existing.

Restraint. Kiri, his sister, had always said his impulsiveness would haunt him.

He scrubbed a hand over his face, the fingers coming away slick with blood. He scowled and went to clean up. The entire way and back, Alexia's tear-filled eyes haunted him, not broken because of the trials she'd endured, but spilling because of him.

He lifted the paints in the corner of the church and cleared her image from his mind by purging it onto the wall, exasperated by the futility of his art. What purpose did it serve? To deepen his wounds and keep the past fresh? Even the flowers he cultivated for his rare inks brought him little peace. Flowers he crushed for these memories. Destruction for torture. He was determined to spill the paint out back and never waste his efforts again...except he couldn't misuse the blood of so many living things. Reluctantly, he dipped his fingers again and finished the scene—the woman who tore his cheek and called him unworthy.

She had been right. He understood that. At her back he outlined a gateway of light, the only way to a safe haven for all of them. Whether he wished to be a leader or not, he owed his people enough to fight. And he would.

Perhaps it was time to try again. Condemning himself to marriage and fatherhood was an excuse to keep from trying. The wrong course. The cut across his face said as much.

Kiren exited the church and aimed straight for the spot where everything had begun.

The gateway.

*** 

Alexia scrubbed her hand in the stream, determined, desperate to get the blood off. The blood that would never come off. Fifty suffering creatures flashed before her eyes, the sword clutched in her hand as she murdered them again and again and again. Men in armor dotting a mountain side, crushed by the debris...

She cried out and picked up a stone, scraping the blood free, scraping until the skin was gone, scraping until her fingers were too numb to continue on.

Kiren. She had scarred Kiren, forever.

It was her.

She collapsed into her folded arms, weeping for the dead and lost. For the misery she'd caused. For the child she'd brought to this age, only to leave her defenseless and alone. For the father she should be drawing near her child, the one who despised her and the little one within her womb.

She curled around her torn flesh.

*** 

Alexia woke with a start. The stream gurgled by next to her, but darkness saturated the land. She'd fallen asleep. Her hand ached...

But her heart ached worse.

She returned to the church as stars blazed above, knowing Kiren's appearance in camp would herald her shame and they must resolve this conflict. All would see what she'd done to him, an action she could hardly explain. She needed to apologize, to beg his forgiveness, to find a way to heal this.

The church was dark. The door was locked and no one answered her knocking, though her raw fist throbbed in the aftermath. She knocked again, harder. Nothing. She pressed an ear to the door, listening for a single creak, an exhaling of breath, anything.

Chirping insects filled the silence.

He was gone.

She turned for camp. Perhaps she had missed him and he'd already joined the others around the fire. Perhaps he had made a villain of her in the eyes of the Passionate. Perhaps he would exact his revenge by revealing her *perceived* treachery and ruining her reputation.

The bushes rustled.

Alexia stopped.

An invisible weight pressed her shoulders. The hairs of her arms stood up. She turned.

Crimson eyes watched her from the shadows—the hungry leer of a predator. She didn't dare move a muscle. Not even to breathe. Alexia brushed mental fingers over the flow of time, prepared to jerk it to a halt. Not that it would help.

She had no idea how to fight this thing, but whatever it was, she must. The weight at her hip—the dagger that could dispatch the Soulless—felt leagues away. One movement, a hundred breaths, a thousand seconds too far from her grasp against an enemy uninhibited by time.

Feet crunched through the underbrush from behind. She whirled, ripping the dagger from its sheath, ready for an attack. Deamus skipped toward her, his face alight with joy. He halted at her weapon.

She turned back, but the eyes were gone.

He cleared his throat and swung his arms, weakly mimicking his delight of a moment ago. "I have found it."

She blinked. "Found what?"

"The location of the gateway!"

Alexia's fingers squeezed into a ball. She glanced back at the darkness she'd felt watching, but the ominous presence was missing. Deamus had attempted to open the gateway twice, and this enmity-suffused presence had appeared around the same time. As much as she wished to dismiss the children's story of souls being eaten, she'd begun to believe it held a seed of truth.

"Your enthusiasm is astounding," Deamus said, voice flat.

"Is it safe to open the gate?"

"Safe?" His jaw flapped. "It is safe on the other side—safer than being hunted by armies and invisible monsters."

Of course it was. Or at least, she hoped it was. The others would be jubilant at the prospect of this new world, and with the Passionate gone, the Soulless would never become. But the society she'd known would cease to exist. Kiren would never become the man she loved.

She forced a smile. "That is incredible news. You can finally go home."

His head tilted. "And you will go with me."

She nodded, but her stomach twisted. "You think we can garner the strength to open the gateway?"

"There is a way, and I know what it is." A grin broke his face and he threw both arms around her. His lips touched her cheek, and she pushed him away.

He frowned.

"Go," she encouraged. "Tell Amos. You are going home!"

Happiness returned to his face.

***

Alexia searched the underbrush, hoping to find evidence of what? An inky cloud? She needed some way to track it, but it left no trace.

She returned to camp slowly, pondering. Deamus's eagerness for this other world turned over and over in her mind. It sang to her: a place where her child could grow without fear of being chased. She loved the idea, but no such utopia could exist.

Utopia. The book had not even been penned. Oh how she missed reading!

Part of her had been dreaming about this new world, and part reasoned that there was no such thing as a perfect world. Surely this new place posed just as many threats or challenges as her current one. She would die in childbirth either place. At least Kiren would eventually know his child if Alexia remained here. She owed him that.

Embers remained of the fires. Dawn would warm the sky shortly, and though she searched every face in the camp, she found no Kiren. Zephaniah lounged among the others, chatting contentedly. He met her gaze, his sharpening with suspicion, but he didn't rouse himself to question her.

Had she done it then? Frightened Kiren away? Condemned herself?

All because she couldn't bear to tell him the truth.

But he couldn't handle the truth—as he'd proven when she'd first allowed him into her memories.

Zephaniah was here. Surely he wouldn't go anywhere without his best friend. He, at least, had something in the world worth remaining for.

# Thirty-Eight

# *Will*

Kiren stopped in the clearing. He hadn't been here in years, not since Kiri disappeared in the middle of the night and he'd returned to try the gateway. It was as he remembered. Mostly. A slight slope to the ground, moss and weeds blanketing the earth between cottonwood and elms.

Wind blustered through, ruffling the ground cover and carrying a hint of rain. The chill scraped over the raw flesh of his face. He pressed a hand to it, agonizing over what he'd said to Alexia again, the accusation that rang false the instant it left his tongue. The hurt in her large eyes. The betrayal and force of her blow.

His skin still burned where her golden ring had raked his flesh. And it wouldn't heal. It didn't matter how he concentrated his energy on the wound, either he was subconsciously fighting to keep the pain—because he deserved it—or traces of gold had infected his lesion, making it impossible to mend.

Guilt squirreled through his gut.

Enough with this. It was time to open the gateway home and set things aright. Deamus said it could be done, and if that was even the slightest bit possible, he had to try. He'd failed the Lost Ones before, but if he succeeded, tonight he could atone for his errors by granting them access to his home. They would join his subjects on the other side. They would be his subjects.

Including Alexia.

His stomach contorted at the idea of bringing her to his world. Even if she forgave him, she could never be his queen. The eyes of all nations would be on him and expectations would wall him in like an elaborate prison. His companions from this world may attest to her purity, but she would be jaded and looked down on as power hungry or morally questionable. The whole world would see her. The whole world would judge her. They would question his wisdom and perhaps even his honor for choosing a companion whose virtue was in doubt. He couldn't do that to her.

Stepping through the gateway was the same as letting her go.

Perhaps he needed to. Alexia had inspired him toward this action, which may have been her purpose all along, the reason God placed her in his path. It didn't matter that the thought of losing her scraped his insides raw.

Kiren inflated his lungs, pulling in more air to compensate for the crushing weight on his chest. Back home. To a kingdom torn apart. To a waiting sister. To his father's throne. Not to the woman he'd allowed far too close to his heart.

He lifted the medallion from around his neck, the key between worlds. He recalled playing with the charm as a child while it hung around his father's neck, never guessing its importance. Kiren had been three years of age when Father slipped the chain free and looped it about his son. *"Keep this safe for me, little prince, and never forget your duty."* It was Kiren's proudest moment. He hadn't known until too late that the charm might have saved his father's life, that it was given to him out of love and not because the king believed Kiren could protect anything.

His arm shook and he steadied it. He had neglected his calling for a time, but he would make it right. This must be done with certainty. Today he would return and save the beings of both worlds from a war that would tear them to pieces.

"Open for me," he commanded with all the conviction of a king.

The sky rumbled.

Clouds trembled overhead and darkened.

Kiren turned the pendant toward the black and pooled the energy into his fist. He aimed the current upward. "Open!"

Lightning snaked through the clouds. It flashed overhead. Thunder boomed, deafening him. Wind gusted into the clearing, tearing at his tunic.

Power rippled through his skin, launching upward, a beam of light.

Kiren gasped. This was going to work! Home was only a breath away. He could already feel the freshness of the air, the energy that saturated the very ground, his sister's rib-crunching embrace.

*Kiri, I am coming.*

Crack.

Power slammed his chest. Light burned his eyes.

Kiren crumpled to his knees. A pike had been shoved through his torso. A pike of energy.

He couldn't breathe.

He pounded one fist to his chest, gasping and sucking for air, leaning on the ground.

He gasped.

Air entered.

He landed on his elbows, panting. He turned to the sky. Clouds thinned out, lightening and calming. The night sky mocked him with the distance between him and his destiny.

He slammed the ground and shoved onto his knees. His necklace lay in the weeds, waiting for him. It mocked him with its weight and the inability to fulfill his obligations. To reach his sister. To save the Neitherlands. To lead these Lost Ones to safety.

Kiren snatched the chain.

He wasn't going home after all.

He lay a long time recovering before shoving to his feet and rubbing his tender chest. He'd sent everything up to the sky, and the sky had sent it back with a vengeance. At least the energy was returned. It hadn't been wasted, but after a blow like that, he needed rest—the traditional kind.

But he couldn't sit still.

An urge tugged at the back of his mind. He should check... A sense of agitation carried him away from the gateway, to the spot where his enemy had been trapped long ago.

The prison was gone.

Air hissed from between his teeth, his lungs refusing its reentry. While he should have been monitoring this spot, he was out gallivanting the world, healing people and frivolously wasting his days.

Somewhere, a great evil was loose, an evil he must put down, and he had no idea where to begin searching.

He dropped to a knee, uttering a desperate prayer for guidance.

Faces flashed in his mind—the hundreds of faces he'd encountered. All in danger. All at risk. Alexia. Her baby.

His head snapped up. He touched the aching gash, the mischief his own arrogance had wrought. He would suffer a hundred such malignments if it meant she was safe, that she would live.

Kiren got to his feet. He forced the panic down and listened, slowing his breathing until he heard the hum of the wind, the soft chirp of insects, the scuttle of rodents and distant song of a stream. The answer was here. He just had to find it.

He bent and brushed a hand across the mulch where the prison had stood. The ground quelled at his touch. It resonated with the energy in his necklace, and an invisible trail bled off the spot, pointing him north, so old it was less than a whisper. At least he had a starting point.

\*\*\*

Deamus jumped as lightning struck Arik and crouched back behind a tree. Well, that was...unexpected. It seemed the gateway liked the High King's heir less than himself.

He'd recognized Arik when they met—the very image of his father. Open the gateway, and the heir could be restored to the throne so easily. But Deamus lacked the key. He'd felt the power surrounding this heir, and now he knew why. More importantly, Arik knew the location of the gateway, and watching closely had paid off. This was the spot.

Foolish of Arik to try opening it without the correct incantation. He now had a slice across his face as a permanent reminder.

Arik had used the key, the necklace. Had he unlocked the gateway? If so, it was now left to Deamus to finish the job. He watched for Arik to leave, shaking his head at the witless move.

Deamus stepped out and assumed the spot where Arik had crushed the weeds. He lifted both hands over his head and muttered the words, a prayer or inquiry, not a command. Would it work this time?

The wind picked up. Clouds swirled around him. The gateway tugged at his energy. He let it have what he'd stored, holding the clasp tight, ready to close off the flow. A pin-hole of darkness split the sky, widening to a well, leaking blackness to the ground like falling stars.

No walls of light.

Deamus let go. It appeared he needed the key after all. He turned back to camp, to find Alexia. She would be pleased to know they had everything they needed, if she could convince Arik to surrender his necklace. Deamus was fairly certain she could convince the heir, although he didn't wish to know the method.

His throat tightened at the idea of her being near Arik, of the sickening endearments they must share. She should have chosen him. She might still. She just didn't know it yet.

# Thirty-Nine

# *Unmasked*

A shiver trailed down Alexia's spine. She could feel eyes on her, but not the welcome kind—predator eyes, like those of a panther. She turned slowly. People milled about the camp, conversing, arguing, preparing for the night. Beyond them, darkness swelled in the trees. An unnatural darkness.

She gripped the medallion and hurried toward it. If the thing was now manifesting, she would stop it. No more deaths. No more suffering. It was why she hadn't mentioned the thing's presence to Amos—because the dagger may work on it. A little closer and she might be able to destroy it. For good.

"Alexia?"

She paused, glancing at Mae and back to the trees.

"This new world," Mae spoke quietly, "Amos told me of your errand. Do you, do you think there is a place for me there?"

Alexia turned to her friend, startled by the desperate, hopeful tone.

"I wish to stop hurting people." Mae bowed her head. "If there truly is a barrier, perhaps it is where I belong."

Alexia's heart broke. She took her friend's hand. "Mae, see." She opened her mind, remembering the inn on scorched earth and the kindly inn keeper who had housed so many of the Passionate needing protection, the woman with cornflower eyes and a terrifying gift. Alexia released her. "I do not know what this other world has to offer, but if you remain, you will find your own peace. You will become great."

Mae took a deep breath, blinking.

Alexia glanced back at the woods. The ominous black was gone. She tilted her head, searching for its essence elsewhere, but couldn't sense it. The entity had vacated.

Alexia extended a hand to her friend. "Come, Mae. Let us try something new with your gift. We shall see if you can push the energy away from yourself and into another being."

\*\*\*

The scream announcing another casualty came hours later than Alexia expected. Ockman lay dead, his neck twisted the wrong direction, eyes wide as if watching the monster that had killed him walk away.

Alexia bowed her head. She might have prevented it—had she approached the darkness instead of calming Mae. But then, perhaps she'd merely have presented herself as a vessel for the enemy to destroy. Even the dagger might not be enough. Had Mae saved her?

***

Panic filled the camp. Alexia leaned over the fire, warming her hands, weighed by Ockman's death. She'd confessed to Amos, and the council held a debate. If the thing could follow them across landmasses, would relocating to another camp do any good? They'd parted without a decision, and Amos had been in his tent all afternoon.

"The knight slipped his bonds to take revenge," Oriel whispered across from her.

"That is absurd. The man is still bound," Silivia said. "It was the thing that killed Murial."

Hammond drummed his knees. "Or the knight's allies have come and are tormenting us from the shadows."

Amos stepped out of his tent. The Passionate quieted. Alexia caught his eyes and he gave her a grim nod. He had reached a decision.

He stopped before the largest fire, and his voice boomed over them. "An evil has come upon us, though whether it be of man or shadow, we cannot say. But we do know one of you has been betraying us to our enemies. Turn yourself in," he demanded, "else we will find you by examining your mind and learning for ourselves."

Shudders spread through the camp. No one could resist the force of the combined council.

"If you run, you admit your guilt, and we do not take treachery lightly." Amos finished, "You have until midnight to reveal yourself."

Tension hung like the scent of dirty flesh: suffocating, constant, thick.

Alexia escaped to the far side of the crumbling wall where the knight rested on his side, eyes closed. She dismissed Sarlic, promising she would find him when she was done speaking with the prisoner.

"You know who it is." She sat beside the knight. "The murderer who betrayed us and has possibly taken up killing our own?"

The man laughed, actually awake despite his appearance. "A wise individual."

Her fists tightened. "You think so?"

He lifted a chin toward the wall. "What do you think they would do if unleashed on a city? On normal, ungifted people?"

"We *are* people," she countered.

136

He huffed.

"My father was a country baron, nothing special about him other than his title." Oh how she missed Father. "But he loved a beautiful, strange woman with a unique heritage." She brushed at a grass stain on her skirt. "Is there any evil in that?"

He lifted his eyes, assessing her. "You do not show the humility of a noble woman."

"No, I do not, because I am more than a noble woman. You stood across from me on the battle field."

He looked away.

"We warriors carry a heavy burden. We fight for causes we would rather shun on behalf of those who need us."

His jaw clenched. She had hit a nerve.

"Even so, I would no sooner hurt one of your kind as one of ours, but I will not see them wiped off the face of the Earth." She nodded at the wall. "Death is a tragedy except when it comes in old age."

The mountain crumbling reared up in her mind, men buried alive. She had killed his men. All of them. Who was she to lecture him about death and war?

"Forgive me for not believing you, my lady."

"Alexia, if you please."

No reply.

"Sir, we live in seclusion. We attack no one, and yet someone has decided we must be hunted and contained. I submit that these mandates are from men who wish to harness our powers and secure their standing against other countries or kings. They would use us, or kill us. Call me evil if you must, but I believe in saving my people from the torture of powerful men. In keeping their gifts from being turned on humanity."

His cheek twitched.

"And now someone is killing my friends, one by one in the night, and I am forced to believe that one of this company is devolving our stability further." She lifted her gaze to his. "Help me, and I will help you."

He half-chuckled and squeezed into a ball, grimacing. "There is no help for me."

Alexia sighed. If only she could win his trust, but that may be an impossible feat seeing how he believed it best for the Passionate to perish.

She waved Sarlic back over and departed.

***

Velia's shadow draped over the flickering coals. Alexia patted the ground next to herself. The mist woman sat reluctantly, half in and out of the fog like always. They had communicated rarely because of Velia's inability to speak, but Alexia always felt a great deal of gratitude for this woman's sacrifice.

137

A chilly hand touched Alexia's, and an image burst over her: a tower prison, drafty, spilling light from chinks in the ceiling and single window. A man stood before her grinning like he was about to get exactly what he wanted. *He is my captor.*

Alexia blinked. "You are in no prison."

*I am always in his prison.*

And suddenly she understood. "You are bonded."

The mist-maiden's head bowed. *I have done many things of which I am not proud, but I am no murderer.*

Alexia stiffened. "Why are you telling me this?"

*Because I believed you would understand.* Velia waved to Alexia's belly.

Oh, Velia… Her heart ached for the woman. To deny a bondmate was near impossible. She'd felt everything Kiren had felt, desired what he desired, needed to please him. But being bonded to a human was worse. Humans weren't susceptible to the bond—meaning they didn't ache to please their companion on instinct. They didn't connect on a subconscious level. They didn't die when their lover died. And sometimes, a lucky one of the Passionate survived their human bondmate's death.

*I am the traitor, but I have not killed anyone.*

Alexia groaned. Velia hadn't killed them directly, but she may as well have held the blade.

*But there is someone missing tonight, someone who appeared shortly before the murders began.* Velia hesitated. *Is he your bondmate?*

She turned on the woman. "He is not a murderer."

The mist-maiden bowed her head. *Shelter me, and I will testify it is not him.*

So it was to be blackmail. Alexia bit down. "He needs no protection. He has no motive. He is innocent."

*Once I was as well.*

Alexia glared. Velia met her stare, a challenge in hers, a threat. Back down or see him defamed. Again.

Alexia would not back down.

The mist maiden scowled and slipped away.

There could be no bargain, no matter how she ached for the woman or Kiren. Alexia's heart sped. It was what the Passionate would all conclude. Kiren was gone. Someone was dead. He had appeared before the first murder and left right before the last. What more evidence did they need? And if Velia vowed she had witnessed Kiren in the act?

Mist collected near Amos, the woman's head bowed. Alexia could almost hear Velia's confession, followed by an accusation. Amos met Alexia's stare from across the camp. His jaw squared.

She could barely breathe. Things were about to become dangerous.

# Forty

## Shine the Light

Kiren whirled as the wagon rattled past.

It wasn't her.

He'd been walking for hours, ever since he woke this morning with a sore back in a hay mound. His sleep was filled with nightmares: the man who stood in the ash, laughing at the remains of a hidden cottage. Mother and Father buried in the cinders, their flesh smoldering as they screamed. Kiren had awakened with a start, tears fresh on his face. The man who had murdered his parents and been imprisoned on this world, he was liberated. Somewhere he wrought havoc. Somewhere he roamed free. And he was certainly coming for Kiren.

But he would find the demented one first.

He had passed straight through the town in pursuit of his enemy, pushing until every ounce of stamina was spent, until his feet had refused to lift, until he'd collapsed into a hay mound. Frustrated with the lost time, Kiren had awoken and trudged on, but when he'd spotted a thistle of thriving green amidst the barren branches, he thought of Alexia's eyes—such a vibrant hue.

A rock cut into his boot, and he glanced back at the wagon and the dark-haired woman he'd briefly mistaken for the succubus of his mind. But Alexia wasn't that anymore. She was a compassionate soul who gave all for her people, even when it should be beyond her capacity. Their servant. Their queen.

And those same Lost Ones had cared for him. She'd made that possible by accepting him—foolish pride and all. Even with the mischief happening around him, he'd been welcome because of her.

Because she kissed him. Because she scarred him. Because she taught him what it meant to give of yourself entirely.

Kiren rubbed a hand over his painful jaw.

He was not going back, could not go back until he'd found his enemy. She would be safe among the others. They would sacrifice themselves on her behalf before any ill could come to her.

He halted.

What if his enemy was wreaking havoc on the Lost Ones? The essence of darkness, the many forced moves, the murders…

Alexia was in the greatest danger.

Her last words haunted him: "*I will torture you no more.*" Had she bid him farewell with that phrase? Because she knew what was coming?

Never hearing her verbally lash him, never feeling the torture of her allure, never drowning in the ambrosia of her skin, he couldn't live that existence.

He turned around, marching with greater purpose than he ever had.

She had pushed him away to protect him. If something happened to her because of him, something he could have prevented or healed, he would never be able to live with himself. She haunted him now, but she would become the wraith that tortured his every thought.

He turned a prayer heavenward: let him not be too late!

# Forty-One

# *Rush*

Alexia stopped in front of the little shop, fixated on her reflection in the window. No proper woman of the eighteenth century would waddle through the streets in this state, but there hardly was a proper here. Velia had confessed to being the traitor and publicly accused Kiren of murder. Amos had accepted the confession freely, but like Alexia, he was skeptical. What possible motive could the healer have? And if Kiren wanted them dead, why had he bothered healing them at all? Tracking him down was the only way to prove his innocence.

She nodded to Regin, Mae, and Amos as they separated amid the town's traffic to find evidence of their quarry. Deamus admitted to having followed Kiren some and pointed them to this town. Alexia hated that they were tracking him like a criminal, but she had no way to disprove his guilt, and he had fled. Because of her.

She uncurled her hand and gazed at the scabbed flesh. No matter how much damage she'd done to herself, she could never sheer away the evidence of her crimes. She was forever chained to this fate. As much as it weighed on her, she finally understood Kiren's plight—her Kiren. The weight of thousands had rested on his shoulders. He'd borne it well, but that tortured silence hung at the back of his mind, the muted need to make right all pains suffered because of him. Now she recognized that place in herself. It was a gap that separated the functional Alexia from the one destroyed by guilt. No going back in time could undo the rift. She was forever fractured.

And if her companions caught Kiren, if they accused him of one more terrible offense, it may be enough to break his confidence forever. She'd argued with Amos about this, but he insisted that to the rest of camp, Kiren looked guilty. And he was right.

Because Kiren had abandoned them. Her child. Herself. All of the Passionate.

An invisible fist squeezed around her heart, one that had been tightening with every thought of him. Her heart pulsed painfully. She'd never considered he might run, and if they couldn't find him—as they likely wouldn't—she'd never have the chance to say goodbye or reveal the truth about his child. She had foolishly squandered their time.

Alexia would forever regret it.

Mae waved from the far end of the lane and stepped around the corner. She had made significant progress in their recent training. She could now direct her siphoning within a controlled scope. Most of the time. Even so, Alexia didn't like them being separated like this. If something happened, she would have no way to reach her friend—unless she was miraculously able to jump back in time. She had attempted it in camp after speaking with Velia, trying to undo the scar and Kiren's flight, but she'd encountered that same inky barrier. The enemy. Outside of time.

Men called behind her and wagons rattled, what seemed like an unusual amount of movement for this small town. She closed her eyes to block them out and listened to her heart, hoping it would direct her toward Kiren.

An iron slapped around her wrist.

She jerked out of her calm.

Someone yanked her around and she stumbled to a halt. Two soldiers grabbed her arms, forcing her to face the man in blue robes before her.

"As you can see, men, her countenance is far superior to the ilk of this town."

She swallowed a gasp.

A nobleman in this small town? And not just any nobleman.

Velia's captor.

A battalion of soldiers marched up the street, aimed toward camp.

Rage curled up inside. Velia was taking her revenge by placing Alexia and the rest of them in the enemy's hands.

Mae screamed. Alexia twisted, but her friend was obscured by buildings. Soldiers filtered between storefronts and peasants, weapons at the ready.

Velia had spurred them on a fool's errand, leaving the Passionate vulnerable!

But Alexia would not give in easily. She felt for the timeline and stifled a smile. No tar wall blocked her. She almost laughed at the fetter around her wrist.

"What is my crime, my lord?" she asked, pretending terror.

"You see how she feigns innocence. They are built for deceit."

Alexia laughed. He was out of his depth, but seeing the man face to face, she knew one thing for certain: they would be hunted forever. Best that they fled this land for the other world.

"Carry her to the wagon and secure her bonds."

Alexia closed her eyes and stretched back through time—relieved it worked. She had worried the tar wall was because of her pregnancy, but it must be as Grandfather said: her enemy had blocked the way. Well, *it* wasn't here now. Even so, she couldn't go too far or she'd be left alone and exposed in this town while her friends were traveling. The last time she'd jumped, hours had been too much. But ten minutes, that should be safe. It would be enough. It had to be.

She reached into the timeline, finding a moment ten minutes back like picking up a shiny pebble. Something cracked. Alexia gasped, pain shooting up her back as the world blacked to nothing, time resetting.

She collapsed to her knees in the street, blinded by the misery racing out to every joint.

Scuffling feet.

Agony.

Wetness down her leg.

# Forty-Two

# Flight

A woman's shout came from the far end of town. Kiren homed in on it, unable to stop the panic suddenly pumping through his veins. He was running before he realized it.

Alexia lay in the middle of the road, blood pooling around her skirt.

She was here.

She was here and she was in trouble.

He reached her in two strides, felt for a heartbeat, and placed a hand on her womb. Her pulse was weakening, as was the child's. He closed his eyes and listened deeper to the flow of blood, escaping from where the baby's sac had prematurely detached. Blood pooled inside Alexia, trickling free.

He pressed his fingers to the bare skin at her collarbone, as close to her heart as he could.

*Slow*, he commanded her heart. Delving deeper, he focused, following the arteries down to where they merged with the womb, where it had torn free. *Fuse.* The cells reached for one another and knit back together, suturing the tear, but blood still welled in her womb. Too much blood. Strength poured through his fingers, wringing him out until he was a dry rag, filling her need.

Kiren sat back, panting hard with Alexia cradled in his arms. Even his healing may not be enough. The guiltiest part of him didn't care if she lost the child, but he needed her to live. She had to survive.

Dark mist exploded down the lane as Amos appeared behind him, mouth set grimly. His eyes widened when they landed on Kiren's cheek.

Kiren brushed the hair back from Alexia's face to show that she still breathed. Regin stepped through the cloud, tugging on gloves, and covered his nose, half-turning away. Mae shadowed him, hands flying to her mouth.

"What have you done to her?" Amos's voice thrummed with a cool rage.

Kiren twisted to him. "Me? I stopped her from dying."

"So much blood," Mae whispered, but her gaze was fixed on Kiren's face instead of the pool.

*That is right. Look now. Get it over with. Soon you will avoid eye contact for fear of offering offense.*

Alexia's hand flattened over Kiren's, pressing it to her cheek, eyes burning into his. *Give me strength.* An inner sob. *I cannot lose this baby.*

Kiren drew from the pendant and gave her more. Her back arched, lips smashed together in pain.

*** 

Alexia blinked her eyes open, her ear cushioned by skin and cloth, fingers cupping her cheek. Oaken honey wafted over her, tinged in sweat. Her eyes flickered open, and she caught a glimpse of his chin and jagged skin. Her Kiren. She was home. Did she dream him? She would happily stay here in his dream arms forever.

"Alexia is too fragile to travel. Where is Velia?" Kiren's voice rumbled against her ear.

"She is detained in the camp," Amos replied. "She is the traitor."

Her limbs felt like noodles, her womb aching as if it had been scraped from the inside. Then she recalled what had happened, how she'd crumbled to the ground, and suddenly Kiren was here, talking to Amos?

He wasn't her Kiren.

She swallowed the disappointment and gathered her strength. Back in camp, Velia had accused Kiren of murder and revealed her own betrayal—which made her case against Kiren stronger. She'd been bound, which meant she must have already told the nobleman where they resided.

Alexia gasped. She tugged Kiren's sleeve. "He is here," she rasped. "Our enemy…"

Silence.

"Is she of a fit mind?" Regin questioned.

Kiren tilted her head back, his thumbs cradling her jaw, and he met her eyes. His had darkened, the night sky right before a storm. The storm was coming. She placed a hand against his torn cheek and forced the memory into him, Lord Ulric, his soldiers, more of them on the horizon.

"We are trapped." Kiren's head jerked up. "The soldiers will be here any moment, so many of them. They are headed to our camp. We must detain them and warn the others."

Everyone stared at him.

"Ask Alexia!" he shouted.

They looked at her. She nodded.

Kiren spoke through his teeth, "Mae, we need a diversion. Amos, you can shelter us all in your haze while I carry Alexia from this place, then obscure Mae and escape. Regin, you must run now and warn the camp. Move them right away. When they are safe, send someone to find us." Before anyone could argue, he hefted Alexia up. "I will keep her whole until then."

She tried to get her feet beneath her in protest, but he slid her hands around his neck, looping his arms around her knees and back. She stiffened.

"Relax and trust me," he whispered in her ear.

She told her body to loosen, but the knot in her stomach tightened, squeezing away her will. She tucked her face into his shoulder and balled her fists, venting the agony into her fingers.

"How do we know you have not brought this enemy down on us?" Amos asked.

Kiren paused. His voice darkened. "You do not." He set off between buildings and into the shadows. His even strides jarred her as Amos's scowl disappeared into the haze. Alexia didn't like it, but with Mae on the offensive, they would be well...she hoped.

*I am not supposed to be weak. I am supposed to protect them!*

Shouts erupted behind them. Alexia cringed, focusing on the rhythm of Kiren's breathing, each flex of a muscle turning into a stab of pain as he raced for freedom.

*Mae, protect them. Amos, keep Mae from going too far...*

\*\*\*

Kiren sprinted as fast as he dared, holding Alexia firmly against him. No matter how even his paces, her body tensed with every footfall. He hoped that any additional damage to her might be easily mended. He'd already given her more than ever offered before, siphoning strength from his necklace—a resource he couldn't spare. Still, her life meant more than the preservation of his reserves. He only prayed they would replenish before he needed them.

No place in the township would be safe—unless he could pass them off as human. But with her glow, it was never going to happen. There was a church just over the rise, a haven he had visited before as a friar when he'd healed the priest's crippled hand. The priest would provide sanctuary.

Shouts carried behind him, growing more distant. He tilted his head, listening for what he dreaded. His senses zoomed backward, to the conflict, creating a net around the heart of the confusion and muffling its noise. Footfalls reverberated off the walls of two alley buildings, growing in volume. Labored breathing—men who must be lugging weapons or armor.

He listened closer. Two sets of feet, one significantly heavier than the other, neither with a gait he recognized.

Pursuers.

Kiren silenced his footfalls and slipped between buildings, carefully cradling Alexia's head to him. The brick church appeared between houses. He sprinted up the steps and into the chapel.

The priest whirled around, back pressed to the altar. His eyes widened at the blood staining Alexia's skirt and now Kiren's robes.

"Brother Arik?" he asked.

Kiren nodded, cringing inwardly at the false name.

"What happened to your face? Who is this?"

He lifted Alexia, who had lost consciousness. "I need sanctuary, and space to heal this woman."

The priest's mouth worked, his eyes traveling up and down the two of them. "She will defile the sanctuary."

"There is nothing more holy than a woman with child, nor the preservation of life." He stepped forward. "I will not deceive you, there are men chasing her for their liege, and should she fall into their hands, she and the child will die."

The priest straightened, fear in his eyes. "Why do they pursue this woman?"

Kiren stepped closer. "You know me."

The man stilled, looking at him, eyes flickering away from his scar.

"I would not protect her without great reason. I am asking for your assistance. Help me."

Lines crinkled around his eyes. "Brother Arik, I know you are not entirely of this Earth, and if you are on God's holy mission, of course I cannot refuse."

Shouts carried from outside.

"The rectory hideaway," Kiren insisted.

The priest waved them forward. "Come."

***

Dust shook free from the rafters overhead as soldiers stomped about the church. Kiren crouched in the cellar hideaway, his shoulders grazing the ceiling. He shaded the candle next to Alexia with his hand, praying the light wasn't noticeable through the floorboards.

Alexia's bleeding had stopped, but she was unconscious on a blanket. Sweat glistened in the candle's flame, beading her forehead and nose. A glimmer of light reflected off the chain links about her neck, drawing his notice to the steady rise and fall of her chest. To distract himself, he dipped a rag into the basin the priest had provided and wrung it out very near the surface, minimizing any noise. It didn't matter. The men stomping around were busy shouting.

"Sirs, this is a holy place," Priest Eli countered. "Lower your voices and be away, lest your actions be construed as sacrilege."

The church quieted. One man cussed under his breath. "The blood trail dried up not far back. We will try a different direction, but if we learn they came this way, Lord Ulric will not be pleased."

"And if the holy pope hears about this, your lord will have his own answers to supply," the priest replied.

"What'd Ulric do to the last man ter cross 'im?" The second soldier asked as they clomped toward the exit.

"Had him strangled, drowned, and hung. Publicly."

Door hinges squealed.

Kiren pressed a hand to Alexia's neck and focused on her inner workings, attuning his senses directly to her womb. The graft held, but a bubble of blood had been trapped against the inner wall. He asked the fibers to pull apart, just

147

enough to discharge the trapped liquids. They loosened, releasing the blood. It seeped into Alexia's skirt.

Kiren sopped the rag again and began cleaning her bloodied feet and ankles. Priest Eli lifted the trap door and peered down into the murk, a clean robe clutched in one hand. He half turned away, gaze stuck on the exposed skin Kiren was cleaning.

"I thought you might be needing this." Eli offered the robe.

Kiren thanked him and took hold of the clothing, but the priest didn't release it. Kiren met his stare.

*...not right, a man and a woman who are not married being holed up together, touching so intimately. Especially in a church. Not right.*

He flinched at the priest's thoughts. If their places were reversed, he would agree. What he must do to save Alexia and her child went beyond any laws of propriety—made worse by the fact he was a man of the cloth. And a man who possessed a wild attraction to her.

But what was the other option? Let her die? Call a midwife who would report their location? Marry Alexia to appease the priest?

He laughed inwardly at the last thought.

He tugged the wool out of the priest's hand and went back to work, but Eli remained, watching him.

He scowled and debated asking the priest to fetch a woman to assist if he was so worried. But bringing anyone here was unwise. The more people who knew of Alexia's presence, the more likely they were to be discovered—and he knew how noblemen worked in this corner of the world. That rat would offer incentives enough to win loyalty from the peasants. A washwoman coming and going with bloody garments would definitely raise a few eyebrows.

No. No one else could know.

He pressed his fingers to Alexia's neck once more, testing her pulse and listening deeper. She was steady.

For all he knew, she was already married and forcibly separated from her husband, or had run from an unspeakable union. Perhaps she'd refused his advances, insinuating it was to protect him, because she was already bonded? If she was, he didn't want her. Couldn't want her. That would be wrong, wouldn't it?

And why was he thinking about this? Being bound to her wasn't an option. He had his father's throne to obtain, and no woman in this world could possibly understand the burden he would place on her shoulders by taking her to wife. It was cruel. And dangerous. For her.

And for himself if he was being honest. Being bonded to another meant opening himself to the possibility of dying if his bondmate met her demise. Placing his life in the hands of another, it terrified him as much as Alexia's death.

As much as.

Not more.

Kiren growled.

Eli jumped in his periphery. "Is something wrong with her? Something I can, um, assist with?"

"Have you ever played the physician, my brother?"

The man's face reddened. "It is not for men of the cloth."

"No, indeed." And yet it was Kiren's gift. "But Christ himself healed the infirm."

The priest retreated into his own thoughts, hands writhing over top one another.

Kiren turned back to Alexia. Marriage was not the path of the priesthood either, and yet the idea of a woman belonging to him, it was intriguing. The thought of Alexia being his set his pulse racing, his mouth salivating.

She was different. Always had been—and not merely because she possessed the blood. Or because he desired her, although that helped. His senses were keener when she was near, even if his mind was constantly clouded by thoughts of her. She focused him on what mattered. The memory of her taunted him when apart. She understood who he would become, and she was talented. A woman who could travel through time would prove an asset beyond reckoning to a king.

He stopped himself. Could he even think of using her so callously?

"We need more water here." He turned to Eli. "If it pleases you to assist."

The man nodded, but his eyes were troubled.

The trap door closed, leaving them to a candle's flicker that painted her face in mysterious shadows as deep as the secrets she harbored from him.

"Take me into your confidence." Kiren brushed the hair from Alexia's face and begged her to wake, calling for adrenaline through his touch.

Her eyes fluttered.

His heart pounded. After the last day, he knew what she meant to him. Could she see it?

Lush eyes met his. "You came back."

Her voice was so weak, a stab to his heart. Had he arrived mere moments later she would not be alive, gazing up at him. But she lived. He'd saved her. A smile puckered his cheeks, unbidden but sincere.

"How did you find us?" she asked. "How did you know?"

"I did not." He wanted to touch her, an intimate graze of fingers that would communicate the tenderness he felt for her, but he stopped himself. "It was luck or fate that saved your life."

She smiled warmly. That single expression flooded his soul with sunlight. He wanted her to be happy, to see her smile like this every day. To make her smile like this every day.

His mouth went dry. "Alexia, I must know. Were you married?"

Her brows lowered, mouth tightening. She nodded.

"Are you still?"

Her nose flared, eyes squeezing at the corners. She looked away. "I am outside my timeline, Kiren."

"And will you return to it?" *To your husband.*

Her shoulders dropped to the floor, brow squeezed in pain. "I am tired."

***

Alexia held in a sob only because he was watching, but her ribs ached with the strain of containing it. How could he sit there and question her about her husband while bearing the man's countenance, voice, and tenderness? The torn rivulet of skin mocked her, so fresh, so painful. She yearned to smooth it away, to stop it from existing! And yet she recalled his words, so crass, so unfeeling. He had believed her a loose woman, and perhaps she was for welcoming him into her affections, for returning his passions under the pretense of training, for allowing this near-stranger to fall into her heart. He must believe her even more so now, knowing of her marriage.

His eyes turned away, mouth tight. "You should rest," he whispered.

She couldn't look at him. His words still hurt. At least now he knew that her condition wasn't the result of whatever ruse he'd imagined. She was a virtuous woman, even if she couldn't resist him.

***

Alexia changed into the priest's robe in the cramped cellar, and Kiren cleaned her sullied dress to the best of his ability. It lay, drying, as he stripped his own robe and tunic free and rinsed blood out. He expected her back was turned while he did so but found her watching him. He allowed it. It flattered him that she cared to look and increased the yearning to have her. To escape temptation, he ventured up into the church and found a tunic that had been gathered to distribute to the poor. It fit tightly, but it was better than insulting Eli's sensibilities when he returned.

If he returned.

The priest's living quarters were humble. An old bed, a sturdy chair, a water basin and chamber pot. A musty scent wafted up from the tunic Kiren had selected, promising a mouse would be saddened to find its bed removed. Kiren peeked into the church. Empty pews lined either side. A large window framed either wall of the altar, dimmed by heavy draperies. A decanter and chalice hid behind the altar, poised on a stool, ready for communion in the morning. A simple building for a simple community.

Kiren wanted to return below, but he didn't know if he could be so close to Alexia and not touch her. And his back ached from bending over.

Alexia's dress had halfway dried by the time Eli entered the rectory, water pail in hand. He moved jerkily.

"Brother Eli?"

150

The priest spoke softly, hesitantly. "There was a terrible disturbance in the town. Men are injured and terrified, speaking of darkness and death touching them." He turned to Kiren, shoulders hunched. "Tell me you did not do this thing?"

"It was not I." Kiren took the pail, meeting the priest's eyes and conveying his concern through a look.

"But you know what did it?" Eli asked.

He steeled himself. "I do."

Eli relented custody of the bucket, and Kiren descended to the hideaway. He offered the pail to Alexia and left her to the privacy of the cellar, returning to the priest who watched him anxiously.

"Will you go to them?" Eli asked. "Heal the men who are in need?"

He faced Eli, gathering his thoughts from his eyes. The man was terrified, thinking demons and angels were raining down on the earth. Kiren almost raised an eyebrow at the belief that he, Kiren, was an angel. He'd seen the insinuation before and never validated or denied it. Having the man believe he was from heaven had proven beneficial today. "I cannot. Not this time."

The priest lowered his voice. "Because of your companion."

Kiren nodded.

"She possesses the glow of an angel and yet she inspires men toward unheavenly thoughts."

Kiren stopped a glare, barely. How dare Eli look upon Alexia and think— what? The same things he had since first meeting her? But that was different. She kissed him. She wanted him. This man dwelling on her unique beauty and imagining the fulfillment of his lusts made Kiren's fists ball with a need to break the priest's face.

Eli continued, "Surely she cannot be of Heaven and heavy with child. It were not possible for an angel to conceive unless she is carrying the spawn of a demon?"

"No one said she is of Heaven," Kiren snapped. Though she may as well be. By action, she would find fitting company among angels.

Eli flinched.

Kiren peered out the window at the setting sun, his hands shaking with the desire to throttle the man…but Eli's suggestion of demon spawn fell right in line with Kiren's own thoughts about Alexia's child. It wasn't right. The child was innocent, the product of marriage—though whether it was a desired or safe marriage, that was another thing.

"This is not the holy war you imagine." Kiren calmed himself. "We are people like any other, struggling to survive. I am not from Heaven or Hell. My companion is a married woman, separated from her husband and fearful for her child's survival."

The priest shrank. "But her countenance…"

Kiren exhaled. He had hoped that explanation would suffice. It was dangerous for Eli to know more, but he was sheltering them. Perhaps he should be trusted. "She is descended from a unique bloodline."

"Like yourself?"

Had he begun to take on her glow from all their shared affections? He eased the tension from his lungs. "Lords and kings desire to control people with gifts like mine, people who marry and raise children and work the land. Lowly friars who travel to bless lives and remain unknown." He bowed his head. "These men of power take what is precious—our families, our possessions, the need to eat—and force us into servitude, waging their wars with powers no mortal should ever possess." Kiren lifted his gaze to the priest. "Though we may not be of Heaven, we possess the ability to wage hell on Earth. In the hands of these men, that is what you would see."

Eli hugged himself, gaze sweeping the floor as if frightened to meet Kiren's stare. "That is what happened today?"

"It is."

"And these men came for you?"

Kiren shook his head. "Not for me." He pointed toward the cellar, indicating Alexia. "She may well be a saint for all I have seen, and I will do what I must to assure her safety and survival."

The priest nodded. "This will take some pondering." He slipped away into the shadows.

Kiren wasn't certain he'd won the man over, but he couldn't take the words back now. Part of him didn't want to win Eli's loyalty. Fury still beat through him. How dare the man consider laying claim to his Alexia, even in thought?

He swallowed hard.

*His* Alexia. Where had that come from?

She pushed the trap door open and took in the church before giving him a confused look.

Kiren turned away. She was not his, but he wanted her to be. Clearly.

# Forty-Three

# *Stirring the Pot*

The entity licked its lips, or the equivalent. The feel of mortal skin housing its every whim was intoxicating. Watching the other potential puppets flit about the camp, absorbing their fear, their anger, their confusion, it was almost enough. Almost. They had been too at ease today. Time to shake their world again and lap up the resulting trauma.

# Forty-Four

# *Angel of Havoc*

Alexia slumbered, her head resting on Kiren's leg as he sat, unable to stop his wild thoughts. Her body had obeyed and mended mostly, but she was still fragile and needed all the calm he could afford her. The stone wall was cool against his back, his mind whirling.

*His* Alexia.

It wasn't an option. She had been taken by another man and was still married in the future. But then, why had she kissed him and allowed him to pursue her? Was it because she feared her husband and willed to be free of him by forming a new bond? To change what was to come? As strong as she was, she could merely reverse time and escape her bonding...yet she hadn't. What else was he to conclude but that she intended to return? To leave him?

Perhaps that was why she refused his deeper affections.

He thumped a fist into the dirt.

Alexia moaned and shifted. He stilled himself, conscious of not upsetting her again.

She was claimed. And he didn't wish to have a wife, a family, extra duties and obligations around what he already owed the Lost Ones.

Or did he?

For a moment he imagined what it would have been like if his parents had lived, if he'd been raised under his father's tutelage. Father would have chosen him a bride, as he'd chosen a future husband for Kiri. There would have been a long-standing betrothal and grand to-do about his wedding: festivities, honors, lavish expenditures, and dignitaries from all corners of the world. If he hadn't cared for the woman Father chose, there would have been little recourse, because she would have been a child of noble birth, one worthy of his station.

Yet here in his lap lay a woman he'd chosen for himself, because she moved him. Because she was selfless. Because she won his respect. Father and Mother would have adored her, but had his parents lived, he never would have entered this world. Never would have met this powerful, compassionate woman. Perhaps all things did happen for a reason. Perhaps God's hand was in his life, even the darkest parts.

Except that Alexia could never be his.

Voices roused him from pondering. Soft voices. Near the entrance to the church and close to the back door. He listened closer, blocking out the whisper of Alexia's breathing.

"...spare the church. I believe both are very dangerous." Eli.

Kiren groaned. He should have let the priest go on believing his own holy delusion. Lesson learned: the Lost Ones should never reveal the truth about their nature, except to one another.

"Weapons at the ready," a gravelly voice called.

"Weapons in a church?" Eli asked, shocked.

"Ye'd have us face them creatures without them?"

Kiren hoped the priest was receiving a royal sum to appease his conscience, because the man would rot for this betrayal.

He shook Alexia awake and pressed a finger to his lips. "The calm was nice while it lasted."

"It never lasts." She gave him a sad smile as he helped her up.

"Ever?"

She reached for the trap door. "We must hurry."

With a gentle shove, the door opened, and she climbed out. He followed, emerging into the rectory. Daylight cut through the curtains, sending dust motes across the space. Alexia crossed to the exit, glancing back at him.

She shouldn't be on her feet after the near loss. Kiren didn't know how she found the strength even now.

The door opened.

Three men froze in the entry. Alexia glanced back at Kiren, mischief painted in her smirk. This was going to be good.

She blurred and stood suddenly behind the men, her fingers clasped about her necklace in an all-too-familiar way. Kiren leaned to the side, but he couldn't get a clear view of her pendant around the three brutes.

Alexia tapped the men on the shoulders, waiting for them to turn before blurring again. All three followed her out of the church. Kiren lost sight of her as men charged through the door behind him, naked swords ready for action. He sprinted after Alexia.

Sunlight hit him in the eyes. Men shouted from behind. Weapons sliced the air. Hissing...

A soft hand grabbed his shoulder and pulled him off balance. He tumbled sideways, an arrow nicking his cheek. Alexia let go of him and whirled forward, grabbing hold of one man's crossbow, blurring as she moved. Her blade whirled in mayhem as she stepped back into the church, slicing a man's belt, chopping a drapery into the enemies' path, flipping a decanter from its stool, and smacking one man in the brow while spattering others in the face with wine.

An angel of havoc—graceful, assured, gorgeous, and his.

He shook that thought away.

Kiren ducked a blade and kicked the man aside.

"Go!" Alexia shouted.

"Not without you!" he called back, dodging a blow to the shoulder.

She spun and knocked a dagger off its trajectory for Kiren's heart. Her eyes speared him, angry eyes. "Move!"

He dodged around a soldier and ducked behind an oncoming wagon. Shouts carried after him, but he fled into the trees. Kiren pressed up against a trunk and calmed his heart, feeling the slow aging of the wood and the calm of nature. It was possible to hide in plain sight from those without a trace of his bloodline, trick their brains, but if any of them possessed even a drop of blood from the Lost Ones…

*There are only trees here.* He projected the message more to himself than anyone. *I am a tree.*

Men darted past him, one or two stopping and looking around. They looked right through him and fanned out. He leaned back around the trunk, searching for Alexia.

\*\*\*

Alexia breathed easier once he disappeared, but now she had thirteen men converging on her. She drew on the medallion again, feeling the supply thin, like too little jam on toast. Had she finally drained the thing completely?

She tugged time to a full stop and escaped through the still limbs and past the raging faces. Time to find Kiren and be done with this. But first…

She smacked her feet into the hardened ground, creating what would be a set of footprints leading off the wrong direction once time resumed and the force of her impact hit. She lightened each step until she was barely tiptoeing and hurried the way Kiren had gone.

The knot in her womb tightened. Pain raced down the back of her neck, and lightning tore through her legs. She paused briefly, panting, but kept going. Her muscles were liquefying. Any moment she would melt into the ground, but she had to get herself and this baby far away from the men.

Instinct led as her vision blacked out behind a wall of agony. Her knees smacked into the earth. Alexia screamed.

Time jolted forward around her. She pulled inward, grating her teeth against the moan that needed to escape. Her womb surged, stealing her breath.

She crawled forward, biting down as the intensity lessened. *Get back up. You have to move. Get on your feet!*

# Forty-Five

# *Almost*

The man who inflicted pain retreated from guard duty, and Leofrik slumped in on himself. His ropes were securely fastened and—while he'd longed to plan an escape—he'd been so exhausted from torture that he'd slept.

Rustling material in the darkness drew his attention to the other prisoner. Velia's shift stood out in the night—a ghost. She was very real, bound by an iron fetter and as solid as she'd been while trapped in his care. She'd been bound across from him since shortly after he heard shouts from the other side of the wall.

A single laugh escaped Leofrik. "I suppose you were discovered?"

She turned her face away.

"I should have known better than to trust your kind."

She laughed. A voice rasped out of her throat—barely a hiss, more like a breathy scraping of wind across eaves. "I will…never see…my daughter again. He will kill…her." Her mirth devolved into sobs. "You should have…stopped me."

"And she speaks, to make all this worse."

She drooped toward the ground.

"At least this way we both die." He groaned. "I do not want to die."

"Nor do…I."

Quiet overtook them.

"Sir knight…my people will…not kill us."

"Then what will they do with us?" he huffed.

"Nothing." Her rasp flickered with uncertainty. "Ulric will…be here soon."

"You betrayed them one last time." Why should it surprise him? Why should he hope that her loyalty at least extended somewhat to these people?

Because that meant there was hope for him. As it was, Ulric would brand him a failure and send him off to some remedial duty rather than back to his brothers. And what would become of this band?

Her head hung. Was she ashamed for her betrayal?

"Were you…a good knight?" she asked.

He groaned. He didn't want to speak with her, but the conversation was better than silence and his continual awareness of aching muscles. "I was raised in London and shipped off to the crusades at the age of thirteen. I fought until it was the only thing I knew. There was no place for me in this country, no battle sufficient to further sully my sword. But then I was discovered by the Knights Templar, a sect of knights who protect pilgrims making peaceful passage through hostile lands. It may be war, but it is war for a good cause. My brotherhood saved me from losing all feeling."

She was quiet. "*He*…used you."

Leofrik rolled to take the pressure off his shoulder. "Lord Ulric wants what Lord Ulric wants, and he has the king's ear."

She placed one hand on top of the other, palms up. "And my…child."

They both quieted. Leofrik didn't bear the woman ill will. She had been miserable because of the same selfish lord, and although he saw her actions in their full treachery, he understood. These creatures deserved death or imprisonment, but to be used as weapons?

***

Leofrik drifted in and out of sleep. It was late when he woke to shouting on the other side of the wall. He strained to hear the words over the nervous chatter of several people.

"…gather your things and do it fast. They will be upon us inside the hour."

A man of eastern descent with narrow eyes, a flat nose, and dressed in monk's robes appeared from around the wall, a man he'd seen several times. Wearing gloves, he unlocked Velia's fetter from the tree.

"You brought this upon us," he said.

Her shoulders dropped and she touched him.

"There is always a choice," he muttered.

She hissed out, "Not when your…bondmate wants something…enough."

He tugged the woman to her feet. "And she speaks. Lie upon lie. There will be no coming back from this. You have overstepped our good graces."

Her eyes grazed over Leofrik as she was dragged away. She passed the inflictor, Sarlic, who returned and stood, hands on hips. "You awake?"

Leofrik shifted onto his rear end.

Sarlic knelt before him. "I would rather leave you here to be found, but we leave no trace, least of all someone who will report our numbers."

Leofrik laughed hoarsely. "You can all rot in a Holy Land desert for all I care."

Sarlic seized Leofrik's ropes and jerked him up. Leofrik tripped and tottered forward as a dagger sliced through the ropes at his ankles. He stumbled, his legs like jelly.

The inflictor steadied him, bearing most of his weight. "You know, I was once like you." The gruff voice was more of a bark than a cadence. "Believed in a cause. Even fought for the holy pope in the First Crusade."

Leofrik flinched. That would make the man at least seventy years old if he went to war fresh into manhood. He didn't look more than five and twenty. Not only were these creatures dangerous, but they lived extended lives.

"I thought it was a holy war," Sarlic continued, "but it was not. The pope, kings, all were interested in trade and resources. Money. Take what you can, fight for the rest."

He shoved Leofrik forward, stomping along behind him. Velia's white back came into view just ahead where she marched next to her captor.

"I landed with a wave of knights whose orders were to take Nicaea," Sarlic continued. "Peasants fought against us—women and children too—until blood ran down the streets. There was no glory in it, only the dead and the men who rose up to take their places. I tired of seeing men murdered simply because a French knight possessed a sword while a Turk did not...but they wouldn't let me abandon my post. Oh no. I was branded so as I would never forget." He pointed to the cross above his eye. "You had best believe I never forgot."

On occasion, a man who loved the Church would brand himself with the holy cross, but never on the face. An arm, a wrist, somewhere that showed his might. Some place on display to fellow soldiers, evident in the heat of battle.

Sarlic seized Leofrik's bound arm and directed him away from the glowing fires of camp. "This mark should be stamped on every man who kills without remorse while wearing the Church's colours."

The knight kept quiet, tasting bitterness at the back of his throat. They followed a line of people who thumped into the coal-black woods beyond camp.

Darkness gathered around his escort. Leofrik wanted to blame it on his exhaustion, or the dimming of his eyes, or the thickness of the shadows, but the heaviness grazed him: the essence of despair, frustration, rage. It seeped into the torturer's skin. Sarlic pushed him out of the line of refugees and into the woods.

"You are a burden at this point. A waste of victuals. And I personally do not like you." He shoved Leofrik to the ground.

Sarlic's skin grayed slightly, and his eyes lit to crimson.

Leofrik scuffled backwards, fixated on the crimson pupils. It was like watching a demon come to life.

"Allow me to show you what is to be done with unnecessary burdens." Sarlic pulled a dagger from his hip.

The knight shouted and twisted onto his knees. He shoved forward. The weapon sliced across his back. Pain raked up his flesh. He whirled and threw a knee into the man's wrist. Sarlic scuffled after the weapon.

Leofrik clambered to his knees, arms still bound, and cursed his fate. Given equal standing, he might have a prayer. This was it, the way he'd die—hogtied and in a heap.

Sarlic latched onto his blade, the weapon glimmering in a pool of starlight.

Leofrik slid backwards until he hit the stump of a tree. Nowhere to go.

The inflictor rose, face hidden in shadow. Only the red of his eyes penetrated the darkness. A djinn from the underworld.

Leofrik glanced left and right for an escape, a weapon, anything. A palm-sized stone sat to his right, one with a sharp edge. Out of reach. He'd have to throw his entire body that direction to snatch the weapon, and even retrieving it was dubious, but trying was better than waiting to be murdered in the dark. What he wouldn't give to have his hands freed rather than trapped behind him! He readied to leap.

Sarlic neared, his blade lifted.

A trickle of sweat dripped down Leofrik's brow.

His torturer jolted forward.

Leofrik ducked beneath the blade and sprung right, slamming into the ground with his back to the rock. His fingers curled around the sharp rim.

Metal pierced his leg. He screamed through his teeth. The man laughed, and pain seeped into Leofrik's every nerve. It ate through him, consuming his energy, robbing him of breath, stealing any hope of survival.

Sarlic stood over him, blade poised.

"Goodbye." The weapon arced down. Light curled across the surface in curious shimmers, incredibly beautiful for being the instrument that would end a man's life. Leofrik cringed, ready for impact. This had been his fate the instant Ulric dragged him away from the Holy Land.

The weapon neared and he closed his eyes.

Weight thumped into his chest.

He gasped, eyes shooting wide.

Velia met his stare, her meager frame pressing into his chest. She was moonlight cutting through a nightmare. A white lady. A spirit. Her head tilted, and she gave him a rueful, sad smile. A trickle of blood escaped the corner of her mouth.

Voices filled the night, but he was fixated on the blood, black in the night.

Her life.

Stark against her pale skin.

A hilt protruded from her back, the blade meant for him.

Her head lolled and her smile faded, eyes dimming. He'd seen it so many times, the life leaving a body, but never when that life had been sacrificed on his behalf—the woman who betrayed him no less.

"Velia," he whispered.

Hands pulled her away, and he reached after her with his all. *Do not take her away. Let her stay with me. Let me thank her properly.*

His attacker lay on the ground across from him, unconscious. Several of these strange, gifted people stood between them. One leaned down and ran a hand over Leofrik's chest, searching for wounds. Another cut his wrists free while yet another examined the wound in his calf. They were talking but the words were fuzz.

Velia lay next to him, her body still, a metal cuff still clasped about her skin. As soon as his wrists were free, he flopped over and cradled her in his arms, not knowing if he would have another chance. "Thank you, dear one, for your gift."

A life cut short. A woman who should have lived. One who had begun to infect his soul, regardless of her heritage.

Whispers carried around him, sad voices he didn't want to associate with people. They weren't people. They were creatures.

But she gave her life for him. Was there a nobler thing in all the world?

Perhaps they were better than any people he'd known. Perhaps he had misjudged them because of his own bias and impatience, because he was too blinded by notions that didn't hold true. Velia said they wouldn't kill him, yet one had tried.

"How badly are you hurt?" the eastern man asked for the third time.

Leofrik shook his head. Fingers grazed his back and he trembled.

"Bandages for him."

"And for her?" another man asked.

The monk was quiet. "Go." He faced Leofrik. "My name is Lucian, and we will restore you to full health. That I promise."

Leofrik glanced again at his attacker, slumbering now. "I should think my demise would have been a relief."

The monk gave him a strange look.

Leofrik blinked.

Lucian lifted a knife. "If you will promise not to harm any here, we will release you, but we cannot have you returning to your lord."

"Ulric is not *my* lord."

They wrapped bandages around his leg according to Lucian's instruction. "Sarlic would never do this. He is angry, yes, but he is not a man of blood."

Leofrik related the strange way the man had changed, the darkness, the red eyes.

The monk nodded. "I see glimpses of the future, and I too saw how he changed. There is an evil following us through this land. It seems it has taken to possessing and slaying our kind. It is a dangerous time."

Leofrik turned to Velia. "She saved me."

"She did."

*Forty-Six*

*Returning*

Alexia's legs shook, but she got them under her.

An arm looped around her and lifted some of her weight. She looked up into eyes as vast as a starry night sky. Kiren's eyebrow rose, asking without a word if she was able to travel. Now that she had him, she was.

She nodded.

He pulled her into the shadow of bush and tree.

\*\*\*

They didn't stop moving except to catch their breath. The motion kept Alexia warm, although she stumbled all too often or had to pause and lean against a tree. Kiren halted with her and regarded her closely, obviously attuned to the exhaustion she was determined to hide.

"It is not much further," he muttered.

*Liar.* Though he offered the words as motivation, she didn't want his falsehoods—even if his truths hurt too much. He had no idea where they were going or the distance it would be to a new camp.

She glanced at the angry red tear across his cheek, worry trembling through her. The last day, or however long she'd been conscious, had been spent in silence—a silence so thick between them, she didn't think it could be breached. There were too many raw feelings. Too many hurtful words and actions. He'd opened up. She couldn't. He said unkind things. She scarred him. He left her.

Kiren exhaled. "Whatever it is you have to ask, ask."

She took a deep breath. "They accused you of murder."

His jaw squared, stretching his scar. "It is no worse than what they have done before."

"Whether you admit it or not, it injures you."

Kiren scowled at her. "Are you so concerned about my injuries in light of your own? Even the ones I have inflicted on you?"

Her cheeks flamed at the memory: the revelation of how he'd viewed her all along. He'd chosen private moments to pursue their affections at first because his attraction to an unwholesome woman shamed him.

Alexia turned straight ahead, unable to banish the sting and yet unwilling to connect it with the man who looked the part of her husband.

"I did not mean what I said." He groaned. "I did not mean any of it."

She held her tongue. He meant at least some of it. The fury behind his words could not have been faked, a resentment long buried by good intentions.

"I opened myself to you, Alexia. All of me. I have never done that with anyone before, and it terrified me—especially knowing I am not the first man to care for you."

Her chest tightened.

"I needed your acceptance. You dismissed my confessions, ready to move on with your life, and I was angry. I still am. I offered myself to you. Do you know how humiliating that was?"

Every statement weighed on her more. Another leaden weight pulling her shoulders down. It was becoming unbearable. "Because embracing a tainted woman would sully you."

He growled. "I have never believed that, even if I wanted to. Do you know what you are to me? Every step away from you emptied my soul. When I found you in the township, I was returning. I could not stay away. You drew me, and when I heard that scream, I knew where you were and that you needed me." He glanced at her sideways.

Alexia bit her lip. Was he bound to her already? "I told you to stop," she whispered. "I said we were not going further."

"Why did we start? How could you have—?" He shook out his hands and blew out a heavy breath. "You are married."

She bowed her head.

"You should have told me," he said.

"Would that have stopped you?"

He eyed her lips, and her heart did a little flip. "Any man who could let you escape him does not deserve you. But how can this work when you are bound to someone else?"

She could barely breathe for the desire melting through his ocean tides. Every word reined with restraint, his fists clenched at his side, the pulse madly ticking in his neck—though from anger or longing, she had no idea.

"It is not *meant* to work," she said.

His hands clamped around her arms, stopping her. "I want to know you, Alexia. I *need* to know you."

His oaken musk rolled over her, and she lost herself to memory—his bare arms wrapped around her, the press of his lips as they traveled her body. But this Kiren didn't know that carnal pleasure. She forced the moment back where it belonged, buried. That was a different man.

"I have to be by your side, if for no other reason than to quash the irrational fear that something awful will happen to you." He stroked her cheek. "You have beguiled me." His lips neared hers and she didn't pull away, didn't back down. His breath was warm against her lips. "Beguile me again."

"Kiren—"

His mouth crushed her weak protest. He kissed her deeper than he ever had, so deep he grazed up against her barrier and she had a hard time remembering why it needed to be there. Why not let him in, let him have all of her? He was her husband…or would be. Was there anything so wrong with giving herself to him in this time?

"My baby." She pulled away. The child would claim her life. It would claim his. She must save him from himself, save him period. "Hate me if you must, but I stand by my decisions." Even so, she was wavering, begging silently for him to respect her words, because she didn't have the restraint to stop him again.

His teeth clenched. He ripped both hands through his hair. In three paces, he whirled away and cut a steady path through the brush. She followed after, tasting his frustration on the wind.

*** 

A shadow dropped over them as Kiren kept pace ahead of Alexia. Wings flapped. He glanced up as she waved at Zephaniah, too enthusiastic that he'd joined them. Kiren had mixed feelings. Zeph could carry Alexia to the heart of safety, but that would mean having her out of his sight. His friend's presence would also ease the awkwardness between them, but Kiren had hoped for another chance to smooth things over.

"Glad you are alive." Zeph smirked at Alexia.

"Is that why you came searching? You thought I might have died along the way? One might believe you descended from carrion crows."

He laughed. "I was more afraid you had taken this simpleton with you." He wrapped an arm around Kiren's neck and muttered quietly, "Even if this bludgeon-head is willing to throw himself in the path of the bull."

Kiren shrugged his friend off. "You should take her to the others. It is safer there."

Zephaniah's head swiveled his direction, and he blinked several times rapidly. He brushed a hand over his own cheek. "Did that happen while saving her?"

"No," he said. "Yes!" Alexia insisted at the same time.

Kiren met gazes with her. How dare she lie when he was willing to bear the shame of his actions?

"That is up for debate," he said, and gave Alexia a head shake. She touched a finger to her lips and hooded her eyes. She wouldn't be revealing his secret. He hadn't realized until this moment it would shame her as well. It was their secret then.

Zeph gave him a look that said they'd be talking soon. "It is not far to the new camp and you look exhausted. I will be back." He caught Alexia and carried her away.

Kiren watched them go, debating how easy it would be to slip away rather than face his friend's interrogation. Zeph would murder him for taking off alone. And his enemy must be hiding near and killing the Lost Ones—according to Alexia. That was the direction he needed to go. He only wished he was better prepared for battle.

Long moments stretched, too solitary with just him and his thoughts.

Zeph dropped next to him on the hilly path. "You left without me."

"It was not planned."

"And that makes it better?" His friend's wings furled. "You could have taken me. I would have gone."

"You did not wish to leave."

"But I would have. Always."

Kiren thanked Zeph silently for his loyalty.

"They think you killed someone."

Kiren nodded. "I know."

Zeph's head was shaking. "But you know who did it?"

"I might."

Silence.

"No accusations for now?"

Kiren lifted one tired foot after another. "Not yet."

Zeph shrugged. "And her? Seems like she is not having you."

Kiren rubbed his healing skin. "Maybe."

# Forty-Seven

# *Leverage*

"Here lies his fortress armament, and there the stables." Leofrik pointed to the dirt outline of Ulric's fortress, leaning back so the crowd of listeners could see more clearly. "The tower is where the child is being held, which will make for some difficulty as there is only one way up or down, a single stairwell."

Amos touched his shoulder. "Are you certain you are willing to do this?"

"I bear no love for the man." He glanced back at Velia's wrapped body, prepared for the funeral rites. His fingers snaked into his pocket and wrapped around the toy wolf. His vow weighed on him more heavily than even his promise to his brethren knights. "And I owe her justice."

Nods and solemn looks passed over the group.

After Velia's death, the block over his mind had disappeared. He'd allowed them to examine his thoughts, because it was better to go peacefully, and he was still overwhelmed by Velia's sacrifice. He hadn't expected them to reciprocate. In return for his compliance, he'd been shown their previous conflicts. He'd seen account after account that mirrored Velia's experience: men appearing unexpectedly, chaining them, killing them, using them. These people had been chased like a rare breed of panther rich men decided they must possess.

But Leofrik was no one's huntsman. Not anymore.

He felt a strange kinship with these vagrants—having been an unwitting pawn in Ulric's war. He would never be used by the nobleman again, and he was determined that they shouldn't be either, whatever the cost.

He resumed. "Although we hope to enter and exit without notice, we must prepare for the worst. We will need to place people along the way to keep our path open. If we breach the fortress by night, we will have to penetrate closed gates. Day will provide less resistance; however, the guards will be in abundance. They carry swords and daggers, making it difficult to attack at a close range."

"We are going to rescue a child, not fight a war," Lucian reminded. "We prefer to take no life."

"Which I admire, but they will not mercifully lay their weapons down. We must prepare, which means we shall have to gather or construct weaponry before engaging the enemy. Have you any skilled in the forge?"

Sarlic stepped forward. "We have no need of a forge. Not with our gifts."

Leofrik shuddered. The inflictor had recovered, and after a thorough searching of his mind, he'd been declared free of external influence.

"We will use what weapons we have then," Leofrik agreed. "But as you have proven, we must be on guard if this, this thing can take hold of anyone at any time. Most of the strong will go with us, and most the weak will remain here until we return—but not all. There must be countermeasures on both fronts." He breathed the reality in. He was really doing this: leading them to the child, and then assassinating a corrupt lord.

And what would become of him? Imprisonment? A quick death? He squeezed the toy wolf and let it go. He didn't know what his fate would be, but he owed Velia her child's freedom. He'd kill Ulric as he'd sworn. If the cost was his life, the cost was his life.

\*\*\*

Kiren and Zephaniah reached camp as the sun dipped below the horizon. Zeph agreed arriving after dark would be better to avoid attention over Kiren's obvious blemish. He would let people believe it was an injury sustained in Alexia's rescue, but he wouldn't like it.

Alexia stood as they arrived, her skin warmed by the campfire. She was surrounded by people who cared for her, all asking her about her adventures and fussing over her comfort. Young Willem even held onto her like he'd decided he was the man in her life.

Warmth filled Kiren's heart. She was loved.

After a quick meal, he escaped to avoid the stares and accusations. The whispered allegations hurt, but not as much as gazing upon Alexia, knowing she had refused him again and would always refuse him. He needed space to think. To grieve.

*His Alexia.*

How had it happened? When? Did it even matter? The heart wanted what the heart wanted, and his would not be silenced. She would have him. She was married in a far distant time, but he could erase that if he married her now and kept her for his own. For all he knew, she wanted that. She would be his. Only his. An extremely powerful woman, a worthy companion, his future queen. The merits couldn't be argued. But if he desired her just because of her gift, he was worse than a snail under a log. Scum not worthy to reside on her boot.

She had no father or brother to negotiate her marriage, which left it to her liege lord. Amos. Surely the old man would see the wisdom in giving Kiren what he wanted.

He made a straight line for their leader. Amos stood over Velia's wrapped body, talking softly with Mae.

"...dead by Sarlic's hand," Mae said. "He was not in his right mind."

Amos turned, bringing the conversation to a halt. His eyes expanded and his shoulders stiffened. "Unless you have come to miraculously bring the dead back to life, we have no business."

No apology then? Kiren exhaled and squared himself. "I think we do. Walk with me?"

\*\*\*

Alexia looked up from Willem when Amos's shadow fell over her. His mouth formed a straight line, hands fisted at his sides. She rose, asking him with a look what was wrong.

He nodded away from the others, into the outskirts of the firelight.

"What is it?" she asked when they reached an appropriate distance.

With a sigh, he turned to face her, eyes on the ground. "Have you considered what will happen to your child if you do not survive childbirth?"

She nodded. "I have asked Mae to watch over her."

He let out a slow breath.

"Amos, speak. Do not withhold what is troubling you."

He groaned. "Perhaps it would be best if you were to marry."

"Marry?" Her eyes darted to the camp, to Kiren sitting next to the fire, laughing with Zeph. His gaze lifted to hers and his smile disappeared.

"Within the bonds of marriage, a man would be required to provide for your child, and as you insist that it will be a girl, she will need a protector."

She turned back to him. "Mae is strong enough to protect my baby."

He nodded. "She is, but—"

"Then why this discussion? And why now? You did not say anything months ago."

"Your time is nearing, Alexia."

She couldn't argue with that.

"Think of it this way. A woman cannot work the land. She cannot plough with a horse and plant. She must spend her time sewing and cooking and raising children. How is Mae to do both when she cannot even eat without a gold cuff? Think about the burden you place on her."

Alexia bit the inside of her lip, hating his words and that she hadn't considered how great a difficulty she left Mae. If they made it to this new world, her friend would be required to provide all for the little one. If they didn't, Alexia had assumed the Passionate would remain together, that her baby would be safe inside their collective strength. But what if they weren't?

"If I marry and then die in childbirth, the bond would claim both of us," she argued.

"Unless you do not consummate your marriage."

He was right. She hated how right he was and knew it was because someone in camp had inquired after her hand.

Amos tugged at the front of his tunic, dusting imaginary dirt free. "You are not required to consummate your union, but to join in matrimony."

"Now it is *required*?"

He shook out his hands, head turning heavenward. "I do not like asking this of you."

"Then do not."

"—but for your child's sake, it must be done."

She bristled and glanced at Kiren again. He appeared engaged in what Zephaniah was saying, but a quick twitch of the eyes her direction said he was listening in.

"He asked you to speak with me."

Amos let out a heavy breath. "Offered to stay permanently and be our healer if I can convince you."

"And you decided *not* to begin with that?"

He dropped a hand on her shoulder. "He requested that I present it as my idea, not his. Do understand, I did not wish to place that burden upon you. You sacrifice so much for us."

Although she appreciated his sentiments, it was this final argument that won her. She could marry Kiren. He would be responsible for the baby. On top of that, he would become the man who loved and cared for the Passionate. It was right. Exactly right. And if she never fully bonded with him, surely he would survive her death. He had been alive in her time which meant it had to be the case.

She huffed. Kiren. She'd known the considerate, cautious version of him, but this determined, fiery soul was almost more fun.

So be it.

He'd get what he asked for—let him deal with the consequences.

Alexia folded her arms and faced Kiren from across the distance. "He will have to ask for himself."

Kiren stood immediately, startling Zeph. With a wave of assurance to his friend, he turned her direction and approached, determination in his lowered brows.

Amos backed away. "Do not allow him to frighten you into this. If you say no, I will uphold your choice."

With a nod of thanks, she turned to the trees and waited for Kiren to arrive. They had barely stepped into the veil of leaves, starlight illuminating his face, when he said, "Be my wife, Alexia."

She blinked. She opened her mouth and closed it. *His* wife? No "Marry me, please" or "Will you do me the honor?" It was no question at all, but a demand.

He crossed his arms. "You have no good argument against it."

"Except for your lack of chivalry." Even so, Alexia could breathe for the first time in ages. The world was right. Kiren wanted her, wholly, completely, forever. This was the sweet man who had lost his family and found it again in her! And if she could survive childbirth, she may actually know what it meant to be his once more. She was ready to crack this brooding demeanor and melt into the haven of his arms—

But why?

The excitement died like a butterfly crushed under a boot heel. Was it just because he couldn't have her? Because she'd refused him enough times? She'd been accused of trusting too easily, and here she stood again on the brink, ready to dive before knowing his motives.

He watched her like he expected an answer this instant.

"Why?" she asked.

He flinched. Did the edges of his new scar turn whiter? One might think she'd slapped him rather than voiced a question.

"Because I asked?"

"You did not. You commanded like a pampered, pompous prince. Do you expect to start a marriage on that foundation?"

He licked his lips and tugged a hand through his hair. With a straightening of the shoulders he said, "Allow me to start again."

She leaned back, waiting.

He grinned. "The truth then: I have thought of you every day since I first saw you." He clasped her hand in both of his, clasped it like she might escape his grasp forever if he didn't keep hold. "You said you would torture me no more when you left me at the church, but not being by your side is torture. Not knowing what you are thinking is torture. Not knowing you are safe or feeling you smile upon me is torture."

"So you wish merely to ease your torment?" she challenged, certain he didn't understand what he was asking. Marriage. Bonding. Eternal commitment. Eternal connection. Eternal dependence.

He lifted her fingers, cradling them between his as if praying. "You make me better, Alexia." He whispered. "Make me want to be better."

She blinked, not expecting so profound a confession.

"You also make me want to scream." He chuckled and she laughed with him. "But that is good for me—the challenge. I have lived enough years without anyone expecting anything. I have been selfish." He brushed her cheek. "You remind me of my purpose."

"Which is?"

"To become the man my father would smile upon."

Alexia shivered. Rarely had he spoken of his father. Bringing up the dead king who was his north star, he had to be serious.

"And here I am, being that selfish man when I say, be my wife." He lifted her fingers to his mouth. "God forgive me, I think I will always be this selfish."

She released a tentative grin. From the fear behind his humor, he really wanted her—even if he didn't know it fully. He was not the man she loved from the future, but he was getting there.

"I am going to die, Kiren. In childbirth. Are you prepared for that?"

"I will keep you alive."

She loved his certainty, but he couldn't know for sure. Only one person did. Alexia closed her eyes and stepped out of time, the shift from everything to nothing. No wind, no pollens, no Kiren. Lester/Grandfather waited for her in the absence, and she had only one question for him:

"Will it kill him? If I say yes, will it kill him?"

The man lifted an eyebrow. "What does yer gut tell you?"

She focused inward, pushing past the awkward knot of nerves and clouding fear. With clarity, she could see smooth fields and blue skies, not knolls and angry cliffs. The way forward looked clear. It felt clear.

"You are a terrible guide," she teased. "I have to discover everything for myself."

Grandfather smirked. "I never claimed to be guidin' no one."

"Will you wish me well in my marriage?"

"Aye, and a whole bit more. I'll wish you joy." He placed a kiss on her brow. The tenderness sank in, and she missed Father for one terrible moment. Father, Sarah, so many others, but strangely, she didn't miss Kiren anymore. She didn't have to.

"Goodbye, Grandfather." She returned to time, standing before Kiren as he watched her expectantly, waiting for an answer. "You will not be allowed to *touch* me." Not in the intimate ways he desired.

"For now." His eyes darkened.

Her breath caught. She didn't know if she could do this. Being near him was one thing, but being married to him and not giving in? She breathed deeply and hoped her future Kiren would forgive her. If he was allowed to be greedy, she was as well. "Would you call me selfish for consenting?"

Kiren caught her shoulders, jaw dangling. "You will?"

"You expected me to say no?"

"Well, I—"

"Then why did you bother asking—nay, demanding?" What was with this confounded man? If he didn't want to marry her, why wouldn't he leave her be?

Various sounds escaped his mouth as he worked to form a response, nothing coherent. A speechless Kiren. Incredible.

She rolled her eyes. "I will be your wife, if you will be *my* husband."

He squirmed under her scrutiny, and she turned her gaze to the navy sky beyond sheltering leaves. He was worse than a child. Tell him he couldn't have something and he'd fight to the death for it. Tell him he could, and he'd fight like a lion against it.

He swallowed, hard. "You understand what that means?"

"That I will be your queen when and if you are restored to your throne? That you will have countless enemies who seek to exploit your weaknesses? That I must be willing and able to win my own battles? Yes, I quite understand."

He blinked at her several times. "I suppose you do."

Alexia crossed her arms. "And you must understand that you will lose me." Else he would have been different. It had to be that way, unless they might somehow rewrite time? Unless they'd already begun to rewrite it? No. The timeline was sure. "Our days together will be limited. That much I know."

"It cannot be prevented?" His voice was very small.

Her poor, tortured love. "I do not need a husband, Kiren." What was she thinking? Let him marry her only to lose her? It was cruel. "And you do not need a wife. We are better this way." It was a complete lie, but she avoided his gaze so he couldn't read the truth.

His hand dropped over both of hers, halting them from fidgeting with her robe. "Stop, Alexia. For me?"

The last two words killed her protest. It was rare to hear him beg.

He took her fingers, teasing warmth into them while his eyes locked onto hers. "I have every confidence you are adequate on your own. Why, I am inclined to believe you might sprout wings and fly if you desired, but I want you firmly bound to the earth because this is where I reside. If you took to the sky, I would stand every day watching for you to pass overhead." His fingers locked into a ring around her wrist. "It is humiliating to admit, but if you will have me, I wish to be the man who holds your chains—even for a short season. You will be my prisoner, and I will be yours."

"That is where you are wrong, Kiren." She brushed a hair from his cheek. "This bonding is not a prison. It gives you the power to take wing. I would have no other flying companion, unless you are determined to remain upon the earth?"

He smirked, meeting her gaze, stars glittering in his firmament. "I have always adored the sky."

"As have I." She grazed a finger across his lips. "It resides in your eyes."

He sucked in a breath. She barely had time to brace before his lips possessed hers. Warmth exploded through her chest, a passion she had trapped and staunched so fiercely it tore at her soul. Compounded by his own, they might light the world aflame. Heat exploded over them both like a fiery sun— the first true sunrise after ages of darkness. She wanted more. She wanted all of him. Needed more. From the way his fingers raked down her body, his blood burned for her as well.

This was going to be impossible.

He pulled away and tugged her through the trees. "Before this campaign at the fortress, before you have room to reason, before another sunrise, I am taking the choice away. Tonight, you are my bride."

"Tonight?" she asked.

He grinned at her, and she lost the power to walk straight. It was exactly what she wanted.

They stumbled into camp where numerous eyes turned to their clasped hands as Kiren dragged her across the encampment. He stopped before Lucian.

"You married Gerbaud and Thiphania when I was..." Kiren stilled. "Before."

"I did. God rest their souls."

Kiren pulled her next to him. "Marry us."

Gasps filled the camp.

Alexia glanced down at her loose hair, her priestly robe, her unwashed hands. She sighed. It seemed her fate. No wonder Kiren had fought so desperately in the future to give her the wedding she deserved—because this certainly wasn't it.

Well, better to marry the man than wait for perfection. Peace settled in her heart and took up permanent residence. Some things were meant to be. She and Kiren were one of them—no matter the time, no matter the circumstances.

People circled them, astonished looks passing from one to another.

Lucian opened his mouth to protest, but at Alexia's encouraging nod, he turned to Kiren. "Dost thou promise in the sight of God that thou wilt keep Alexia as thy wife; that thou wilt have her and hold her in faith and fidelity, in health and sickness, and in all other misfortunes; and that either for better or for worse, thou wilt not replace her with another, all the days of thy life?"

"That I can promise."

Lucian turned to her. "Alexia, dost thou promise in the sight of God that thou wilt keep him as thy husband; that thou wilt have him and hold him in faith and fidelity, in health and sickness, and in all other misfortunes; and that either for better or for worse, thou wilt not replace him with another, all the days of thy life?"

"It is my vow, yes."

Kiren lifted an eyebrow at her. She could almost hear the question in his stare—that she would marry another one day and make this very same pledge. How could she mean it? Although she wished to enlighten him, she held her tongue.

He loosened the girder about his tunic, took her hand, and wrapped the rope around their wrists. She steadied, readying for the rush of the binding.

A gentle warmth settled upon her, like the touch of cherubs, but not the enveloping rapture of her first marriage. Kiren gulped, his chest rising and falling as though he'd swum the entire English Channel. The glow of Alexia's skin seeped into his wrist and spread, and with it, her awareness of him—like opening her eyes for the first time. She saw all of him. The trepidation in his soul grazed her heart—the uncertainty brought on by this step, the need for her, the hope and fear for keeping her alive. He profoundly adored her. She couldn't look on him as ignorantly as she had, and she couldn't look upon his scarred cheek at all.

She hated that she'd done that to him. Her eyes stung with tears.

Kiren lifted her chin, tenderness filling his sea. He shone, like when they first met, a light that elevated him in a dark world, one that set him apart.

She gasped. He had been married to her all along. Those years he watched her grow, he knew he was gazing upon his wife, even if she hadn't yet been married to him. How it must have tortured him! As it had tortured her these last months.

She reached out and traced his jaw, the pucker of skin, the permanent damage she had done. His breath tickled her skin. It hitched.

"Finish it." His brows lowered.

He wasn't speaking to her. Alexia glanced at Lucian, his mouth hanging open.

Light permeated the camp, like a miniature sun had taken residence in their bound wrists. They two put the fires to shame like a pair of fallen angels. Everyone watched them, eyes wide.

"M-may God confirm the marriage contracted between you. You are now man and wife."

Kiren pulled Alexia near, grinning, and kissed her hard for everyone to see.

# Forty-Eight

## *To War*

Kiren was a fool. A complete fool. A brainless bobbywagger who'd pledged his soul for an hour of gratification.

He kissed Alexia deeper, running a hand down the curve of her hip. Fool or no, he wouldn't reverse his decision today. They were alone in the silence of the trees, but he didn't care if they occupied the highest spire of the Vatican. He'd want her just as badly.

Alexia pulled free, panting. "Much more of that and we will fall too far to rise."

"I will fall with you." He chased her lips and she backed away, pulling his wrist with her. They were still tied together. Under tradition, a couple was bound until their relationship had been consummated, until they were truly one. He hadn't thought about that either before promising Amos he would agree to these terms.

She believed she would die when the baby was born. She feared her death would bring about his. He respected that. He stomached it because she was wrong. And when she survived, when he'd saved them both, there would be no barrier between them, no reason to withhold anything.

It was time to begin dispelling mysteries. He reached for her necklace, curious to see what she'd been so valiantly hiding from him. Alexia caught his wrist, her eyes wide.

"I will show mine, if you will show me yours." He waggled his eyebrows.

She scowled and stepped away, the rope again pulling at his wrist.

Or perhaps she would cling to her secrets longer. Kiren tugged the cord free from their wrists.

Alexia placed a hand over his. "What are you doing?"

"We cannot go into combat bound together like this."

"But it is dishonest. People will assume—"

"We are married." He slid a lock of hair behind her ear. "Let them assume."

Her cheeks flamed red. The tie slipped free and he felt strangely naked without it. She was right. It wasn't meant to be removed until they were one. He wanted to push her over the precipice with physical persuasions, but he wouldn't. No more selfishness. Except in one thing.

"I do not want you going into battle with us." He bowed his head.

"Is that why you married me? So you could order me around? I warn you, it will not work."

"I am thinking of the baby." He placed a hand on her womb and stepped up so their bodies pressed together. "And you."

"And I am thinking of everyone else, including you." She slid around him, back toward the camp. "Why is it you think that I lead our forces?"

*Because you are marvelous.*

"Hm?" she asked.

He hadn't realized she was expecting an answer. "You are a skilled warrior."

"Because I can change time, Kiren. I can stop a tragedy from happening and orchestrate our efforts so we conquer or withdraw without loss."

He wrapped an arm around her, spreading his fingers over her enlarged girth. "Even while birthing a child?"

Her spine stiffened.

"That was another aspect of my discussion with Amos. Your time is near. He agrees it is unwise for you to lead us in your state. It has compromised you before."

"Traitor!"

He grinned. "Mae thinks so as well. And Regin. And Lucian. Did I miss any of the votes bearing weight?" It had been easy enough to plant the idea in their minds through innocent conversation. Amos had agreed it would be best for the knight to lead the march.

"Deamus."

"Ah." The bumbling scroll reader who thought he had a prayer of winning Alexia. "As Deamus is absent, I suppose he forfeits the opportunity to voice his opinion, but I wholeheartedly believe he would join the others."

She glared.

"It really is for the best, Alexia. Amos has agreed that you should remain behind this time. I think that wise."

"And if you are injured? If you die while I am here?"

He laughed. "You tell me. Will I die?"

Her angry grimace said it all. She knew he would not.

$$***$$

Weapons were tucked under jerkins and hidden under sleeves and in boots. If they resorted to needing those weapons, they were in trouble.

*It is no different than any of our rescues*, Alexia told herself again as she slipped her Soulless-slaying dagger into her belt. Except it was. She wouldn't be leading the charge—upon Kiren's insistence. An entity that would become the Soulless may appear in the conflict. Or in camp. No one else understood it. No one else had a weapon to subdue it. Kiren and the others were entering a lair of vipers, and if this thing was as intelligent as it seemed to be, it would manifest. Those in camp could run. Men and women in the heat of battle would be trapped. She needed to be there.

The chosen warriors set out, following Leofrik's lead. Alexia took a deep breath and fell into line.

"No." Kiren barred her way.

She rolled her eyes.

"You think you can stop me?" she challenged.

He lifted an eyebrow. "Will you force my hand?"

"I have had enough of men telling me what I can and cannot do. You may disapprove, but you cannot change my decision, and I would rather be honest with you, so stand aside."

His jaw clenched. Fingers slid around her arms, tightening and loosening. "I love you, Alexia."

Her anger deflated. He'd said the words. He'd actually said the words.

Kiren continued, "I have suspected for days that you planned to sneak along. And if you did, who would know until it was too late?"

She folded her arms across her chest. "Without Velia to whisk people to safety, I am the last line of defense."

"We have Zeph."

"Zeph is wonderful, but he is not nearly wonderful enough. He is restricted by time and space. A single arrow could take him out of action."

He rubbed her arm tenderly. "A single arrow could take *you* out of action." The softening of his voice reminded her that she expected to depart from this life shortly.

She matched his tone. "I am not that easy to kill."

"And yet you insist you will die soon."

They were both quiet.

"What would you have me do?" she asked. "Stay here and agonize about whether any of us will be lost today?"

He bowed his head. "Better than birthing an infant on the battlefield only to leave her motherless after the conflict is ended."

Heat rushed to Alexia's face. Now that he voiced his fear, she was plagued by the expectation that this would be the cause of her demise.

Kiren tugged her into his arms and pressed his lips to her brow. "We will return triumphant. I will see to it."

"And if this is it? What if you go and we are besieged while you are away? What if I labor while you are away and that is how I die?"

His eyes widened. "You will not. I have only just found you. You are not to leave me so soon. Do you understand?"

She wished his command was enough to deny fate.

He pulled a hand through his hair, then a second one. "Come with me then, but you are to remain on the fringe of the battle. You must be safe, Alexia."

"We are stronger together."

His cheek tugged upward. "And yet I have never been so terrified."

She patted his face. "You will live, Kiren."

"Yes, but will you?"

# Forty-Nine

# *Locked Away*

Late afternoon rays threaded a sunset as Alexia stumbled into a township. A row of permanent, one-story buildings lined the thoroughfare, their wooden fronts weathered and rustic. Smoke rose from various chimneys—warmth she ached to experience. Kiren shot her a look and hurried forward. They had come in groups, small ones so as to not raise any concern. Their entire force was now within a short radius of the fort that towered over the town.

The scent of baking bread and roasting venison made her mouth water, countered by the stench of refuse and unwashed bodies. Beyond a single row of buildings stood the gray fortress against the grayer sky. Alexia was growing to detest that color, with a vengeance. It meant shackles. It meant prison. It meant rain.

She counted the number of men, women, and children still milling around the fortifications. Potential casualties. The very idea made her sick. Fires circled the building, along with tents, the soldiers of the fief lord who took pleasure in caging the Passionate.

The idea was a precision attack. Go in. Grab the child. Behead the serpent who led the people. Get out.

Metal clanged against metal—the timbre of blade on blade. She yanked the seconds to a halt and hurried forward. Let it be a smithy. Soldiers practicing in the yard. Anything but…

Silivia's weapon reflected sunlight, deflected by a knight's blade.

Alexia reached through time to go back a couple minutes and stop the conflict from happening. She pressed up against the inky barrier and groaned. As feared, the enemy was present.

Goodbye, surprise.

Goodbye, precision.

Hello, war.

She unsheathed her dagger, grabbed the charm about her neck, and dashed forward. Her womb contracted. She slowed.

Carefully then.

People surged around her, heeding the call to arms. Alexia slipped between them. Sarlic, Regin, Amos, Willem, and Mae made an intimidating line, pressing their way forward.

Alexia drew on the medallion, slowing the world to a crawl as she walked straight for the gate. Any moment, the enemy would close the giant wooden doors to the fortress, and then this battle would grow far more interesting than she could condone. Not even she would be able to reopen them.

Darkness exploded over the battlefield in waves.

*Well done, Amos,* she thought. *At least now they will not see us coming.*

She stepped by Regin who was casually reaching for a man whose sword had momentarily lowered. Mae had unclasped her armlet. Sarlic held both hands out, inflicting pain on an entire line of armored men.

Alexia entered the shadow of the gate. Two soldiers were running for one door in slow motion. Another man shoved at the other door by himself, but he was not nearly strong enough to move it. Alexia placed a hand on the man's chest and gave him a slight shove. His mouth flew open as he sailed backward and slammed into the stone archway.

She cringed as his head smacked the wall.

The two soldiers slowed, but she aimed straight for them. The first she knocked into another wall. The second ducked and side-stepped. She slipped a foot in front of his and lifted up, bending his knee. He tripped forward, landing on his face.

She let go of time.

Shouts filled the air, feet pounding toward her from outside the walls. Alexia pulled on the pendant once more, but stopped when Kiren appeared. His scar caught the light, followed by his ocean-deep eyes.

"I thought you were staying *behind. Away* from the danger."

She knocked on the wooden barrier. "Just holding the doors for you."

His head tilted, mouth opening.

Alexia nodded him forward. "We have a child to rescue, do we not?"

In they went, to the courtyard. A man here or there rushed for the gate, but they hadn't enough time to gather or arm themselves. She used time to knock them unconscious. If Kiren got to them first, he fought them until she arrived. Leofrik appeared amidst the skirmish, shouting orders and rushing forward, sword pointed. They followed him.

"The child is in the tower. Guard me!"

Zeph, Mae, and Sarlic fell into formation.

Darkness engulfed the gate and stood firm—Amos's darkness. As planned, Amos and Regin would hold the gate until everyone could escape with the child. Shouts abruptly cut off and turned to snores within the gloom. Alexia grinned.

Kiren tugged her away from the courtyard and through two heavy doors. Scuffling and a shout deafened her. Two guards dropped to the ground—both at Mae's feet. She reclasped her armlet. Their practice was paying off, and Alexia couldn't be prouder. Mae met her eyes, relief and a tentative hope in hers.

A single torch turned the narrow hallway golden brown, and a staircase twisted off to one side. Zeph and Sarlic tugged the unconscious men behind the edge of the stairs, and Mae waved them on. She took up her position at the exit.

Shouts and confused voices reverberated toward them. Any moment more people would appear. Alexia and her company took the stairs single file, Leofrik's armor echoing ominously against the stone as he led the way.

Urine and mold stained the air. Alexia wrinkled her nose and tried not to breathe deep.

A scraping of boots carried down from several floors above. Sarlic lifted both hands, the lines around his face tightening as he readied for an assault.

Leofrik led them off the first landing and into a hall rather than continue toward whatever force awaited them. Slits of light cut across the stone floor from glassless windows, lighting a wall of doors. Leofrik motioned them forward, all the way to the end of the hall which bent right and opened to an inner corridor of the fortress. Torches lit the dark expanse and outlined doors. In the corner nearest them, another stairwell spiraled upward.

Boots and naked blades appeared on the stairs. Alexia turned to retreat and yanked time to a stop. A sword hung mid-swing toward her neck.

The man must have come from one of the rooms they'd passed.

She ducked and tapped his blade upward while slowly releasing time, throwing his trajectory. The weapon smacked into the ceiling. Kiren leapt forward and slammed his hand into the man's throat. The enemy's eyes rolled back, limbs shaking.

Kiren dropped him like he'd been stung.

Sarlic yelled and the last man fell. Five bodies littered the hall. He and Zephaniah moved the unconscious aside.

Kiren stood frozen, staring at his hand.

Alexia touched his arm. "We must move."

"I took it."

"Took what?"

"Life." His eyes met hers. "I have never…" He swallowed hard. "Always given, never…"

"But he lives." Alexia pointed out the rise and fall of the man's chest.

"Barely." He pulled her to him. "I saw him attack you and I—I do not know what happened."

"Oy!" Sarlic stood at the base of the stairs, Zeph and Leofrik already pounding their way up. He nodded them up and crossed his arms, taking his predetermined position and glancing nervously past them down the hall.

Alexia tugged Kiren after her. He let her drag him, a true testament to his shock.

They rounded the curve and caught up to Zeph. He stood several steps below Leofrik as the knight raked his blade across an enemy's weapon.

"Stand aside!" Alexia ordered.

Zephaniah flattened to the wall, and Leofrik twisted as close to the stone as possible. Alexia gripped her necklace and slowed time, lifting one foot then the other through the stilled minutes. Three enemies filled the stairwell above her. She pushed the nearest one squarely in the chest and watched as he flew backward in slow motion, smacking into the two behind him and falling to one elbow on the stairs. The man directly behind him lost his footing and tumbled onto his rear. The third backed up two steps and held a knife at the ready.

She released time and Leofrik surged forward, dancing past the fallen and engaging the last man. Zeph leapt forward and knocked out the man who had fallen to his rump. Kiren shoved a hand against the other man's throat and visibly cringed. The man fell unconscious. Kiren shared a look with Zeph and a nod, but neither spoke. He wouldn't look at Alexia.

They chased after Leofrik and arrived at a landing where he'd cornered the last man, his blade pressed close to the enemy's neck. He shoved the man toward the stairs. "Go. Do not get in our way."

The man nodded emphatically and turned to the stairs.

"Sarlic will get him," Zeph said.

One more curve of stairs and they came to a rickety door. Leofrik tried the handle. It didn't give. He stood back and kicked it in.

A small room appeared with a single window across the way.

A squeal pierced their ears. Alexia hurried forward, pushing past the men and into the room. A little girl leapt at her. Jangling chains. Light flashed up.

Not light. *A blade*, Alexia realized too late.

Startled eyes pierced into her as fire raced down her side, pain radiating out from where the dagger burrowed between her ribs.

Alexia gasped.

Heat spilled from the wound, the warmth of life, escaping quickly.

Reality crashed in with nauseating force. Alexia dropped to her knees and onto her side, the blow reverberating through her womb, tearing something free.

# Fifty

# Fated

Kiren sucked in a hard breath, his side aching with phantom pain. He elbowed Zeph and the knight aside. Alexia lay on the floor, her robe changing color from a sage brown to rich-damp soil. Except that wasn't water.

He wrapped an arm around her shoulder and touched the blade, unable to grasp what it was doing there, why it protruded from his beloved wife.

The murmur of voices agitated him, background noise to the buzzing in his brain.

Alexia was injured. His greatest fears were coming true, and no matter how he'd vowed to keep her safe, she was going to die. He'd condemned her by allowing her to come. No, he'd condemned her by claiming her, just as he'd condemned all he loved. He couldn't draw in enough breath. His lungs were failing.

No, not his. Hers.

Her palm touched his cheek, her lips moving. He focused on them: "Heal me."

He shook the stupor free and focused inward. The knife had punctured her lung. He tugged the blade free and called for the tissue to mend. Power surged through him and into her chest. The room swam.

Alexia's back arched, and her grip tightened around his arm. Sweat beaded her brow. She panted and screamed.

Kiren held her, fighting dizziness and listening for her heart to slow, but it didn't. It was pumping faster. He didn't understand. Her lung was whole. She should be mended.

Unless...

He placed a hand over her womb. Blood pooled beneath the surface. She was bleeding internally. Again. Her fall had ruptured her previously healed wounds. This wasn't something he could heal in a prison tower. He'd already given her all he could spare. The injury would take all he had and expose their entire party to capture.

"Sleep." He drew on the chemicals in the brain that would force her to rest, to slow, to minimize the danger. He ripped a blanket from the straw bed and tied it around his wife, at an angle that would put the most pressure on the rupture, holding it together. "Zeph, you have to take her. Take her somewhere safe and then come get me."

His friend's wings unfurled.

The little girl gasped.

"Go now. Fast as you can. Faster than you have ever flown!"

Zephaniah squeezed through the window and reached back for Alexia. Kiren and Leofrik carefully maneuvered her out. An arrow hissed past Zeph's wing. Kiren met his friend's wide eyes, catching his thought: *Waesucks! That was close.*

"Go!"

Zeph grabbed Alexia and flew straight up.

Kiren watched him disappear, heart thundering an ominous foreboding. This was it. This was when he'd fail her.

He vaguely registered Leofrik's voice, a soothing coo. "Your mother sent me. We have come to bring you to her."

"But what I did to that woman…" The girl's voice faltered, her eyes fixed on the window.

"Child, Velia wished your freedom, and I have vowed to make it so, but we must leave."

"You know her name," the girl whispered. "She really did send you. But my father—"

"You saw the man with wings? The man who healed the knife wound before you? They are like you. There are others. Your father will not stop us."

Kiren turned as the girl nodded up at the knight. She lifted her arm to expose her chain. Leofrik pulled his blade and smacked the hilt of his weapon into the cuff once, twice, three times.

"That will not work," Kiren promised. He pulled a seed out of his pocket and placed it in the locking mechanism. Leofrik backed away as Kiren held his fingers over the opening and felt for the seed. It waited. He offered it life, growth, energy. It lapped up his offering and burst outward. Metal cracked under the sudden pressure of a tiny tree.

Ironwood.

Kiren knocked the wood free, and the shackle dropped to the floor. Instant color flooded the child's face.

Leofrik offered a hand and she took it. He led her toward the exit.

Decision time.

Kiren glanced out the window, back after the girl and knight, out the window… He could take his chances waiting here for Zeph to return, or help the others escape. His gut was a knotted rope, twisting tighter under the weight of Alexia's dangling life.

He could do no good here. Remaining was a guarantee of his eventual capture. He followed the two out the door—the same instant a shout carried up at them. He shared a look with Leofrik, and they sped down the steps.

Sarlic was bent over at the waist, chest heaving as he held both hands in front of himself. He could inflict on a single person without issue, but each mind he touched simultaneously multiplied his efforts. He'd already employed his gift on so many. Three men lay crumpled at his feet, but more thundered down the hall.

They were trapped.

# Fifty-One

# *Waylaid*

Kiren pulled his dagger and readied for impact. Bodies blocked out the torchlight, undoubtedly drawn by Alexia's scream. Sarlic stumbled back, his feet hitting the lowest stair, sweat spilling down his face. Leofrik loosed his sword, poised for combat.

The child retreated back up the steps.

Three of them against a fort full of humans. Amos and Regin likely faced the same odds, and Mae… They should have brought more people, or never come. Kiren understood the tactic. It had been a strategic move as much as a compassionate one. Velia's daughter would one day be a powerful tool and asset, but for Alexia's sake, they should have chosen another way.

Alexia would die because he couldn't escape this. Not in time. He'd put the life of Velia's child, a girl he didn't even know, over all he cherished. And yet, Alexia would want this. Were she here, she would stop time and whisk the girl to safety before thinking for an instant of herself.

Kiren stepped squarely to the center of the stairwell, blocking the passage as men filled the crossroads of corridors, cornering them.

Leofrik stepped forward, sword swinging. It clashed against the first combatants. The hallway was too narrow for anyone to pass their whirling blades. Back and forth they went, losing a step, gaining one, muscles straining. Every second more of the enemy flooded in. And Alexia was that much closer to death.

Wind whooshed past Kiren's shoulder. A crossbow bolt embedded itself in the mortar behind him. He turned on the crowd and found the weapon. The man who had shot at him was loading another bolt. Kiren lifted his dagger, the only shield he possessed. The crossbowman raised his weapon up once more, taking aim.

Sarlic stepped in front of Kiren, reaching out. The man howled, his hands crinkling at odd angles, the crossbow dropping from his grasp.

*Whunk!*

Leofrik cried out. His weapon scraped along the stone wall and caught in the mortar, trapped. He ducked a blow. The enemy swung again.

Sarlic growled, knuckles popping in his hand, shoulders lifted and tense. The attacker grabbed his head and screamed, tumbling to the floor. Others spilled forward. Leofrik dodged their weapons, falling back into the stairwell.

Blades lifted toward Leofrik's and Sarlic's throats. The crossbow had been retrieved and was now pointed squarely at Kiren's head.

*I know I have not been the truest of servants, Holy Father,* Kiren muttered silently, *but spare me, and I will serve until I can give no more. I will give all I am. Like Alexia.*

His throat tightened. His Alexia, who might even at this moment be dead.

*I beg thee,* he pleaded. *Beg thee.* "Let her live" was how he longed to end the prayer, but he couldn't mutter the words, knowing it was impossible. God heard his heart. God would do as he had designed, and Kiren would have to trust that no matter how his heart broke, it was the right solution.

# Fifty-Two

# *Abandoned*

Muscles screamed, balling so tightly Alexia knew they would break her. She panted through it, feeling blindly for someone, anyone. She was alone.

Rotting wood filled her nose, along with the stink of rodents. She forced her eyes open. Gaping floorboards cut into her shoulder, sunlight streaming through narrow slats overhead. She must be in an old barn or abandoned house, one that had long since been empty.

Her lower extremities seized. Pain melted in and out through bouts of intensity.

Tightening. Agony. Loosening. Panting for breath.

Silence.

She was going to die. This was it. She'd known it was coming all along, but not like this. Alone. Abandoned. She didn't want to die alone.

"Yer not alone."

She blinked her eyes open, and there stood Grandfather. Outside of time? Within regular time? She couldn't tell. He wrapped an arm around her shoulders and gave her a tender smile. "None of us what alter time do anything alone. I am here. Always."

# Fifty-Three

# *Abandoned*

Kiren lifted his chin and looked the crossbowman in the eye. If it was his time, he would face it bravely…or he could duck out of the way and live another hour. He liked that option.

Alexia said he would live centuries. This was not the end for him, but that didn't mean he could avoid being caught, bound, thrown in a prison, and becoming a new toy for the lord of the fort.

All while the woman he loved faded from this world.

Kiren reached up slowly and wrapped a hand around his pendant. He had drawn life out of a man. It made his gut rot, but perhaps with the aid of the necklace, he could give his companions a fighting chance.

One soldier near the crossroads of hallways dropped. Straight down. Onto his face. Another dropped. A third. Five down.

Men turned to the other hall, facing something on the other side of the bend, beyond Kiren's view. An entire ring of men trembled and fell. The rest backed away, their hearts filling Kiren's ears with a symphony of terror.

Mae emerged from around the corner. She clasped and unclasped the cuff around her arm.

A crossbow bolt shot toward her. She stepped aside. The shooter crumbled to the floor. Men ran away, the ones who still could. Two faltered and dropped in their frenzied escape. The rest remained on the ground, their skin graying, dark energy swirling from their collapsed forms toward the woman's skirts.

Mae firmly clasped the bracelet. She turned toward them. "I thought you might need some help."

Sarlic stumbled forward, dancing between collapsed bodies. "I could kiss you right now."

"And join them?" She pointed to the fallen. "Heavens, no."

He stopped short.

Leofrik pulled his sword free and retreated back up the stairs as Kiren waded forward, past the reaper. "If ever I wished for an ally in battle, I would take you."

Her face pinked.

He continued. "You truly are breathtaking in your own element—and look how you preserved them without taking a single life!"

Leofrik ducked down the stairs with the little girl.

Mae clasped both hands before her. "And there she is, the precious little one. Come, child. No one will harm you further."

The girl eyed the fallen with something between wonder and fear as Leofrik guided her forward. He halted and knelt to face the child. "You must go with them now."

"But what about you?"

He lifted his head, gaze fixed down the hallway where the men had retreated. "I have one final thing to do."

Her little head bowed.

*I wonder, will Alexia's child be like this one—so fragile and small?* Kiren pondered. He shook the thought free. Her babe would not survive, nor would its mother if he didn't find a way to her right now.

"Come!" He waved everyone forward. Mae fell into step next to the child, and Sarlic took up the rear. The little girl kept glancing backward to where Leofrik watched them, until he turned and paced down the dark hallway, alone.

***

Men crowded the courtyard, rallying around the plume of midnight at the gate. A wall of slumbering bodies hedged the exit in. Both stood between Kiren and freedom—the advantage being that none of the soldiers were paying attention to him and his companions.

"Mae," he muttered, "Perhaps Regin could use your assistance."

She loosened her cuff and pointed to the battlement walls. "Up there for safety."

Kiren seized the little girl's hand, and Sarlic guarded them as they climbed the stairs to the top of the wall.

One by one, the men fell. A collective gasp filled the courtyard along with a couple shrieks as realization hit. Mae walked forward, hands out to her sides as the essence of energy sizzled into her limbs from the fallen. She reached the wall of sleeping men and reattached her bracelet.

Kiren peered over the battlement at the other side.

More men rallied on the outside of the gate. He hated how exposed this action had made his people.

His people.

When had he begun thinking of them that way? Already he was planning the future, how they'd go to ground and slowly blend in with humanity, placing a person here, a person there, each with a strong communication system to keep watch on their enemies.

All because Alexia insisted he lead. Because she opened his heart. Because he'd promised to stay if she agreed to be his.

Wings flapped in the distance—gray-green wings. His pulse jumped. Zeph. Kiren eyed the men below, the number of bows present. Terrible odds.

"Mae, press through the gate!" he called.

The gates inched open. Regin appeared from the darkness below, backing away from the murk. Amos also appeared. The darkness faded. Men surged toward the small opening. True to fashion, they began collapsing, unconscious.

Zeph's figure could no longer be mistaken as a bird, but the men below were too distracted to notice.

Kiren turned to Sarlic and the little girl. "I must leave now. Sarlic, protect her. Flee with the others, and I will join you when Alexia is whole."

The branded man took the little girl's hand. "Save our Alexia."

Kiren gave him a nod, and hands latched under his arms, hefting him into the air and away.

# Fifty-Four

## Ulric

Leofrik pressed the door open into the large chamber where Ulric had summoned him not long ago. The nobleman sat in a high-backed chair, fully dressed for war, pondering his hands. "And I thought perhaps you were dead." He rested an elbow on the chair. "If only I were so lucky."

"You will wish it was so by the end of this day."

Ulric lifted his head, his eyes burning cinders through Leofrik's chest. "Oh, I wish it now. Attack."

Footfalls thudded behind him, three sets. Leofrik whirled and blocked a blade.

# Fifty-Five

# New Life

Kiren landed before the old barn, repulsed by the stink of rodent feces. The building was well away from the roads, so far from notice that no one would come this way. And yet the idea of Alexia giving birth here…

He hurried forward. "Zeph, go for clean water and cloths."

Wings flapped, wind stirring around him and kicking dust into the entry. Kiren shielded his eyes and stepped through. Alexia lay in a crimson puddle, her life ebbing slowly away, but he couldn't move. He'd been kicked in the gut. Twice.

Draped around her neck, fully exposed on the floor next to her head was a pendant.

A flat pewter diamond with ancient symbols: a large Z with a cross stroke and rounded tail, encircled by a ring of smaller characters.

His pendant.

And yet his necklace weighed against his chest, safely tucked away.

She *had* come from the future.

He'd never surrender the medallion, which meant in her time, he must be dead. Had she come through time to stop his tragic end from occurring? But for her to bear the necklace, she would have to be of the royal bloodline. A blood relative.

His stomach roiled like an egg in a skillet.

Alexia whimpered. Her skin was white, so pale he feared she would slip away into the next life. Kiren dropped to her side, fumbling through his horror to find her injury.

She must be his or Kiri's granddaughter. Blood. And he'd forced her hand…

This must be the great secret she was shielding him from. He could make it right. He could pretend he never knew, cover the truth and live out a lifetime of bitter-sweetness.

"Oh, twisted man that I am," he barely whispered. "Reviling flesh." His gaze turned heavenward. "This is my punishment for forsaking the cloth, is it not?"

She was dying. Was it wrong that he loved her, that he would do anything for her, even if being her husband was the greatest perversion of his existence? She'd been a test for him. One he'd failed.

He pressed a hand to her womb. She screamed. Blood oozed from inside, her heart pumping weakly around the loss. *"In thy graciousness,"* he pleaded quietly with God, swallowing down panic, *"let her stay with me, right or wrong, just a little longer."*

She grabbed his arm. Her eyes flashed up at him, a desperate green slowly leaking of vitality, filled with memories, her final hurrah with life:

*She curled into the warmth of his side, a hand resting on her center. "And if she despises penmanship like I did, how shall we curb her resistance?"*

*Kiren's chuckle pulled her gaze to his face, the jagged scar, the merriment dancing in his ocean swells. He was the most beautiful thing she'd ever seen.*

*He twisted a lock of her hair around his finger. "We can always ask Edward to make her think she adores penmanship."*

*She gasped and slapped his shoulder. "We will do no such thing."*

*"He would not be able to convince her regardless. She will possess your determination and my mental steel."*

*"You mean your stubbornness?" Alexia giggled. "Then she is doomed for certain."*

Alexia let go of his arm. She whimpered and tensed.

Kiren couldn't breathe. Couldn't move. He'd forgotten how or had been completely disconnected from his muscles. That had been himself in her thoughts—just as he was now.

Alexia whispered, "Save my baby."

Reality came crashing down like a freezing rain, like all the stones of a castle suddenly slamming into place, like he'd been dropped onto the pinnacle of a tower and could abruptly see the entire valley below.

He clasped her hand. *"Our* baby?"

She smiled. It flooded his soul with sunlight, the truest moment of sunrise when all doubt washed away with the darkness.

"I will save you both," he vowed.

Her entire body stiffened, and her grip on his fingers stopped the circulation. "I love you, Kiren."

She must be delusional, mistaking him for this future Kiren. He brushed a mix of white and near-black hair away from her face, tenderness flooding his soul while he dosed her with strength. She carried his child. All along. He had been callous, terrible to her, and she had only ever loved him—but not him, the him who would be.

"I love you," he repeated to appease her, startled how vehemently he meant the words. They may only be the seed of something greater, but they nestled at the core of his being, impossible to uproot. How could he not love a woman so selfless she would give up her happiness to save a rag-tag group of Lost Ones? She embodied everything he wanted to be, and more. She was the mother of his child. The person he thought of before closing his eyes and upon first opening them.

His Alexia.

"You are both going to live." He pressed his palms to her womb and closed his eyes, siphoning the strength from his body, from the pendant, from the world around him. "Live!"

***

Alexia fled to the absence of time and back between surges to catch her breath. Hours turned into days as she fought through pain, terror, and guilt. This was it. Her final day. She hadn't stopped the Soulless from becoming. She'd failed. Each touch from Kiren was a boon, not the caring caress of the husband she'd left behind, but an adequate farewell. At some point Mae entered and began to assist. She calmed Kiren, and Alexia was grateful to have so dear a friend near in her final moments.

She sat in the absence of time, rolling her thumbs over one another. Grandfather sat in the distance, eyes closed as if sleeping.

"I failed," she finally said.

One eye perked open. "What were that?"

"I did not stop the Soulless."

Lester frowned.

"I have burdened the man I love with a child he is not ready for and helped bring the Passionate together with promises of a better life, all while they're being murdered in the dark. How could I have been so wrong?"

"Hm."

"And now I will die in childbirth, and the Soulless will be born, just as they were."

Lester grunted. "Are you all that important then—what the world can't turn without?"

Alexia swiveled to him, shocked.

"Don't forget, Sparrow, the world was before you and it will go on after. We do the best what we can in the little time we're allowed."

"I am not ready to die."

"Then don't."

She scowled at him. "But how can I prevent it?"

He smirked. "Heal faster."

*Faster.* Alexia knew she could speed time, but her mother had warned against it as she couldn't control the world around her and risked dying in the process. But what if she could do it only for herself—speed only her own clock?

"Is that possible?"

"And much, much more."

She may still be able to do it, to save the Passionate by stopping the Soulless—but she would have to be strong. So much stronger than the time remaining dictated.

Lester nodded. "You've a baby to birth. Go to it."

***

Alexia screamed and pushed. Kiren wished he could ease her pain, that he could do more than kneel at her side and pray.

"Little more now," Mae encouraged, poised to catch the infant with gloved hands. Kiren held Alexia's fingers, brushing sweaty hair back from her face. His skin was stained in blood, her blood, but the only thing he could see was her, the woman he felt certain he was about to lose.

She gasped for air, chin tilted toward the ceiling.

He gasped along with her, unable to adequately catch his breath, like his lungs were being crushed by the weight of what he knew was coming. He'd heard stories of his people and their births. Often either mother or baby did not survive. But he wasn't willing to lose Alexia, and if she thought she was going to leave him alone with an infant in his arms, she was sorely mistaken.

"Once more," Mae called, and Alexia bore down. "I have a head!"

Kiren leaned forward, curious. Mae gave him dagger eyes. He backed away and wrapped an arm around Alexia's shoulders, bracing her up. "You are almost done. You can do this."

She nodded, lips pinched in determination.

One more surge and the infant was free. Kiren watched in awe as Mae twirled and slapped the tiny thing on the rump. Its mouth opened in a wail.

"Do you hear that?" Kiren asked. "That is your baby."

But Alexia wasn't listening. Her head drooped back, mouth cracked open, skin pallid. Kiren shook her. Her head wobbled, uncontrolled.

# Fifty-Six

# *Crossed Swords*

Leofrik kicked the final man aside, leaving three unconscious and bleeding men on the floor.

A battle cry came from behind. He turned and lifted his blade, arms weak from dispatching the three assailants. A heavy blade slammed into his, knocking him back a step.

Ulric's clenched teeth caught the torchlight. "I could make you great." He whirled in and swung again.

Leofrik barely deflected the blow.

"A knight of your own realm. Rich."

Another jab. Leofrik blocked, jolting his weary arms. He held his ground.

"All you have to do is bring them to me." Ulric slammed his weapon down, catching Leofrik's blade in a cross. "We will be more powerful than you can imagine, more than even the holy Church!"

The sword raked free. They circled.

"What is your response to that?" Ulric asked. "Two powerful men shaping the world in their image. You and me."

It could be his—the power of these immortals. He'd seen through Velia's mind how Ulric had controlled her, even against her will. She'd had to obey, even if she fought his orders. An unwilling but obedient slave. How much good could he do with the gifts he'd seen exercised while in their camp? Cloaking darkness. Putting people to sleep. Inflicting pain. Altering time.

Leofrik ingested the reality. It was one he'd been facing since the moment he glimpsed Velia, first felt her vulnerability in his carefully laid trap. How amazing it had been to transport an army across continents without the use of ships or coin! How fantastic to feel the freedom of being anywhere in the blink of an eye. He could conquer the world.

But Velia was dead. She'd spared his life, then sacrificed her own for him—even after he imprisoned her and forced her hand. Despite her mental enslavement to Ulric, she'd found the power to defy him, enough to keep her people from being captured, even while having to obey him. She wanted only one thing: freedom for her child.

Leofrik saw his opening. He caught Ulric's retreating foot with his own and tripped him, throwing the nobleman on his back. Ulric's weapon clattered across the stone.

Leofrik pressed his sword to the man's neck. "You are not worthy to lead."

Ulric grinned. "So kill me. When word of your betrayal reaches your fellows in Jerusalem, they will come after you themselves. You will be hunted for slaying me. Hunted, punished, stripped of your title."

Instead of wielding a sword with the Church's backing, he'd become a criminal. Leofrik cringed at the truth. He hadn't anticipated surviving this, but he just might. Now that he'd met Velia's child, he wanted to live. He wanted to care for her and protect her among her kind. She would be his own daughter.

"It is a price I will have to pay." Leofrik readied to thrust.

Inky coldness seeped up from the floor. It lapped over his feet in waves of blackness and gushed into Ulric's nose, mouth, and ears. The nobleman's body shook, eyes rolling back in their sockets.

Leofrik backed away, terrified of being tainted. The smoke disappeared into his enemy, and the man rose to his feet, his skin a shade grayer. His eyes popped open, glowing a vibrant crimson. He grinned like a jackal. The very essence of evil saturated the air, so thick it clogged Leofrik's throat.

Ulric snatched up his sword. His voice echoed with a timbre far deeper than the man's. "Face me, knight."

# Fifty-Seven

## *The End*

"No! Alexia, no." Kiren felt for a pulse. It was fleeting, slowly dimming. "Stay with me!"

No response.

Kiren delved, following the flow of blood as it stilled. All was in proper order, the organs intact, her wound from earlier adequately healed, but her heart continued to slow. And then he felt it.

A subtle jolt—an electrical surge that counteracted her hearts efforts, strangling the muscle. He traced the energy to its source and his eyes popped open.

The medallion.

It couldn't be worn by anyone except his direct bloodline, and Alexia no longer carried his child.

He tore the necklace from around her neck and Alexia gasped. Her heart thundered again in his ears. She reached up and touched something on his cheek, something wet. Tears.

She smiled and leaned into his embrace.

***

Tiny fingers slipped through Alexia's as she marveled at the little wonder in her arms. A tangle of fiery hair curled from the babe's scalp, her nose so petite, her mouth open as her head shifted.

Alexia laughed. Her baby. This tiny wonder had come from her, and here it lay, the most incredible thing in the world.

Kiren knelt beside her, gazing in awe at the bundle. He had done she-didn't-know-what to help her heal, but she felt amazing, even more amazing from the astonishment and unbridled love in his wide eyes as he examined the child. Mae had exited for fresh water, leaving them alone.

Kiren knew now. Perhaps she should have kept the truth from him, but it was too late. She was not going through childbirth again just to keep him from realizing he had a child.

He touched the little girl's face. "What will we call her?"

*We.* Her heart jolted at the word. They were a we at last. She wanted to name her Sarah, but doing so felt like conceding that her sister was dead for good. No, their child needed a name that reflected this moment, the crowning change brought to both her parents, the most amazing thing Alexia had ever done. She knew the name before she'd even considered it, for she had met her daughter in the future. "Corona."

His eyes met hers, smile slipping. "How can you place that burden upon such a tiny thing?"

Alexia timidly slipped a hand onto his forearm, unable to meet his gaze. "She will not have a burden to bear so long as her father lives."

He hissed in air.

Quiet.

A long silence.

She finally looked up at him. His brow scrunched inward, eyes worried. He swallowed loudly.

"You will become a worthy king, a man of the people."

He opened his mouth to protest.

She lifted a hand. "That is not fair to you, but regardless of how you feel about it"—she tickled the little one's cheek—"Corona bears your heritage and your blood. If you refuse the throne, it will fall to her." Alexia wrapped the babe a little tighter. "When I am gone—"

"You are not going anywhere."

She sighed. "If it will ease your burden, I shall place her in someone else's care."

"No." He trailed fingers through the baby's twisted locks. "She is mine." A vein in his neck pulsed, his jaw flexing and loosening. "You both are. I will raise her, and so will you." His eyes burned into her, brows low, daring her to counter his statement.

She gave him a weak smile. "I should rest now."

He took the child from her arms and rose. She felt like she'd been robbed. Whatever precious few moments she had with her daughter, this may be it. She didn't want to sleep. Didn't want to let the infant go. But her body weighed like bricks, her eyelids leaden and drooping.

Darkness claimed her consciousness.

\*\*\*

Kiren held his sleeping baby girl, astonished that anything so small and perfect could exist. Flesh of his flesh, bone of his bone, and terrifyingly vulnerable. He cradled her closer and paced slowly across the old barn. His boot smacked something. It skidded to a halt three steps before him.

The pendant Alexia had worn.

It was his. From the future. It made sense now. She had carried his child, his blood, and thus she'd been able to bear the thing, but the instant his child was no longer within her, the medallion had attacked. Now it was a hazard—two of the exact same necklaces? How could it even be possible? He felt that one should melt away and cease to exist, but it remained, staring up at him.

Corona wheezed. He glanced down at the infant, so dangerously defenseless. The necklace. The baby.

He crouched and wrapped his fingers about the cool metal. A subtle energy tremored through the chain. Kiren wrapped the links over the child's head.

The necklace shrank.

He blinked twice, forcing his eyes wider. It was no mistake. The chain had become tiny, just right to fit around the infant's neck. Rightly so. It was hers now.

# Fifty-Eight

## *Kneel*

Leofrik hefted his sword between the entity-possessed Ulric and himself, every muscle in his back and arms burning in protest. "What are you?" he asked.

The thing laughed. "Fear." It stepped forward. "Hate." It advanced again. "Malice." Another step. "Chaos."

Leofrik backed away and hit the wall. Cornered. This was the thing that had taken control of Sarlic and claimed Velia's life. This was the true enemy.

The monster swelled the air around him, not just inside the possessed lord. "I am the hunger that consumes men to destroy, the rage that turns women on their children, the force that hovers without, waiting to control all. I am eternal. Unending. Unstoppable."

*Unstoppable.* Leofrik doubted that. Anything could be stopped—even time. He needed to figure out this riddle, to win a few more moments for his brain to work. "Where did you come from?"

Ulric-non-Ulric grinned, his crimson eyes the thing of nightmares. "The in-between."

"I do not understand."

"The lock is broken. The worlds will merge once more. The Unnatural cracked the seal, my prison, and now I will reign over this earth until it is only fire and ash."

Possessed Ulric stopped right in front of Leofrik. The air stilled. The world chilled to a winter's night. Hope bled away from him in waves. This was it. The creature would consume him and exert its will through him.

"What do you want of me?" Leofrik choked out.

"Your service."

"In helping you destroy the world?"

"It is destroyed. You cannot see it now, but you will."

No! He would not give in to despair! Leofrik shoved his blade upward, through chainmail and straight into Ulric's gut.

Ulric/the entity calmly looked down at the weapon protruding from its belly and back up at Leofrik. Ulric's body dropped.

A cold wind washed over Leofrik, and then came the night.

# Fifty-Nine

# *Forever*

Kiren worried over Alexia as she slept. She woke only to feed her baby, and then dove back into a leaden slumber. He cleaned the old barn while she rested, dosing her with energy every few minutes. He paced. He held the baby. He ran through all the reasons she slept through three straight days, and could quantify none of them.

Mae stopped in to report that Amos and Regin had returned to camp, pleased with their campaign. They carried word that Lord Ulric had been slain and the castle raid was blamed on a rivaling Baron.

Now people were preparing to depart for the gateway Deamus insisted he could open. Though part of him hoped, Kiren knew it was impossible. And even if it wasn't, he had to be here for Alexia.

He listened to Mae's updates with half a heart, budging only to accept food from Zeph. Alexia's body healed far too rapidly. Kiren wished he could claim her rapid recovery as his doing, but he was not the master behind it. Mae didn't know how to substantiate the rate at which Alexia was mending either, but she affirmed that her dear friend had "healed in a matter of days what normally takes six months."

There had been no more deaths in camp as everyone was watching, and no one traveled alone, even for water. On the third day, a small group appeared at the barn to see the baby and inquire about Alexia. Kiren kept the visit short.

After they left, he placed his head in his hands, praying silently for his wife.

\*\*\*

Alexia woke to Kiren kneeling over her in the darkness, staring earnestly into her eyes—like he had so many times upon waking in their shared bed.

"How long have I been…?"

"Four days. You should eat." He lifted a bowl of porridge, something she recalled being spoon fed between slumbering.

She sat and took the earthenware from him with thanks. While she ate, Mae arrived. Kiren spoke with the woman quietly, then handed their slumbering child over. Alexia rose to protest until he turned to her. His eyes brimmed with oscillating emotions: fear, relief, joy, such longing…

\*\*\*

Kiren fastened the door behind Mae, who was taking the babe to meet the Lost Ones. He left everything but his wife outside.

The child was alive. Alexia had survived. His wife and his child lived, and now he had promises to fulfill.

Alexia watched him, her chest rising and falling in the light through the rafters. There would be no moon tonight. The perfect time for bonding. Light glistened over her wild curls, turning them half golden. All else faded to darkness around her. She was his angel. His redeeming soulmate. His forever.

They rushed to one another in the same instant. Bodies collided. Mouths locked. Teeth clicked and teased in play so elegant it could only be called art: the art of two souls as they merged to one.

*How?* he asked. How was she whole?

*Time traveler's secrets,* she teased.

Kiren slipped Alexia's clothing free, marveling at the feel of her skin, shivering with anticipation, his own and hers. At last he would claim her entirely. She would be his.

She laughed and leaned back. "Yes, and you are mine."

"But you chose me. How did that come about?"

"Shall I show you?" She pressed up against him, lighting his skin on fire.

The whole world existed within her embrace. He was lost in the darkened forest of her eyes, and yet all this paled to what she offered him now. The truth. The future. A priceless chalice filled with her secrets.

But something irked him. She had been seen, known by another man. Another him. The idea made him want to burst into flame. She should be his entirely, not shared by some shadow from a time to come. He ground his teeth together. "What kind of husband am I in the future to abandon you to this fate?"

Her gaze lifted to his mouth. "The kind who listens to his wife. Now fulfill your promise, or I will be forced to fulfill it for you."

Desire trampled through him—hers, the suppressed longing from the last many weeks—its potency dragging him beneath the swells of a consuming ocean. He was drowning in it and she was his only lifeline. He gave into the hunger, battling with his rage. Each touch drew him deeper, each brush with her mind lulling him closer until he'd lost himself completely, not knowing where he ended and she began. Her mind, her soul opened to him and he saw all: a young Alexia terrified and fascinated by the blue-eyed man who haunted her dreams. How she sought him out to discover the truth about the Passionate and sacrificed her sister in order to preserve his life. She had loved him so deeply—

the patient man who was willing to risk everything for her and his people—that she gave up her entire life to become part of his.

Was it possible to cheat on himself?

The final image of her leaving him for the purpose of saving so many lives, it broke him completely. She'd given up the thing she wanted most for the good of all the Lost Ones. Worse, he knew she must be correct after all he'd seen. She would die in this time.

His throat tightened, and he held her tighter as they lay together. "How is it possible for me to continue on if you...?"

She gave him a sad smile. "It must be because I am out of proper time. I will not be born for many centuries yet to come."

Centuries. The magnitude of what she'd told him sank in. She would be gone shortly, and he would not see her, touch her, speak with her again for *centuries*. His heart squeezed. She didn't deserve to have her fate decided before she'd even been conceived. This noble, independent woman should have the freedom to choose what she would become. He wanted that. He wanted so much, but most of all, her happiness. What had a life with him given her—a baby? A death sentence far from her home and loved ones?

Condemned. He had condemned her the instant they first touched. She deserved to live. He wanted her to live.

Perhaps if he could stay away from her, she would have a chance for true happiness. Perhaps it might be what kept her alive. He needed it to be what kept her alive because...

He loved her.

Loved her with all his heart.

He held perfectly still, lips nearly grazing hers. "How could you not have told me?"

Alexia traced his collarbone, leaving a trail of fire. "You were not my Kiren, and you were not ready for me. How would you have reacted if I had claimed I carried your child?"

He frowned. "I would like to think I would have taken you to wife a great deal sooner, but I am afraid I would have behaved badly."

"As if you did not behave badly enough."

He laughed and brushed his lips across her cheek. "You wanted every kiss."

"I did." A raspy breath escaped her.

"But?"

"Not for the reasons you kissed me." She nipped at his ear, fingers tracing the sensitive skin of his neck and stoking the inferno to a new blaze. It wasn't fair that she knew all his weaknesses and he knew none of hers. "You would have felt obligated to care for me based solely on the baby, and I did not want you bound by your future."

"Perhaps you should have asked my opinion on the matter."

Over the next hour she told him about her family and home, about her childhood and the appearances he made throughout it, how her memories were taken at Father's insistence. She outlined her mission to stop the Soulless. He could hardly fathom a fate more terrifying than becoming one of these undying creatures, but as she detailed each aspect of their existence, he concluded along with her that these monsters must never exist, and that he must do all in his power to aid her. Even if it meant losing her.

She slid her fingers through his. "In the future, it is you who will shield me from what is in your heart and mind…and I am afraid you must."

"And why is that?"

She rubbed his arm, tracing the muscles. "Just as you were not ready to know your fate, neither shall I be. I must discover for myself the truths of this life. Knowing will destroy me. You cannot tell me any of what is to come when we meet."

"It would not have been easier for you—"

Her head was already shaking. "Kiren, promise me you will keep our secret."

The weight of her words rang through their bond. She believed them entirely.

It pained him to utter the oath she needed to hear. "You have my word."

"I did not want this for you." She toyed with her ring. "Secrets bring about mischief, but there is a time for keeping them. You will become a master keeper."

"That sounds like a happy time."

A single laugh escaped her. "There will definitely be joy." Her eyes raked up him longingly. "And other things."

He met her yearning with a deep, fire-inducing kiss.

She pushed him back. "One more thing."

"Anything." *Just stop talking so I can have my way with you.*

"Do I detect impatience?"

He growled.

"Kiren." He met her serious eyes. Her mouth puckered with emotion. "The Passionate need you."

"The what?"

"The Passionate. Our kindred."

The description fit better than anything he'd yet heard—a people so driven by emotions, needs, and powers that the world bent around them. It far outstripped the depressing title of Lost Ones he'd adopted.

"You have seen what becomes of them under your rule from my memories. They need you." She cupped his face. "I need you."

His breath caught. It was true. In the age she was born, he'd been leading the Passionate. And though there was conflict, the infrastructure of their secret government had concealed and protected her until she was ready to become his. Could he do it? Could he overcome past failure and doubts? Could he govern a people who even now may be poisoned against him?

"I know you," she whispered. "You are capable. Most will follow you, and you will be honored and revered."

Like his father. He had new purpose, a reason to be in this world and a long-standing promise to seek her out one distant day and pave the way for her survival.

"So be it," he said. "I will strive to become the man you love." His sister would have to hold her own in the other world until these vows were fulfilled.

Her grin brightened, and with it, his soul.

Alexia wrapped her arms around him. "No matter the time or age, I have always loved you. Always."

"Alexia," he drew her close, tucking his lips next to her ear.

She stopped him. "There is something I need to tell you about our daughter—"

Pounding on the door ripped them out of each other's arms.

"Arik, Alexia! God forgive me." It was Mae.

Kiren pulled on his tunic and hurried to the door. Alexia slipped on her robe as he cracked the door open.

Mae wrung her hands, face a wild mess of panic. "The baby is gone. I do not know what has happened to her. She is just gone!"

# Sixty

# Taken

The blackness cleared as Leofrik entered camp, wondering how he'd arrived there. A brick of ice hung in his chest, a chill he couldn't escape. The last thing he recalled was facing Ulric.

The immortal ones rejoiced around a fire, the scent of roast venison and crispy greens making his mouth water while toasts rang through the air. This new camp backed against a cliff of boulders. He overheard conversations of a new world and this being a final meal.

Regin wrapped an arm around his neck. "To our hero, slayin' collectors and provin' himself an ally and brother!" He lifted his waterskin, which smelled suspiciously of berry wine.

Cheers echoed his.

Regin sobered and spoke softly. "Now Velia is true and goodly avenged."

At mention of the woman, Leofrik's eyes snapped to her child, wrapped in a blanket on the far side of camp, sitting and studying the ground. He escaped the man's grasp and walked straight for the girl. She shifted up straighter, her frown fading.

"Child, it pleases me much to see you safe." He crouched down to her level.

She threw her arms around his neck. Leofrik blinked away the shock and slipped an arm around her back. Even the warmth of her embrace could not dissipate the frost around his heart.

"Mama said she would send someone. She told me he would be a knight."

Velia had never stopped believing he would fulfill his word. He squeezed the girl tighter. "I do not even know your name little one."

"Nor I yours, brave knight." She let him go, bowing her head. "I have no name."

"None? How then are you addressed?"

"Papa called me 'Poppet.'"

Leofrik scowled. "That is no kind of proper name for a child. Hm. I think from now on you shall be known as Ilaria. It was my sister's name."

Her face lit, her whole body lifting an inch from its depressed slump. "Was she beautiful?"

"Aye, but not nearly as beautiful as you shall one day be." He pulled a hand through her white gold hair, recalling her mother. "And I will be here to see it done."

Her face lit. "What does it mean, sir knight? What does my name mean?"

"Joyful or happy—for you, little Ilaria, will be a joy to me, and you shall be happy, I am determined." He slid the wooden wolf from his pocket and placed it into her grasp.

Her face lit. It dimmed just as quickly. "Everyone is leaving soon, going somewhere strange or away on their own. You will stay with me? Mama could never stay."

"I will. Always."

## Sixty-One

## Complete

Deamus accepted the babe from the knight and pulled back her swaddling to reveal the necklace. It hummed with energy. Now he had all he needed.

"Thank you, Leofrik."

The knight lifted his head, and crimson eyes speared Deamus through. Deamus shivered. Those eyes resurrected a memory, something more than the recent attacks and the entity in the darkness. A force. It had taken possession of his mother when she threw herself at Father, scraping at his arms and face with her bare nails as he fought through the final incantation to seal the gateway. Neither Deamus nor his brother had been able to restrain her.

Deamus shifted backward. "Are you my ally or enemy?"

The thing in the knight's skin tilted its head. "I am whatever you make me." Its voice weighed like stone, with a cadence of rushing water. "You uttered the words that broke my seal. You have a choice."

Deamus clenched a fist, holding himself perfectly still. "Then be my ally."

It stared at him longer. "Open the gate."

He turned to obey, leaving the thing in the field and fleeing to the clearing where thirteen Passionate waited for "entry" to the other world

# Sixty-Two

## *Wrong*

Leofrik shuddered awake. He stood in a field, his arms cold where a weight had recently left them. He twisted, confused and strangely empty. One moment he'd been speaking with Ilaria, and now here he was. The ice in his lungs was gone. He felt entirely himself, albeit he couldn't staunch this sense that something was wrong. Terribly wrong.

# Sixty-Three

# *Saturate*

No matter how they sprinted, leaving Zeph to retrieve Mae, it wasn't fast enough. Alexia held in a shattered cry as she skidded to a halt in camp.

"Corona…"

The space was empty. Wisps of smoke curled from an extinguished fire. The Passionate were all gone. All of them—the remaining twenty-three.

Alexia fell to her knees. "My baby…" She could be anywhere—spread to the far winds with any of the departed. Mae had confessed handing off the child to Oriel, who passed the babe to Silivia, who shared her with Lucian until she'd lost track of the little one. Everyone had wanted to see the child. It was an innocent mistake.

A costly one.

Something hard pressed against her knee. Alexia unearthed a sword that looked like Leofrik's. Why would he leave his sword behind?

Kiren landed at her side, his soul equally pained. "She has to be…she cannot be far. Come on." He tugged at her arm, getting to his feet. "We will find her. She is out there."

Alexia nodded and got up, taking the sword with her. She strapped it at her side and turned in a circle. "Which way?"

Kiren turned to the horizon. "I have a feeling…"

"The gateway," they said in unison.

Kiren grabbed her hand and yanked her forward.

***

Every second was killing her. Alexia took Kiren's hand and pulled him into slowed time, running faster than she'd ever run. She'd done this once before, to save his life. They could share their gifts through the bond, but he was so caught up in his determined gait, his cool rage seeping through their connection, that he didn't say anything.

Kiren squeezed her fingers and she glanced at him. His jaw clenched with determination, his eyes lances of fiery ice. This was the side of him she'd ached to see, the purpose and focus, his direction sure. He was going to save their child.

Voices carried through the trees—a low bass hum. Alexia's heart leapt. Perhaps they weren't too late. Perhaps her child was on the other side of those trees!

She let go of time, and they burst through the shrubbery. Kiren yanked her to a stop. Seven men on horseback turned their direction. Soldiers.

They must have followed Leofrik or the others.

Kiren's grip on her hand tightened. He backed away. Alexia followed, watching the men warily. Hands rested on weapons, heads tilted. Two horses left the group, circling around them.

"We have no time for this," Kiren muttered.

"Ho there, and where be ye runnin' so fast?" one man asked.

Alexia readied to stop time, to slow it, something, when Kiren tugged her arms around him. He clasped a fist around his medallion and brought the other hand down at a sharp angle. The sky boomed. Electricity cut through the clouds and pummeled into the ground. Men flew every direction. The earth heaved. Alexia clung to Kiren, his knees steady as the world shook about them. Horses screamed and hooves pounded away.

Quiet filled the grove. She looked up. Men lay sprawled across the forest floor, one or two on their knees, trembling and cowering.

Kiren groaned. "I was saving that for whoever took Corona."

She turned to him. "Have you always been able to do that?"

He leaned back. "And you profess to know me."

She took his hand and they hurried forward.

"It struck me last time," he said. "I didn't know if it would work the way I asked."

Alexia smiled.

"I have just wasted our only weapon."

"Not our only one." She shook her head.

No reply. His eyes were fixed straight ahead.

Light burst through the trees before them, a pillar of brilliance stretching beyond their view into the heavens.

Something yanked at her chest, tugging her forward as if she were tethered to a rope on a pulley. Kiren gasped. One hand flew to his sternum.

The gateway.

If Kiren's only weapon had been utilized, he was no good to her, and fearing for his safety would only hinder her. Alexia froze time, pressed a kiss to his still lips, and tore through the distance. Air fell heavily in her lungs, moving like putty, but she forced it to flow. The stillness parted for her, creating a tunnel of freedom. She had never been so alive, so free. This must be what Lester felt when he ran—that the world was his to control.

Branches parted.

Alexia froze. People knelt or lay prostrate, writhing, their faces contorted in pain. Skin had shriveled, forms thinned to a structure of bone and flesh until she barely recognized them—like how she'd first discovered Mae. A stream of something translucent tugged from their chests to Deamus's open hand where he stood, silhouetted by light, *holding her baby* and funneling power into the gateway.

Thirteen of the Passionate. Amos. Sarlic. Oriel. Filia. Oluchi. Silivia. Beatrice. So many others. No Regin, Willem, or Lucian...

She wobbled forward, Deamus's face coming into focus. He was grinning like a lunatic.

A madman.

The Soulless were born because thirteen souls gave themselves into the hands of a madman. It was happening. This was the moment.

Alexia stepped closer and froze. A barely visible ribbon hung in the air before her nose, coursing from the trees beyond, straight to Deamus. She squinted and focused on several other streams, eleven thicker sources. Each of the remaining Passionate. But there were more, narrower threads, hundreds of them stretching beyond her senses.

The gateway had been open mere seconds, and already Amos and Oriel looked close to death.

Deamus was using them to get home. He either didn't intend to bring them with him or was blind to what he was doing—controlled by the entity. The Passionate would be dead before he finished his escape.

All of them.

Had he been using them all along? Using her? She'd trusted him entirely, believed in him, even considered him a friend. This must be the entity's doing.

Her nails cut into her palms. Somehow she could stop him, keep him from destroying the Passionate. And she would.

Alexia stalked forward, fists balled, ready to shatter Deamus's nose if that was what it took to put him down.

A chilly breeze curled around her wrist.

She twisted around, startled. Nothing filled the space but a murky cloud, yet in the cloud she sensed something more: Intelligence. Malice. Despair.

The Soul Eater.

It reared up in front of her, creating a wall. Its tentacles spread across the space before her, reaching out and touching each of the dying Passionate. Sinister joy filled its presence.

Alexia stumbled backward. She had no weapon to fight this. A dagger could not wound something without a body. It was not bound by the laws of time like every other foe she'd faced. She could feel the thing grinning at her as each tentacle became a hook. They slammed into the thirteen Passionate like daggers. Their bodies jolted.

"Stop!" she begged.

The blackness pulsed with glee, mocking her.

She had to stop it. What had Grandfather told her?

That she would need Mae.

Alexia swiveled around, but her friend was not among the prostrate nor in the woods beyond.

The Passionate were doomed.

The black cloud lifted a limb over Alexia, the end forming a barb. She dodged to the left, releasing time and rolling onto the ground. Strength surged from her center, sucked free. She shrieked.

Deamus's head turned her direction. His grin widened. He licked his lips.

Alexia curled into the mossy ground, helpless against the foe. No, not helpless. Even if every advantage was ripped away, she would save her baby, the Passionate, her husband.

She had to stop Deamus.

Alexia's limbs trembled. She was freezing, like the marrow had been sucked out of her bones as surely as when the Soulless attacked. She didn't have much left. She could stop time again and face the monstrous essence that would take possession of her soul. But there was no escape.

This was always where she'd been meant to die.

She should have brought Kiren with her. At least then she'd have someone to turn to in the end, a way to confess her eternal love, her remorse, to beg his forgiveness for sacrificing herself so foolishly.

Now that it was here, she didn't want to die.

# Sixty-Four

# *Inside*

Alexia lifted her sword. She needed Mae. She had to save her baby. She had to save the Passionate!

Every desperate instinct balled in her chest and tightened. They squeezed and twisted in such a fury of need that they tore at her very cells.

Her desperation exploded. The world shattered around her like glass, the fragments dancing outward and freezing. They hung suspended around her in a vast nothingness. No ground beneath her feet. No sky above her head. She floated with the fragments, but she wasn't outside of time. She hadn't slowed or stopped time.

Each shard of reality depicted a different moment, a different person, a completely different reality. In one, John held Sarah's hand as her sister stared into the eyes of their surviving baby. In another, Father played peek-a-boo with toddler Corona. Another showed Miles living in a country cottage where his children played while his parents stood on either side of him, beaming. Each of her friends and loved ones dangled about her, all with their happiest possible life.

"Where am I?" she muttered.

"Yer inside time," Grandfather's voice echoed.

She twisted and found his face reflected in one of the fragments.

"You have slowed time, sped it, escaped it, and altered it. You've stepped outside before, but now yer at its core. Breathe it in, Sparrow." He grinned. "You *are* the Maiden of Time."

She closed her eyes and stretched out her hands, relaxing and inhaling. Her mind burst wide open and she saw everything: a beautiful queen giving birth to Kiren, a giant explosion on the yet unknown American continent in the far future, the birth of the Soulless… Not only could she see everything, she could feel every possibility. In the blink of a second, all was laid before her. What would happen if Kiren were never born? His father would die in a war, leaving no heir. The far distant explosion in America would mark a new era for peace and world order that the Passionate couldn't even begin to imagine. And the Soulless…

The Soul Eater. It was the essence of the Soulless. It would be contained within thirteen of the most selfless Passionate. But what if it wasn't? Alexia watched as the darkness infested the leaders of each nation, one by one, turning them on each other. Mass genocide. War and fires. Destruction. The annihilation of one kingdom after another until the final man pressed a button and burned the Earth to nothing with a weapon too horrifying to exist.

But must the Soulless exist? There had to be another way.

She tweaked time so that she didn't liberate Deamus from his tree prison. The darkness was freed by someone in the other world, and when the gateway opened between worlds, it slipped through and destroyed everything.

She went back and placed Mae at the gateway when the thing entered. Her friend absorbed the entity's strength and stopped it from reaching its goal. All was well. But Mae started lashing out at people. Small things at first: snapping at perceived offenses, stealing bits of energy to silence people she didn't like, consuming greater quantities of power for the high it gave her. In time she was clearing entire villages for the joy of people's screams. Then she was razing the Earth.

Alexia tried again, destroying both of Kiren's medallions so that the gateway could never be opened. Ages went by. Kiren lost his purpose, even the desire to lead the Passionate. He was tired. Eventually he and several of the Passionate fell into the hands of future doctors, then scientists. These men and women prodded and poked until they tapped into the source of Passionate power. After decades of experiments, they pulled so hard on a primal force that they tore a hole in the seam between worlds. The darkness leaked through.

She explored infinite possibilities and every single one resulted in chaos winning. Except for one.

The Soulless must become.

If the darkness was trapped within the breast of thirteen of the purest Passionate who lacked access to their gifts, the rest of the world would live. The rest of the Passionate would live. These thirteen would become the eternal embodiment of the Soul Eater's monstrous appetite. Corporeal prisons.

The lesser of evils.

Alexia came back in time not to stop the Soulless, but to create them. She had always been destined to do this.

And of her baby… A lifetime rushed upon her: she left the darkness behind and fled with her husband and child to this other world. She listened to Kiren sing lullabies to Corona every night, swelled with pride over her little girl's first word, rejoiced over her daughter's first step, ached when Corona fell and broke her first bone, dressed her daughter up in beautiful gowns, and thought her heart would explode with love when a little brother was born. Each success and failure filled her heart. Her young ones grew. They began to use eloquent language, fulfilling the role of princess and prince while their father ruled the land, always guided and consoled by Alexia. The children matured into stunning young people. They married. They brought the greatest joy to Alexia through grandchildren. Her life was beautiful and so full. Kiren's smile lines deepened with time, but he never aged, and she remained youthful along with him—whether because of their bond or her natural gifts, they never knew or cared. And then the day it all ended. When the man destroyed the Earth, her world burned as well. It melted from the inside out because of the metaphysical bond between worlds.

Alexia could barely breathe for the sweetness and sorrow of all she'd experienced. It was a full life, and it was hers. She could have it if she wished.

But there was another possibility. Many years of pain, loneliness, and suffering stretched out before her, but in the end, grievances would be answered. Mae would marry. Miles would find love. And Sarah…

She squinted into the murk of possibilities.

Her sister, her best friend, the one person she couldn't stand to have lost…

Alexia stood in Mae's inn the day Sarah had taken her own life after the stillbirth of her child. John set Sarah's dead body at Alexia's feet. She crumpled over her sister, tracing the raven curls that hid sightless eyes. Tears spilled down her cheeks. It didn't matter that it had happened a year ago but not for another five hundred years. The pain was here and now. Alexia remembered the squeal of joy as two young girls gallivanted through Father's gardens, mucking their dress hems and shoes. She felt the press of down blankets while a storm lashed at the windows, Sarah's protective arms wrapped around her. She grinned into the mirror as Sarah pulled a brush through her hair, their discussion of prospective beaus both disgruntling and hilarious.

Alexia touched her sister's unmoving breast. Borrowing unintentionally from Kiren's gift, she found Sarah's heart, stilled because it had bled out after being pierced with a dagger that could kill the Soulless. Her sister who had been the most vibrant person she knew. So full of life. Now empty.

But it didn't have to be that way. "I can still save Sarah."

Time rearranged itself to Mae's hidden cellar as Sarah lifted the dagger to her chest. Alexia reach out on instinct, not knowing what she was doing or how, and tapped her sister's brow. Sarah's mind froze. Her heart stopped instantly, her life essence lifting free and hanging, suspended within time. The dagger pierced Sarah's skin, but it did not penetrate to her heart. It stopped shy and, though her body appeared dead, she lived.

Inside time.

Alexia sped to the night John went to bury Sarah. Her brother-in-law stood, stars mocking him from above, looking down on his lifeless wife. He lifted the shovel to dig an inelegant hole, and crumpled. He couldn't do it. He wept over her for hours until at last, he rose and faced the cold stars, his jaw set with rage. He stomped away. Alexia pushed her sister's life back into her and touched Kiren's mind. "Give her strength. Save her. But you cannot let me know. I must go back. You know I must."

Kiren emerged from the inn, scratching his head. He saw Sarah's prone body. Following Alexia's guidance, he touched her.

And Sarah gasped, eyes launching wide.

Alexia withdrew from the future/past and found herself back inside time, all realities twinkling around her. Sarah would live. That single assurance filled her with so much joy she could barely contain it. But what about herself? Was being inside of time what would cost her life?

Snatches of life created a hallway, glimmers of playing with Sarah in her father's woods, meeting Bellezza in a dark cellar and finding Baron Galedrew dead, Kiren kissing her on Father's roof as the sunrise filtered around them… Every moment flickered before her—snippets she'd forgotten, times she'd dreaded being a woman, the tension and joys of finally learning her identity… All things she recalled. Nothing new.

A door appeared between fragments. It was detailed by three swirling vortexes, each with moving hands like the face of a different clock. Intricate lattice work had her reaching for the wood and metal frame before she'd realized it.

"Stop!"

She paused.

Grandfather's voice echoed over her shoulder. "That door be what leads to the end of time."

"I only wished to know what will become of me."

"Alexia, step through that door and you'll end time."

She backed away. "But my pathway leads to this door."

"Not yet."

She glanced back at him, a face in a sliver of glass. "I am destined to end time?"

"It's the end of *yer* time."

She was definitely not ready for that.

Off to save both worlds and begin the reign of the Soulless then. No wonder Kiren had called their death a release. It was a release from their guardianship of terrors no mortal could bear. They gave all people the greatest service through their unending misery. Truly, their death was a mercy, a well-earned mercy. So long as there were enough Soulless to fragment the Soul Eater, it would never gain its freedom.

They would sacrifice all, and Alexia only had to offer…her daughter.

These memories inside of time would have to be enough for her aching mother-heart. "I am so sorry, Corona." Her baby would not have her parents as she grew. It was the only way.

Time for the Soulless to be born.

Alexia settled into Kiren's arms in the barn an hour earlier. Mae stood at the door, a hand clenched at her collar after announcing that Corona was missing. Kiren sped out into the night. Alexia paused beside her friend. "You must go to the field where the others went, to the gateway. Keep your distance. When I arrive, come to me. Remember what we practiced? Pushing energy away from you?"

Mae turned sad eyes on her, startled. She gave a firm nod.

"Tonight we prove you. Tonight we birth the Soulless."

And then Alexia returned. From inside time.

Screams and flickering energy clogged the air, set against a backdrop of light where she lay sprawled on the ground, life bleeding from her and into Deamus's gateway. The entity created an impenetrable net between Alexia and the gateway.

Moment of truth.

# Sixty-Five

# Reaper

Feet stopped next to Alexia's face. Mae crouched over her, the gateway siphon pulling from her chest as well—except she had the power to pull back. She gave Alexia a nod and unclasped her bracelet.

Nothing happened.

Ironic. All that effort, all her hope… Perhaps the vision had been a wishful thing, not a reality.

The veil of darkness shivered.

*Or perhaps not.*

The pitch wobbled and fell to the ground, a writhing mist, snakes of smoke.

"It must go into them." Alexia waved to the thirteen.

Mae's brow crinkled as she focused, grunting as she pushed outward with both hands. The snakes continued to squirm. A voiceless laugh swirled through the air.

Mae was losing.

Abruptly, the laugh stopped. Mists grated across the ground, forcefully slipping toward the thirteen, like grains of black sugar through a funnel. The darkness entered each body, and their friends jolted in protest.

Deamus stood above all this, focused on the incandescence before him, hardly aware that he still held Corona.

Alexia lifted her head. With the chaos contained, she had to save her child and send Corona off to her fate. Time to fight for her baby.

The gateway illuminated Deamus's face as he tilted his head back, washing away the shadows and irradiating his utter look of bliss. Did he know what he was doing? If he was still possessed by the entity and stepped into this other world, he would carry that monster with him. Unwittingly. She had to stop him.

His foot lifted and he stepped forward.

Alexia slid the sword from her belt and lifted onto her elbows, grating her teeth as her lungs crushed together.

Deamus's leg disappeared into the light, his body swaying forward.

"Alexia!"

Her name registered, but she hadn't the strength to acknowledge it, only enough stamina to freeze time.

Deamus's back slipped into the brilliance.

She yanked the seconds to a growing stillness and shoved off the ground, weapon clutched in one fist. She surged forward.

A mist of ebony reared up before her, all that remained of the malicious cloud. She sliced through it with her saber, rending it like a slicing a sheer drapery. The shreds grazed her arms, clawing at her like dying insects as she sprinted for the light. The air vibrated with a silent wail as the onyx smog slithered free of her skin and faded.

Luminescence shimmered before her, humming with energy. Its ethereal glow began to dim.

Alexia leapt at it.

# Sixty-Six

# *Walls of Light*

Warmth sheered over Alexia, like passing through glass as it scraped at her skin, closing in. She shoved through it.

Her ears popped.

Relief. Calm.

Like being in the absence of time.

Her lungs expanded. Panting hard, she tightened her grip on the sword as strength returned to her limbs. Walls of light encircled her, shrinking existence to a ring thrice as wide as she was tall.

Deamus stood with his back to her—the only shadow in the tunnel of brilliance.

He turned, his grin widening. "Ah, you decided to join me." It was Deamus's voice, but it boomed with confidence he'd never had. He must be infested by the darkness.

His features morphed, reflected in glistening waves of light. His overt nose melted down to slightly larger than average. His receded chin broadened as his cheekbones sharpened. His skin warmed to peachy rather than pasty, and she was staring into the assured smirk of a man with perfect teeth. Hair melted from dark blonde to midnight black. His eyes were the biggest difference: pits as deep and dark as eternity, his spectacles crushed beneath his foot. Here stood a stranger.

She'd seen that face before. It gripped something inside her, shortening her breath, but she couldn't recall why.

Alexia held her sword between them, focused on the bundle in his arms. Corona hadn't stirred. "Who are you?"

"You do not recognize me?"

She couldn't decide if the entity inhabited him, but no red glow appeared in his eyes. "Deamus?"

"Yes, that is my name." He scratched his nose.

"You used me? Used all of us?"

He shrugged. "I could not very well explain that everyone had to die in order to open the gate, now could I?" His shoulders sagged, face twisting in a timid grimace that reminded her of her Deamus, even on this stranger's face. "...I...I...I need your lives to go home!"

Her mouth fell open. Her airways constricted, this reality too painful to consider. It had been an act, his clumsiness, his bumbling, his endearing need for her. He had been deceiving her all along. She shook her head, conflicted whether to be angry or sad.

"Do not fear it now, Alexia. I always believed you would make a worthy companion on the other side. You may still, even if you did choose *him*." He sneered.

That sneer. Memory rushed in, the face she'd seen in Kiren's nightmares time and time again, the man who stood in the ashes of a burned home, laughing as Kiren cringed with his twin sister, only children in the giant's shadow. The man her husband feared. The man he hated. The man who took everything from him.

Her breath caught. "You killed his family."

He waved a dismissive hand, the one not holding her baby. "Death is part of life. If I stopped for every bleeding heart or sobbing child, I would be as noble and dead as the High King."

Her blade had begun to dip. She straightened it between them and reached for the threads of time. The High King had been Kiren's father, a title he would inherit one day.

Deamus lifted long fingers in a staying gesture. "I can feel that, Alexia. The energy shifts so subtly, but it whispers to me. I feel everything."

She froze.

"The babe sleeps, and she will stay that way forever unless I wake her. Let us have a reasonable discussion without you using your powers and me having to make a terrible mess."

Not only had he deceived her about his nature, but his power. The glint in his eye said he could flick his wrist and cut her thread.

She licked her lips. "Why would you kill the High King?"

"Have you not figured it out yet? I gave you all the clues."

Thoughts bounced frantically. He'd been there when the gateway opened the first time. It was opened by a man with two sons, a powerful man who controlled the elements.

"You are one of the sons."

He pointed. "I knew you would reach it eventually. But which one am I, Alexia? Good or evil? Cunning or loyal?"

*Cunning. Broken. Wrong.*

"Say it out loud. Do not tell me your courage has failed you," he teased.

If he was so cunning and wicked, why wasn't he attacking her? He wanted something from her. Or needed. "Give me my baby, Deamus, and tell me what you want. We will figure out how to make it work."

"Can you give me my birthright?" His voice drooped with mocking sorrow. "It seems Daddy did not think I would play nice with his toys."

"What do you want with me?"

"You?" His face twisted in disbelief and then softened. "Tut, tut. You mistook my adoration for affection." He placed a hand to his chest, sarcastically tender. "You are beautiful because of your power, Alexia, not your intellect."

Her knuckles popped around the sword's hilt.

"I had planned to bring you with me to become one of my allies. Can you imagine it? The power? A world that is yours to mold?"

The beauty of the land she'd seen had haunted her dreams since he gave her a glimpse. It taunted her now: the world where she could raise her family. The place she had experienced a lifetime of joy.

He extended a hand. "I offered this world to you many times, and you refused. Yet here you are."

"Because you stole my child."

He grinned. "I needed her key." He turned the sleeping Corona to show the necklace looped about the child's neck. It caught the light.

Alexia's blood froze.

"It could have been you," he continued smugly. "You could have been the key and ruled at my side, but I am not great at sharing. Especially another man's wife. It is better this way."

"What way?" The words were barely a whisper. Why hadn't he given her Corona yet? He didn't need her further.

"The infant is so much more malleable, weak mind and all. Still, you have my thanks for her, else I may have had to blackmail one of you into assisting me."

She stepped forward. "Deamus, give me my baby."

"Come with me." He took a step back, toward the light, the infant cradled close. "It will be better if you do. For her."

Alexia's windpipe closed. He wanted to take her child to this other world and keep her as a pet or slave? "Why do you want her?"

"Your lack of foresight is appalling." He sneered. "I will not meet any resistance with her by my side. She is, after all, an heir."

"Just take the key."

He clicked his tongue. "You know I cannot. Only the High King's bloodline can carry it. She bears the key for me. I will give her to you." He clutched the child tighter. "And in exchange for the babe's compliance, you will be given a palace, servants, jewels and fine food, everything you could desire, but—"

Alexia braced for it.

"—you will have to sever your bond. Otherwise you will die when I kill your husband."

She rubbed sweaty palms on her robe. "There is no way to break the bond."

He lifted an eyebrow.

That wasn't true. There was one. Bellezza had proven it time and time again. Alexia's throat caught, the air far too thin. "You want me to kill my husband?"

He grinned charmingly, if one could call a snake's grin charming. "You bonded yourself to my enemy. I warned you against it." He shrugged as if she'd decided to eat dung instead of berries and was experiencing the resulting discomfort.

"Why?" The sob caught in her throat. "What has he ever done to you?"

Deamus waved with his free hand. "He stole my birthright, of course. He stands between me and the heritage that should rightfully be mine. Oh, and he trapped me as a tree for years. Not forgiving that one lightly."

Kiren had offended him merely by being born. "You want this other world—why not simply take it?"

He laughed. "I do not want this other world. It never should have existed. It is a perversion."

"You wish to destroy it?"

"Once I have secured a stock of your kind to feed my cravings, yes. I will cross back over to this world and watch that one burn."

She straightened up, taking notice of the shimmering walls which had begun to thin.

He paced around her. "Choose quickly. That annoyance you call a husband will soon be dead, and here you are, safe with me…so long as you choose to break the bond." He waved a circle in the air. "His sun is setting, Alexia. Kill him now and raise your child, or say goodbye."

Her heart seized. She closed her eyes. Deamus held all the cards. She must obey, or leave both her husband and baby to a worse fate. And what would become of the Passionate? If this mad man could open the gateway whenever he pleased because she aided him with Corona, he would destroy the one bastion of wholeness and peace that remained for the Passionate: this other world. A whole world. There had to be another way!

She kept the weapon between them, letting her shoulders drop. "How do I know the gateway will remain open long enough for me to return?"

He shrugged. "It only makes things easier for me."

"That is no assurance." She tucked her sword in her belt and extended her hands. "Give me my baby. I cannot wake her without your assistance, and your spell will destroy my husband whether I kill him or not. Either I die and she remains by my side, or I return with her and the chance to live. You only have to return and snatch her from my lifeless fingers if I fail."

Deamus tapped his chin. "You make an intriguing proposal. Will she return? Will she not? How else will she try to betray me? Will she sacrifice her child's life simply to stop me?"

Her cheeks heated with rage. "You have beaten me, Deamus. You have beaten all of us! What more do you want?"

His brows shot up. "Baiting me with anger. That is a good tactic, but," he tapped the side of his head, "I am quite certain I made our differences clear. Kill him and return."

She bowed her head. "I will have to manipulate time to keep from being drained while I…"

"Yes, you will." He was back to grinning. "Go to it then."

He lifted his free hand.

Alexia yanked the threads of time and lunged forward.

# Sixty-Seven

# *Close*

Energy smacked Alexia's blade, but she held firm. Inside time. There he stood, a minion of the moments. A spinning shard in the carousel of possibilities. No match for her.

Alexia circled about him and lifted her babe from his arms. She stared into her little one's face. The infant slumbered on.

She had to get Corona far away from here. Far from him. If only Alexia could hand the babe to Grandfather outside of time and stop Deamus for good!

For what she must do, she couldn't keep Corona. Alexia had to say goodbye.

She relived again that reality where she and Kiren raised their child. It was so beautiful. So right. But within time she saw a hundred possibilities. Keep the babe with her, and she would fall in battle with Deamus. Return the infant to Kiren and the recently turned Soulless, and they would both be claimed by the hungry wraiths.

Kiren had a war before him, fighting off the starving Soulless. He would escape. He would even save the other Passionate, including Mae. She saw it. But it would be close.

There was only one option.

Velia's daughter. She would take their baby to safety, but be injured by falling out of the mist while crossing paths with Deiliey—a man who nullified Passionate gifts. The girl would lose her memory. Deiliey would find them both, infant and girl on a snowy mountain ledge. His presence would counteract the spell on her child, suspending it only as long as he was near. Velia's daughter would travel with him and the babe, searching for Corona's parents until many years had passed. Until Kiren found them. Until Mae absorbed the spell on Corona.

It was the best of possibilities.

She kissed her baby's cheek and snuggled her close, not ready to surrender her precious bundle. Tears spilled freely. "Oh my child, you will not remember me, but I will never stop thinking of you. Forgive me, my Corona. When it is safe, your father will find you. I promise."

She stepped through the walls of light into frozen time, past stilled bodies, past her husband who knelt on the ground, yelling desperately after her.

He was the one who had called her name.

She lingered, wishing to smooth away his fear, but she couldn't.

The girl hid in the trees, eyes wide with terror. Velia's child. Mist curled off her disintegrating arms. Extreme passions could bring out Passionate gifts prematurely, and this child had certainly been through more than her share of horrors. She was going to disappear, but before she went...

Alexia stopped next to her and touched the girl's cheek. *Take my babe to safety.*

She hugged her little one close once more, inhaling apple blossom and rubbing her cheek across the infant's soft skin. Even having said farewell, she couldn't let the child go.

*I must.*

Alexia slipped Corona into the girl's arms, securing her dagger into the baby's bundle—a weapon to fight the Soulless. One to keep her safe.

Her heart tore, a piece remaining in that bundle. "I will find you again one day, my little one."

Her cheeks were slick with tears, but she didn't wipe them away. It was time to go. She returned the way she'd come, halting at Kiren's side. She crouched and pressed a kiss to his brow.

"Goodbye, my Kiren. I will save you. I will save them all, somehow."

Alexia faced the tunnel again and took a deep breath.

She was ready for this. She could do this. It was time.

# Sixty-Eight

# *Finale*

The air burst from Kiren's lungs, the desperate cry tearing from the inside out, but it didn't change how her body lay on the ground, littered among the others.

His wife. His family. His life.

His knees smacked into the ground. Strength leeched from his core, flowing into the vortex of radiance, robbing the last of the power stored within his medallion.

Light exploded.

Kiren shielded his eyes.

Death touched his skin, searching for its next meal. He shoved backward, further, further, away from its reach and scrambled to his feet, sprinting blindly away.

Kiren stopped at the tree line and turned back. A single form stood in the midst of the devastation, skirts twirling about her in the wind, both fists lifted and clenched.

He gasped.

He could feel it—the earth crying out to him, shrieking as it bled into her. The vortex had been consumed by the same being.

Mae.

Her fists dropped, chest heaving.

Kiren stepped toward her, crossing an invisible line. The emptiness in the air hit him like an arctic gale. There was no life. Emptiness. It was dead. All of it. The earth, the connection, the gateway.

Thirteen decimated bodies littered the ground, little more than skeletons. Unmoving.

Something told him he should be able to locate Alexia, but there was a void. A nothingness. Her body had simply disappeared. Gone.

Mae turned to him, her eyes wide and searching. "Who is there? Who is it?"

He stopped right in front of her. She looked through him, squinting as if trying to break through a barrier.

"Mae."

She jolted backward. "I cannot see you. I cannot see!"

He placed a hand on her shoulder to steady her, expecting the hungry demons to latch on and suck him dry. They never came.

"What did you do?" His voice broke.

She straightened up. "I took it all. I stopped that monster from consuming everything and everyone. It is inside of them now..." Her eyes dropped to the ground as if searching for the fallen Passionate.

"What monster?"

"The darkness."

"You trapped it *inside* them?"

"As Alexia instructed me."

He swallowed hard. "And Alexia?"

No reply.

An egg lodged in his throat. "Where is she?"

Mae's head shook. She reached out and caught hold of his face. "I can touch you. I am not hurting you and I can touch you!"

He backed away, shaking. Alexia was gone. Completely gone. Not even her body remained. It was as if she'd never existed at all except for in his mind.

A glint of light hit his eye from where the portal had been. He hurried toward the glint and crouched.

A sword lay in the blackened soil, its red-wrapped handle accented by the blood staining its edge. Leofrik's sword. The one Alexia had carried.

He cradled it to his chest, holding in the scream, the wail, the mad laughter that was bubbling up. This was what remained? He ripped both hands through his hair. The torture, the fighting, the desperate hope, and this was what remained!

His mouth fell open and a shout tore from his lungs. It stole every ounce of air. It deflated him until he was a lifeless lump on the ground, panting.

A blackened corpse shifted next to Kiren's foot.

He twisted toward the movement.

Another twitched.

That wasn't possible! The thing was dead.

Its skeletal hand dropped over his ankle. He shoved away and got to his feet. "They still live?" He glanced at Mae.

Her lips were pressed tight. "They will always live."

"What are they?"

"The Soulless."

# Sixty-Nine

## Ages

Kiren and Mae fled. As soon as they crossed the ring of deadness, scorched earth, Mae's gift returned.

They gathered up all the Passionate they could find and set out for a new home. Kiren's heart was heavy, but he held in his hands the promise that Alexia would return. The sword. The only conclusion he could reach was that Mae's hunger had consumed his wife's body. One moment she had been lying on the ground, the next, an explosion of light and everything was dead. He wasn't willing to consider the other possibility, one that featured blood on a silver blade.

The next moonless night, he came face to face with two withered creatures, Amos—who was decidedly not Amos—and a being he'd never met. The air stilled. The temperature dropped. He lifted his pendant and prayed for safety. Light glimmered off his necklace. Amos fled. The other creature opened its hungry mouth and soaked in the radiance, then dropped to the ground. Dead.

Years disappeared. Kiren brought the Passionate together and kept them safe from the Soulless, but no matter what he did, the undead ranks of the Soulless grew.

One day he found three of the Passionate wandering in the Alps and discovered his second sliver of hope. She had Alexia's eyes, her mouth, her build, and her dagger... Corona was seventeen.

The mist child, Ilaria, at last had her memories restored. She had served as Corona's nanny all these years, and whenever his daughter left Deiliey's side, she fell into a deep sleep, until they took her to Mae.

Corona followed Kiren closely, trying to learn his ways and attempting to forgive. His absence had wrought an injury deep in her heart. She found it difficult to trust. They reached a sense of peace, if not a comfortable silence between them. He told her what he could of her mother, but she was never satisfied by the shortage of answers.

Neither was he.

Zeph aged slowly, but he grew into a rightful old man, leaving a son behind. It was an exceptionally difficult season for Kiren.

Deiliey died in a skirmish with the Turks. Corona mourned.

In time, they stumbled across men of power like Ulric who fancied themselves "collectors" or slavers of the Passionate. Kiren infiltrated the hierarchy of the Church and became a cardinal. He exerted his influence to relieve these "collectors" of station and fortune, and replaced rumors of witches and demons with stories of "saints." Corona followed him in disguise and used Church resources to experiment in breeding the most powerful Passionate. Men and women died at her hand in the most grievous ways. When Kiren discovered her efforts, he revealed her to the other clergy: a woman pretending to be an archbishop. She was to be executed. He thwarted the execution and sent her away with her mother's dagger. The peace between them ended.

She adopted Deiliey's name. It took two centuries to crush the rebellion she incited within the Passionate, and insurrection remained. After she lost, she disappeared.

As each sunrise presented its challenges, Kiren watched and strove to be worthy of the woman who possessed his heart. He gathered and taught the Passionate. He protected and loved. He governed and served.

The night he held Dana's child in his arms, he knew like never before that he would finally be complete. She had come back to him, his Alexia.

# Seventy

# *Saying Goodbye: 1849*

Kiren lifted his Bible toward the sky, comparing the star sketch on the inner cover to the alignment of stars. He showed the sketch to Sarah. "This is it," he said. "Six hundred years of waiting to go home, and at last it is time."

She stiffened next to him, and he couldn't decide if she was fighting her hunger or upset by the news.

"This will be the last time we see one another, and I wanted to thank you. Thank you for standing by me, even from inside the ranks of the Soulless." He turned to go but hesitated. "I only wish Alexia had known that she succeeded in saving you—but somewhere in time, she must."

Sarah caught his wrist, and even through her glove, her skin burned his. "You gave me more time with her. I wish I could do the same for you."

The instant Alexia had jumped back through time to stop the Soulless, he had known she wouldn't return, but part of him had hoped. He wouldn't see his precious wife, his queen, again, but he would rule worthily in her absence—just as she would have him do.

"I would like to see you off," Sarah said.

Kiren tucked the book in his pocket and offered an arm. "I am honored."

\*\*\*

The journey back to scorched earth passed in an instant and lasted forever at the same time. This was it, the final stretch. Kiren had endured well and now would fill his father's charge. Duty called.

The inn he'd built with Mae stood to mark the space where the gateway would open, maintained by its immortal caretaker. Kiren recalled fighting with Mae over how many windows, how many floors, and how many rooms the inn should have. She'd won. Every battle. It was what she did.

Corona Deiliey waited at the border of scorched earth. As did Miles. Kiren was grateful they'd come.

Corona offered his necklace as he approached. He took it gladly and energy buzzed down his elbow and into his core. It was like filling up a dry well, a well he'd not realized was empty.

"Are you certain you trust me to lead them?" Corona asked.

Kiren glanced at Miles who gave him a grim nod. Corona had been hidden among the Soulless for the last century and a half, leading them, trying to keep them under control with her ability to alter wills. Mostly she succeeded. Since a vast number had been trapped in the rubble of their hive, their threat had been diminished, but those that remained free were out there and dangerous. Once he and Corona had settled their differences, Kiren had acknowledged her before the Passionate, and Miles had agreed to stand at her side to govern their people. She still departed every moonless night to hold the Soulless in check, except for tonight. Precautions had been established for the Passionate in preparation for this evening.

"It is a singularly terrifying thing to lead." Kiren placed the false pendant around his daughter's neck. "But I believe you will do well. Give them your heart."

She nodded.

The four of them descended to the inn. Out back they found Mae, Regin, Ethel, Edward, Nelly, and Lester. Kiren presented Deiliey. "I give you my successor."

Hands were shaken and words exchanged, and while the others were distracted, Kiren took a moment to say his private farewells. He first spoke to Edward, then tugged Regin aside and whispered, "Has Mae consented yet?"

"Naw, but she will. That ring was bonnie brilliant."

He patted the man on the shoulder, keeping his voice down. "See that you do not give up. She is stubborn, but you make her happy."

"Aye. I'll not be backin' off."

Lester tapped the side of his nose as the two men returned and gave them a knowing wink. Kiren clasped forearms with him.

The runner squeezed his arm. "Tis not the last time we'll meet."

Nelly stepped forward, licked a thumb, and wiped it at a spot on his cheek. "What are you going to do without a rightful cook at your beck and call?"

"That is a good question. Perhaps you had better come with me?" He waved toward the heart of scorched earth.

Her cheeks bloomed bright red. "I couldn't do that."

"Yes, Nelly, you could."

Her perma-grin dropped. "I do believe I could. Would you welcome me in that realm?"

"Indeed, I would."

She fussed with her skirts and hair as he spoke with Ethel, and then Mae caught him.

"It has been a long journey," the reaper said. "Be a good king." She pulled him down and kissed his cheek.

"For you, I will be the best."

She wiped a tear away rather than following up with a jibe, and he was forced again to acknowledge how difficult this was for all of them. But it was time to go to his sister. It was time to relieve her suffering.

Miles stood between him and the place where the gate would open. He pulled the lad into a hug. Emotion caught in Kiren's chest. He had always felt that Miles was the closest he would have to a son: his protégé, his greatest success, his best friend.

He pulled away, breathing the tears down. "You keep her on the right path."

Miles saluted.

Kiren turned his back to them before he crumbled and focused on steadying his steps. Toward the future. Toward the gateway. Toward his destiny. Nelly padded along behind him.

He lifted his pendant toward the sky and called for the gateway to open.

Light burst into the night, a tunnel of radiance.

Kiren exhaled. This was it. For all his adventures and seasons of calm, all his joys and sorrows, the world and people he had known for six centuries, it was truly time to leave.

A sliver of fear twisted in his heart. What he remembered of the other side may have entirely changed. There was no knowing what awaited him, but he had to face it. He clutched a fist around his medallion. He would become the king his father desired.

He stepped toward the brilliance.

A hint of pomegranate and sunshine touched his nose. He shook the scent free. It was a wishful remembrance of happiness he would never experience again. A kindly remembrance. It made him smile.

A silhouette appeared in the light.

He paused, smile dropping.

Had Kiri come for him? Someone else? An enemy perhaps? He lifted a hand to shade his eyes and squinted.

She leapt free of the gateway, dressed in gray monk's robes. Her face was dirty, hair wild and free, cheeks flushed as though fresh from battle.

Jungle-deep eyes met his, and his heart stopped.

# Seventy-One

# *Ever After*

Alexia skidded to a stop and spread her arms wide to regain her balance, startled that Kiren stood right before her. Not Deamus. Kiren. She bent over, hands on knees and caught her breath, puzzling together how it was possible.

She had faced Deamus inside the gateway, sword poised. Deamus had lifted his hand to attack, and she'd launched forward, shoving her sword through his chest. Metal scraped bone. His scream pierced her ears. He'd thrown his arms down and the weapon flew free, blasted outward. She'd soared backward, smacking into the wall of light. The radiance burned around her skin, holding her fast until she pressed through it and nearly stumbled into Kiren.

"What happened?" she asked. "How did I...?"

His brows lowered, head tilting. And then she noticed the inn behind him. The inn.

Kiren's clothes were all wrong—clean and far too modern, a cut she'd never seen before. Behind him stood Nelly, Edward, Miles...

She stumbled backward, reaching for support.

Kiren's arms curled around her, gently holding her to him.

A sob caught in her throat. The truth, the reality, it couldn't be. She couldn't be home. This couldn't be her Kiren, the man who had lived centuries looking forward to her arrival. The man who had sacrificed. The man who cared too deeply.

As his oaken musk sank into her, she knew it was. She had never been more certain of anything. And yet, a piece of her heart remained in the past, with a man who had only just learned what it meant to lead, to love. Connecting the two seemed impossible. Twins. Two different men, and yet one.

"This is... I do not understand. How can I be...?" She turned tear-filled eyes on his face, startled by the confusion in his stare. Old English. She was speaking Old English. She focused on using modern language rather than her tongue for the last six months. "*When* are we?"

"The year of our lord, eighteen forty-nine." His voice was the same in either time, that rich baritone—although it lacked its usual emotion.

"Eighteen..." She pressed a hand to her mouth. Nearly seventy years since she'd left him behind. A full six-hundred years since she'd stood side by side with her beloved Passionate survivors. What had become of her loved ones? Of her family? Her throat tightened. "Father...?"

"Passed away twenty-nine years ago. Peacefully."

She nodded, biting down. Her heart was crying. She knew she'd not see him again when she stepped through time, but being here now, the loss was new. How had it happened? How had she missed so much, been absent for all that mattered? She twisted to the gate shimmering behind her. Six hundred years. Was it possible? Had she been trapped in the gateway all this time? It felt but an instant. Part of her ached to go back. Part of her knew this was where she belonged.

"The battle," she barely uttered, "we won the battle?"

He circled in front of her and placed a hand on either side of her face. Fierce blue tides wrapped her in their caress, an aching so deep the rest of existence was but a dream. "Are you real?"

The sob caught in her chest escaped. She touched him, running her fingers down his scar, so well healed but a permanent reminder of her place in his life. The fissure. The rift she'd created that altered him forever. Tears cut lines down her cheeks. He was the same in either time. This was her husband. The man she loved. Her heart.

She lifted trembling lips toward his. He closed the distance and cradled the back of her head with a hand, trapping her to him as he took possession of her mouth.

His tears mingled with hers as warmth filled them both. Her chest inflated with the life he brought to her, the life that belonged to them both. His crystal palace, his mental prison burst into existence, and she inhabited the tallest tower with him, looking out over a verdant landscape, a world blooming with the first rays of dawn, hope. She took his hand and her feet left the ground, pulling him with her. They floated into the heavens, hovering over the palace that would never serve as a prison again. From now on, they would fly. Together.

Kiren's lips left hers. She stared into his eyes, a night sky of constellations and promise.

"As much as I wish to keep you to myself..." He turned and waved a hand at their audience.

Her face flamed. Of course they had an audience.

Nelly squealed and caught her in a rib-bruising hug. Alexia laughed—as soon as she could breathe—and asked, "But you were buried in the earth, with the Soulless."

"Alexia, child, the earth is my bread. Those creatures are still trapped there, but it could never hold me."

She opened her mouth to respond, but Sarah's voice cut her off.

"How is it that the little cook receives the first hug when *I* came back from death to see you?" The raven-haired beauty uncrossed her arms and stepped forward. Her crimson eyes gave Alexia pause, but this was Sarah. She was alive!

Tears continued to flow as she embraced her sister. Soulless or not, Alexia's passage through time had accomplished something. Her best friend lived!

One of her best friends.

Miles watched her, his gray eyes far too knowing. She gave him a stern look over Sarah's shoulder and his gaze dropped. He shrugged apologetically. She released her sister and pulled him into an awkward hug.

"Listen in if you want, you buffoon. There is only happiness in my heart to share."

He brushed a finger across her cheek and showed her the wetness, tilting his head in an *is-that-so?* gesture. She shoved him playfully, laughing.

His face had lengthened out, his shoulders were broader, and his skin held a vague glow. Though it had been seventy years, he only looked ten older.

Mae wrapped an arm through hers, and Regin gave her an appreciative nod. Ethel placed a kiss on her cheek while Edward patted her hand, beaming. Lester, Grandfather—the great sneak—approached.

"The Sparrow returns."

"Careful, old crow, or I shall tell them what your caw truly means."

He placed a hand on his chest. "Why, Sparrow, methinks you've taken one too many punches while runnin' through time. Mayhaps ye be needin' to mend." He waved her toward the last member of the party.

Her smile dropped.

Corona Deiliey.

All grown up. Alexia had missed her baby's entire life.

The woman stood at Alexia's height, her eyes a mirror reflection. Her hair was mostly pulled up with ringlets dangling around her face. It was not the uninterpretable tones Alexia had glimpsed in the Soulless cave, but a deep auburn. The red of her father's bloodline. She was beautiful, exactly as she was meant to be.

"My precious girl…" Alexia reached out, worried about how she'd be received.

Corona's eyes filled with uncertainty, and she looked to her feet, shifting back and forth.

Alexia lifted one of her daughter's curls. "My heart breaks in pieces when I think of what you have suffered. I am so sorry, my Corona. It killed me to send you away." She touched her daughter's cheek and opened her mind, showing her that instant on the battlefield, the gateway glowing in the distance as darkness writhed through the air and the Passionate littered the ground. Tenderly she had placed her child in Ilaria's arms, barely able to see through her tears.

Corona's eyes lifted to hers.

"It would have killed you," Alexia whispered, "for me to keep you. For your father to keep you. My greatest regret is that you grew not knowing how deeply loved you are." Again, she opened her mind. She showed Corona her birth, the way both she and Kiren had rejoiced. She showed her what might have been if

Alexia had chosen to raise her and let the worlds be destroyed. "I am forever sorry." She pulled her daughter into her embrace and there was no resistance. "I have watched you from inside time. I have seen everything, and I am overwhelmed by your strength and resilience. You are and will always be the most precious thing in this world to me."

A throat cleared. They pulled apart and there stood Kiren.

"Do go on. At least I know my place now." He winked.

Alexia grabbed him and pulled him into stilled time. "Husband mine, you are causing me some difficulty now, for I know not whether to spend this moment acquainting myself with my daughter, or kissing you senseless."

"Well, as you have been so kind as to suspend the moment…"

She laughed. "Precisely."

He slipped both arms around her waist, crushing her to him and reminding her lips that they had a perfect equal. They remained, locked in a physical reunion until both believed the veracity of the other. At last his hold relaxed.

She laced her fingers into his hair and pulled him closer, deepening their connection. *I am not done with you yet.*

He laughed. *Take whatever you want. I am all yours.*

She giggled against his mouth. After all they'd been through, he had better be—no more regrets or secrets. Through their connection, she showed him how she'd defeated Deamus. He shared glimpses of the last half-century, including her father's final moments, surrounded by those he loved. He'd left the world at peace.

*It is time for me to go home*, Kiren whispered to her mind.

She laughed. *Time holds no meaning. We can stay here for the next ten years and then come back to this moment. Remember, you are married to the Maiden of Time.*

Alexia released the seconds, but kept Kiren's hand in hers. She turned to Corona. "And now, dearest daughter, I wish to know everything. Tell me about yourself." She lifted her gaze to Kiren. "We are finally a family."

Life and death. A perfect balance. And for now, she was ready to embrace life, all of it—the good, the bad, the pain, the joy. Whether she believed in Kiren's God or not, she shared one sentiment: All things happened for a reason. The reason may be to test her, to prove her, to build her up, but she would embrace each moment and find the lesson in it. The sacrifices had been made, the world had been saved, and now it was her turn.

She was going to live.

# A Note to the Reader

Dear fabulous you,

Thank you for reading TIMELESS! I hope you enjoyed it, and if you did, leave me a review! I promise virtual cheese and good karma for the rest of the week. If you liked what you read, I offer regular freebies – and not just *my* books – to newsletter subscribers, plus articles of encouragement and reviews on books I love. Sign up and share the readerly joy!

# Acknowledgements

"The third book is done. The trilogy is complete. Breathe!" I've been repeating these things for the last 6 months and still can't believe it. This is an incredible day and I'm so grateful for everyone who has made it possible.

First and foremost—you readers who have nudged, hinted, and outright badgered me about getting my rear in action, thank you. You are the fire behind my fingers.

Next to my fabulous critique group who not only suffered through the third book of the trilogy without reading the first, but who did it on the clock. I am baffled by your generosity.

REVIEWERS, you are the life blood of an author. Even if all you have time to give is one sentence, you make my writerly heart beat. Thank you!

Gratitude as epic as cheese goes to the best husband in the world who read the book 3 times, and agonized with me through a complete rewrite. (Yes, Matt, I mean you. Love you to eternity and back!)

Huge thanks to my editor, Bethany, at A Little Red Inc., for her incredible eye.

To my fabulous critique partner, thank you, Rachel Hert.

My amazing sister who made time to read for me around raising 4 young kids, Cindy, you are the best.

All my blogging pals, thank you TONZ for helping me spread the word and being your fabulous selves. You rock!

To my rockin' Write On Build On writers, and IWSG clan, love you +10! Couldn't have done it without your daily support and encouragement.

My amazing kids… You brainstorm with me, read passages when I'm so excited I can't wait to share, and patiently do your thing when Mom is lost in a story world. I love you the mostest in the whole world! (Other than your dad.)

# About the Author:

Crystal Collier is a young adult author who pens clean fantasy, historical, and romance hybrids. She can be found practicing her brother-induced ninja skills while teaching children or madly typing about fantastic and impossible creatures. She has lived from coast to coast and now calls Florida home with her creative husband, three littles, and "friend" (a.k.a. the zombie locked in her closet). Secretly, she dreams of world domination and a bottomless supply of cheese.

You can find her on her blog, follow her on Twitter, or visit her on Facebook. Subscribe to her newsletter to receive freebies and learn about exciting new developments.

http://crystal-collier.com/